The Lime Kiln and Other Enchanted Spaces

The Lime Kiln
and
Other Enchanted Spaces

POEMS AND TALES

Geoffrey Reiter

Hippocampus Press

New York

Publication history: See p. 249.

Published by Hippocampus Press
P.O. Box 641, New York, NY 10156.
www.hippocampuspress.com
All rights reserved.

Cover art and design by Daniel V. Sauer, dansauerdesign.com.
Hippocampus Press logo designed by Anastasia Damianakos.

First Edition
1 3 5 7 9 8 6 4 2

ISBN 978-1-61498-466-5 (paperback)
ISBN 978-1-61498-470-2 (ebook)

Contents

Testing the Spirits 9

Permian-Triassic 20

A Hellish Thing 21

What if Atlantis . . . ? 34

Adept 35

A Voice in the Night 49

Arbitress of Tides 50

Star Dust 55

Big Sky 56

The Nightmare 77

Quartz Contentment 78

The Absence 83

Désirée 84

Eternal Night 90

MacAdam 91

An Edwardian Quartet 105

A Green Shade 108

A Word 119

The Folly 120

Termination Shock 155

A Glint amid the Corn 157

The Lady in the Wood 174

The Ache of Bone and Joist and Page 177

The Mermaids Keep Their Own Counsel 183

The Lime Kiln 184

Through Enchantment 203

The Cartographer 204
Acknowledgements 247
Publication History 249

To all those who have supported me in my work,
and especially to my sister Alisa, loyal friend and supporter.

I come not lonely to the page. Beside
Me travel all my fellow questers, all
The pilgrims who have walked these roads, who guide
My paths to keep my feet more free from fall.
These are the ancient scribes and sages, mages
And wonder-workers casting forth their spells
Of goodness, truth, and beauty, while the wages
The wild world barters buy abyssal hells.
My people past and present, blood and spirit
In watchful witness-host enclouding me,
Support, sustain my work to bear it, hear it,
To share the fear and frolics that I see.
Before eternity, I stand along,
Among my fellow singers of the song.

I never can be tied to raw, new things,
For I first saw the light in an old town,
Where from my window huddled roofs sloped down
To a quaint harbour rich with visionings.
Streets with carved doorways where the sunset beams
Flooded old fanlights and small window-panes,
And Georgian steeples topped with gilded vanes—
These were the sights that shaped my childhood dreams.

Such treasures, left from times of cautious leaven,
Cannot but loose the hold of flimsier wraiths
That flit with shifting ways and muddled faiths
Across the changeless walls of earth and heaven.
They cut the moment's thongs and leave me free
To stand alone before eternity.

    —H. P. Lovecraft, "Background," *Fungi from Yuggoth*

By blood we live, the hot, the cold
To ravage and redeem the world:
There is no bloodless myth will hold.

    —Geoffrey Hill, "Genesis"

Let me start with the enchanted world, the world of spirits, demons, moral forces which our predecessors acknowledged. The process of disenchantment is the disappearance of this world, and the substitution of what we live today: a world in which the only locus of thoughts, feelings, spiritual élan is what we call minds; the only minds in the cosmos are those of humans . . . and minds are bounded, so that these thoughts, feelings, etc., are situated "within" them.

    —Charles Taylor, *A Secular Age*

. . . man is made a mystery for mysteries and visions, for the realization in his consciousness of ineffable bliss, for a great joy that transmutes the whole world, for a joy that surpasses all joys and overcomes all sorrows.

    —Arthur Machen, "A Fragment of Life"

TESTING THE SPIRITS

Σιγησάτω πᾶσα σὰρξ βροτεία, καὶ στήτω μετὰ φόβου καὶ τρόμου,
καὶ μηδὲν γήϊνον ἐν ἑαυτῇ λογιζέσθω.

—Divine Liturgy of St. James

"Are you ready for me to lock you in?" asked Pastor Brian, gesturing toward the door with his phone.

The four songwriters eyed that door warily, though Gage grinned while tickling out a C major chord on his guitar. "Let's do this!" he enjoined.

Next to him on the dingy brown pleather sofa, Greg tapped his pen and rolled his eyes. "A lock-in, Brian? Seriously, what are we, twelve?"

Brian issued a symmetrical, lacquered smile, an expression that had served him well in his tenure as Executive Associate Pastor. "No. You're adults who happen to be staff at EmPassion Chapel and who need a worship song ready to go by the twenty-third. A song that, to the best of my knowledge, you don't yet have a single line for."

From the far corner Jen began to roll *her* eyes before thinking better of it. "Shows you what you know. We've got two verses down."

"One verse," Darren cut in, his steel-gray hair and his steel-gray eyes belying the fiery earnestness of his voice. "We've already discussed this. The second verse doesn't fit Pastor Jason's teaching."

"We can get into that later," Greg said. "But yeah, at the very least we don't have a chorus or a bridge."

Brian nodded. "Right." He surveyed them all with his unflappable gaze. "Look, we all know Pastor Jason's vision for EmPassion. His strength is his teaching, and with the tools of today's information ecosystems, that teaching can go out to millions of listeners beyond this campus. And the music has to be part of that shared vision."

Darren smiled with his trademark intensity. "That's the vision God's laid on our heart too, Brian. The young people of today need music they can relate to, and old songs are like old wineskins. The Lord has blessed this church with so many gifted sons of Asaph, so why shouldn't we be creating our own praise music?"

"Exactly. That's why I want you to listen to Pastor Jason's sermons while you're here, so your lyrics can be in alignment with this series on 1 John." The smile then slid off his face momentarily. "But if we're ever going to be able to deliver this product to scale, we'll need to have lyrics and music done in time for the full band to practice, so that the whole worship set runs smoothly."

Greg squeezed the bridge of his nose and shut his eyes. "I still can't believe you want us to write an original song on a specific theme and have it ready to go for church on a couple of weeks' turnaround time. That's just not possible." Seeing Darren about to speak, he grunted, "And don't you dare quote Philippians 4:13 to me!"

"Stay on mission, Greg," Pastor Brian insisted, his voice running smooth like syrup. "This is your chance to make something you're proud of."

"We've got this, Brian," Gage reiterated, strumming the feathers of his forearm's eagle tattoo with the guitar pick.

"Great. People are going to talk about this night years from now, guys. This is where it all began."

"The room where it happened?" sighed Jen, chuckling.

"Okay, this is it," Pastor Brian said. "When I leave, the room locks. You'll have no choice but to get this song done. I'll see you in the morning."

He saluted them, then walked out of the big metal door with the little glass window, and a moment later, the light above the latch turned red. It was a reasonably spacious room, all told. Many years earlier the building had been a home improvement store, and when it went bankrupt the fledgling church bought the property. They chased out the mourning doves and the sparrows, and what had once been a space of tools and products became a vast and trendy downtown sanctuary. The room they now occupied had been Accounting; it was bigger than the room that had been the manager's office, which perhaps said something about how the store had regarded its money—for all the good it had done them in the end.

Greg ran his hands through his graying hair. "Seriously, though, guys, we can agree this is kind of ridiculous, right? I don't know about you all, but this isn't exactly in my contract."

Darren regarded him quizzically. "Contract, Greg? We're working as unto the Lord. This is a calling, not a job."

"Yeah, I mean, I get that. Look, I've been with EmPassion since the beginning. I've worked plenty of late nights. But I've got a wife at home with a teenage son and a daughter in diapers, and after all these years, yet again, here I am."

Jen strolled out of the corner and joined the rest of them, slumping into the couch beside Greg, fidgeting with the orange silk scarf around her neck. "Look, I totally understand, Greg," she told him. "But think about it. How many times over the years have you complained about the songs we play? No, really, I mean it. So Pastor Brian was right about that. This is your chance, *our* chance. We get to *make* the songs."

Greg pursed his lips. "Fine. Fine. Let's get this done."

Darren motioned for them to circle up, and everyone stood. He grabbed Gage's hand, then Jen's, leaving Greg to catch their hands on the other side. Darren bowed his head, and they could all hear his deep breathing, as though he were returning from a sports practice or a military drill.

"Dear Lord, I thank you for this group, this family. I ask, Lord, that you would shower blessings upon us this night and place a hedge of protection upon us. Let your mighty hand, O Lord, guide our work as warriors wielding the sword of your word. May the words of our mouths and the meditations of our hearts be acceptable to you, Lord. Amen."

Gage's emphatic echo drowned out the mumbled "Amens" of Greg and Jen. Then he dashed over to the particle-board desk and yanked open the first box of pizza. "Okay, what did we get? Looks like pepperoni here! Any takers?"

Greg ambled over, pulling out the next box. "Meat lovers here. Bottom one looks like plain cheese. Seriously, guys? I know not to expect Greek pizza, but no vegetarian?"

Darren eyed him quizzically. "Since when have we ever ordered vegetarian pizzas, Greg? Don't tell me you go in for that kind of thing."

"I go in for what will lose me a belt size or two, Darren," he retorted. "Not that a few green peppers would counteract a slice of Luigi's. Well, cheese it is."

He pulled out a massive, drooping slice of plain cheese pizza, took a large bite, then got it onto a paper plate—but not before a rogue glob got caught on his face. Darren strode over beside Gage and surgically removed a slice, though a spatter of tomato paste landed on his palm in the process.

"Well, give it here," Jen said and muscled in between them to grab a meat lovers slice.

They returned to their seats while Darren walked over to an adjoining desk, where he had set down his tablet. With a few quick strokes he called forth the video of the past week's sermon. Pastor Jason Wage appeared on the screen. He wore a black polo shirt, unbuttoned and untucked, above his acid-washed jeans. While he paced about the podium and looked down at the audience, his fists clenched and unclenched, as did his carefully stubble-shadowed face. His voice changed registers rapidly, from throaty whisper to thunderous shout. Blazing out from the stage in front of him and off-camera, the key light immersed his body in a passionate red.

"In this passage, dear brothers and sisters, John is speaking out against bad teachers. And this can be scary, because in our evil age there are so many false teachers, so many wolves in sheep's clothing. But you know what? We're not alone in this fight! We've got an ally. The Spirit of God is on our side. He's the one this passage is talking about when it says that we have overcome—past tense, we *'have overcome'*—the world.

"And how do we recognize this spirit, God's spirit in us? We test each spirit, to discern whether it is a spirit of truth or a spirit of Antichrist. And God's spirit is found in those who obey, those who his church can spot right away: 'We are from God, and whoever knows God listens to us; but whoever is not from God does not listen to us.'"

Jen finished her last bite of crust and washed it down with a swig of grape soda. "I know we're supposed to be supporting the sermon series," she said, "but isn't it a bit distracting to have the sermon playing *while we're writing?*"

Darren nodded slightly, though he was not looking at her. "I understand, Jen, but I also don't want us to miss the inspiration. I'll turn the volume down some."

Jen shrugged, recognizing that this was the best concession she would get from him. Squirming, she removed her phone from her back pocket and, with a quick hopeless glance at the clock, tossed it beside her on the cushion. Greg, meanwhile, had his second slice of pizza in his left hand, while in his right he now held his little pen, emblazoned with the logo of the local used bookstore. He started to tap the pen on his pad of paper.

"Okay, we've got to come up with something. Gage, what was that tune you had worked out?"

Gage set down a slice, wiped his fingers, and picked up his guitar. He began strumming out a 1-5-6-4 chord progression in C major.

"Okay, and who wrote down the lyrics that we have so far?"

Jen passed her laptop to Greg, who scowled.

"You can't say this. 'His grace reigns down on us'?"

Gage shrugged. "What's wrong with that? It's a metaphor. Like God is a great cloud bursting with grace, until that grace comes pouring out. I thought you liked metaphors."

"That would be *rain*, r-a-i-n. This is like saying that his grace rules down on us. Do you even know the difference?"

Darren stepped in and put an arm on Greg's shoulder. "It's okay, Greg. It's just a spelling issue. Correct it, and let's move on."

Greg grumbled but acquiesced, deleting the offending verb on

Jen's computer and replacing it with the correct one. "It's still not a good metaphor," he mumbled, though no one seemed to hear him. Scrolling down, he pointed to the next lines. "I like what you put here, Jen," he observed. "This parent image is poignant, probably the best thing in this song so far."

"That's why it's so important to have a woman writing with us," Darren interjected. "We need someone who can be alive to that emotional side of the faith."

Jen crossed her arms. "Yeah, you know, that's exactly why I majored in Feelings at Bible college. Glad it's paying off."

Her pizza slice finished, she got up off the couch and traveled to the old drum set. Once upon a time it had stood on the stage before being replaced by a five-piece set with clear drumheads. Now it languished in this room, its coating worn almost threadbare. Its tarnished cymbals had been too thick, stricken too hard and too often, and now they hung cracked and jagged. Still, Jen took a couple of sticks and began hammering out a simple beat.

Gage grinned. "That's good! I think it could go with that chorus I wrote."

"I thought we didn't have a chorus," Jen noted, still drumming lightly.

"No, I put it in the document," Gage insisted. "I mean, it may need work, of course, but—"

Greg groaned, almost spat, and shifted in his seat as he read it. "For real? I swear, you guys are going to be the end of me."

"What's wrong?"

"What's wrong? Honestly, what language do you even speak, Gage? On what planet does 'awesome' rhyme with 'sovereign'?"

Gage strummed awkwardly, staring down at the mahogany of his concert cutaway guitar, then further down to the dingy linoleum tiles that hadn't yet been carpeted.

"What do you mean Greg?" he muttered plaintively. "They both have that 'ah-uh' sound, sort of. That's like a rhyme."

Greg clenched his fists in something that looked quite like rage, almost breaking the pen in his right hand. "No, Gage, that's actually nothing like a rhyme. That's like two overused words that sound nothing alike. And what exactly is this?"

Gage leaned over to see where Greg was pointing on the screen, then looked back at Greg, perplexed. "'Woah'—it's part of the chorus."

"W-h-o-a—it's spelled w-h-o-a. Barbarians. And how exactly is this supposed to be sung?"

Gage brightened at the query, which he interpreted as an invitation. "Right! Listen to this!" He started playing a tune similar to the beat Jen had been toying with, and after a few chords, his tenor broke into an earnest "Whoa-oh-oh-oh," which he then repeated twice.

Darren rubbed a hand on the back on Gage's neck. "Good. That's a good place to build on."

Jen lowered her arms and shrugged. "Yeah, it's not bad."

"I can't believe I'm hearing this," Greg objected. "On a screen, that's just going to look like a big 'whoa'—apparently a misspelled one. How's a congregation supposed to know what they're singing? Like 'Whooooooa!' on a roller coaster? Or like, 'Whoa, dude, sovereign God is totally awesome'?"

Darren slid over to the couch and sat beside Greg, folding his hands. "I'm sensing a spirit of resistance in you," he said softly, his voice barely audible over the undercurrent of Pastor Jason's sermon, still humming from the tablet at the back desk.

Greg shook his head and brought a hand to his sweaty brow. "Sorry, you're right, Darren. It's just . . . well, I don't love this set-up here, but it *is* my chance to finally contribute something to Christian worship, something that endures, something beautiful."

"Our Lord *is* beautiful, and anything written in praise of him will be a joyful noise," Darren replied.

"Emphasis on the noise. He's beautiful, so he deserves beauty. We shouldn't be creating another generic, cookie-cutter piece of drivel."

For a moment no one spoke, and Greg's words hung heavy in the air like incense, though Pastor Jason's words behind them spumed thicker still. Darren licked his lips and tilted his head, as if listening for the wind, but no such breath of air could enter that sealed inner room. Gage looked poised to strum a new chord; his fingers hovered over the strings without quite touching them. Jen fidgeted nervously with the drumsticks, keeping her lips shut.

Darren moved swiftly then, like a falcon. He snatched the pen from Greg's hand, causing Greg to tumble backward in the couch and drop the laptop onto the floor. Wordlessly, with all the force and speed of a mechanism, Darren pushed Greg's head backward on the stained sofa and plunged the point of the pen into his eye, so deep that it disappeared. There was no opportunity for flailing or scream-ing: one moment, Greg had been a breathing man sitting on a cush-ion, the next his body was transformed into an empty, motionless husk, limbs loosely sprawled, one eye glassily staring, the other re-placed by a welling of blood.

Jen shrank back, covering her mouth with her hand, though Gage stood still, lips agape. He let go of his precious guitar, which rattled on the mottled white tile floor.

Darren, metallic eyes, grown molten, looked up from Greg's body, his gaze sliding back and forth between Jen and Gage. Darren's breathing was terrifyingly regular, while his countenance had the not-quite-placid look of calm waters beneath which predators are hunting.

"Phinehas, son of Aaron, was zealous for the Lord's honor," Dar-ren said implacably. "He turned away God's wrath with his zeal. Do you see how this is our Phinehas moment? I've turned the Father's wrath away from us, and we can get back to the business of praising him in song."

Jen, her hands lost in the pockets of her salmon capris, eyed Dar-ren, forcing her gaze at him and not the prospective exits in the room.

"How—how did that"—she couldn't help glancing at Greg—"turn away God's wrath?"

Darren smiled with a hard igneous warmth, though he looked puzzled as well. "He had a spirit of discord in him, Jen. You could hear it too, I assume. He wasn't authentically pursuing Christ with his whole heart; he wasn't sold out to Jesus."

"Sure," sputtered Gage, his gawky frame trembling mercilessly, "but man . . . I mean, there are things we could do, you know? Talk to him, or whatever, but . . . Like, that was really not cool."

Darren for the moment forgot Jen and, cocking his head, fixed a smoldering regard on Gage, his eyes now appearing the gray of ash. "I sincerely mourn his passing. But he was a wolf among sheep. I could sense it—without words, just the still, small voice of the Lord, telling me to cleanse his temple from all impurity."

"I get it," Gage replied, "and yeah, Greg was annoying sometimes. I know Jesus warned us about wolves and all that. But he didn't go . . . wolf-hunting. He didn't *kill* the moneychangers at the temple."

Standing beside Greg's limp body, Darren hesitated for a moment, his features pensive yet still fixed on Gage, who couldn't keep from peering at the corpse on the sofa. Gage kept tapping his foot on the floor and rubbing his fingertips together. At last Darren spoke again, more to himself than either of the others.

"His feet were like bronze glowing in a furnace, and his voice was like the sound of rushing waters. In his right hand he held seven stars, and coming out of his mouth was a sharp, double-edged sword. His face was like the sun shining in all its brilliance." Darren's eyes lost their sheen of distraction, blazing sharply again. "Jesus came as our sacrifice the first time. But that same Jesus now stands as judge and mighty warrior. We're soldiers in his army. And we don't do battle against flesh and blood."

"Then why did you do battle against Greg's flesh and blood?" Gage asked, barely able to force the query out through the twitching of his jaw.

"You look frightened, Gage," Darren observed. "The Lord didn't give us a spirit of fear. Perfect love casts out fear."

Gage's eyes glanced, from Darren to Greg to Jen to the red light that glowed on the office door. "I'm not scared," he insisted, his voice cracking. "It's just a lot, you know? Just a little surprising, not quite the night I had in mind."

Darren responded by racing toward Gage, who stumbled backward and ran for the door. He tried to twist the handle, but the bolt held fast in place. Darren, meanwhile, had scooped up Gage's guitar by the neck. With an inhuman velocity Darren closed the gap between them and swung the instrument, as a batter in baseball might. Gage was just turning away from the door to move toward a new location as Darren swung, and the guitar's body struck him with full force in the head, the room echoing with a crack of wood and bone. The impact sent Gage straight to the hard floor, where his temple collided with the tile. Darren nudged Gage's flank with his wingtip shoe; seeing no movement, he dropped the guitar, which clattered hollowly to the ground.

Looking up, Darren spotted Jen, inching toward the other side of the room, hands still in her pockets. "I didn't expect this evening to go like this," he mused.

"That makes two of us," Jen muttered. Tentatively she added, "So what now?"

"Do you have any ideas for a chorus?" he inquired. "I agree with you that Gage's contribution was solid, but we need more lyrics."

Jen couldn't keep her mouth from falling open, though she snapped it shut again at once. "Yeah," she nodded, "sure. We need more words. Let's—let's think of something."

"I think that this song, at its heart, is about the Holy Spirit."

Jen slid back to the drum set and began to play out the rhythm she had worked out just a few minutes prior, though the muscles in her arms were taut as tension wire. She started to sing, her voice scarcely a whisper. "Whoa-oh-oh, Holy Spirit, Whoa-oh-oh, can you hear it?"

Darren blinked once and glared. "What is that?"

Jen swallowed. "I'm just trying to do what you suggested, Darren," she maintained. "Trying to come up with a chorus. That's all."

"You're not trying at all," he sighed, striding her way. "You have the same spirit of Antichrist as the other two."

"I swear I don't," Jen began to say, but already he was sprinting across the room toward her. She thrust the drumsticks at his face; they were blunt but hard, and one hit him in the eye like a plank. He stumbled back momentarily, and Jen tried to run. But Darren lashed out his left hand and grabbed her by the ankle, so that she fell to the tile. She kicked at him frantically, but he positioned himself over her and grabbed at her scarf, tightening it around her neck.

"Narrow is the road that leads to life," he grunted as she clawed at his hands. "I wish I had realized sooner just how narrow."

"Darren, please stop," she gasped. "I can't breathe . . ."

He said nothing more but wound the scarf tighter and tighter against her flesh. Her face grew red as she flailed her arms. At last, in desperation, she caught hold of the dilapidated drum set and with a yank sent it clattering to the floor beside her. Darren ignored the instruments strewn around them. But with her left hand, Jen was able to reach out and grab the jagged old cymbal, which had come clattering to the earth. With a final surge of strength, she swung her left arm out in a sudden arc, and the serrated edge of the tarnished bronze sliced through Darren's throat, before she dropped it back down with a clang.

Darren released Jen, who rolled away from him. She watched as he grabbed at his neck, where a surprising flow of blood was now issuing forth. He opened his mouth wordlessly, a horrified infantile burbling the only noise he could articulate. His hard eyes softened, clouded over like fog, as he collapsed, moaning and whimpering for a time before at last falling silent.

Jen tried to stand, but a darkness was closing in around her field of vision. She staggered toward the exit, trying without success to cry out for help. She reached toward the desk for her phone to call out, but her fingers had grown loose and weak through the assault. Retching and waving out frenetically, she dragged herself toward the door in hope of escape before collapsing, blacking out just shy of the handle.

And so the bodies in the room lay motionless in their still quietus, sprawled about and surrounded by broken instruments. The only remaining noise came from the desk near the door: it was the voice of Pastor Jason Wage, still shouting in deep passion, a red light still glowering from the tablet screen.

PERMIAN-TRIASSIC

They died. The million hosts of species starved
For oxygen in Panthalassa's deep,
Or bodies burning as the magma carved
Its brutal hieroglyphic scarring. Weep
For *Gorgonops,* a corpse dried on the shore,
Dicynodon's deep dying sigh, the blight
Of hot anoxic seas whose poison tore
Into the lonely last dead trilobite.
This was the Dying, vast Earth's gurgling gasp
As red-toothed Nature, careless of the type,
Ensnared all flesh within its ghastly grasp.
But yet, behind a fringe of ferns, a stripe,
Gray-green, a boxy *Lystrosaur,* as day
Dawns new, and once again Life finds a way.

A Hellish Thing

When the storm had passed and the wind had at last died down, the four of them left the camp behind to begin prospecting at Mount Kirkpatrick. The Scott tents of the camp, once again bustling with activity, stood red against the new-fallen sheen of snow, rising from the ground like miniatures of the old pyramids in which the bones of pharaohs were housed. Glancing back, Gareth thought of his journey thus far: from Cardiff to "town" at McMurdo station, then to this temporary little village 600 kilometers from the south pole. Now they were leaving even that vestige of human civilization, at least for the day.

He imagined the terrain as it would have been in the early Jurassic, almost 200 million years ago. They would be descending into a warm, dry wood, great bursts of green spurting from the trunks of cycads and conifers, casting deep shadows across the grassless ground. Lurking in those shadows might be the scaly, mottled form of a *Cryolophosaurus,* stalking the wood like a fierce, crested dragon.

The region was different now. The arid heat of the early Mesozoic was replaced by the sharp, stinging cold of today's Antarctic. Gareth knew it could be much colder; he'd felt worse every so often in the harshest of Welsh winters. Still, even after the storm a bitter breeze continued to lash at any piece of exposed skin. Behind him the snow stretched long and white, with a near-blinding sheen of sunlight distended across it. But ahead, as they drew nearer the mountain itself, the snow thinned out, and they could see the sedimentary strata beneath it. Here were swaths of deep, ragged gray, and though this desolation was natural, it reminded him of the strip-mined hillsides he would see gouged out in the countryside when driving to visit his grandmother in Llantrisant.

"Here, hold my phone."

Startled, Gareth turned to see Arkady beside him, proffering his device with his left hand. He was speaking in an exaggerated faux-American accent that sounded somewhere between southern and midwestern, the kind of voice he used when he was getting ready to preen.

"Why do you have it?" Gareth asked, though he knew the answer. "Who exactly are you going to call out here?"

Arkady scowled, an expression that Gareth once would have taken for fury but now knew to be Slavic good humor. "This one is for the website, and I want it to look professional, so no selfies."

"Why not get Denise to do it?"

From his left-hand side Denise grunted, "Hell, no. You know how I feel about these videos."

"It's educational," retorted Arkady. "This is all for science. Now hold it up, Gareth. I promise it will only be a minute."

In the end Gareth shrugged, set down his bag, and held up the phone. Looking into the screen, he adjusted the positioning assiduously until Arkady's meticulously tousled black-gray hair stood out against the stark, pale-blushed blue expanse of the polar sky, with Mount Kirkpatrick looming like rubble behind him. Arkady grinned ingratiatingly as Gareth began recording.

"We're here at Mount Kirkpatrick, looking for fossils," he proclaimed, almost breathless with excitement or cold or exertion. "The life forms that lived here hundreds of millions of years ago survived one of the great extinction events. Today, as changing climates threaten our own world, we can look to the past to find clues to our future."

Arkady gave a thumbs-up sign, and Gareth ended the recording. On the other side of Denise, Mei looked over at him. "I thought we were here to find dinosaur bones."

Denise, nodding, added, "And pterosaurs . . . and cynodonts . . ."

"I'm here for the ferns," Gareth interjected, handing Arkady back his phone. "I guess my question is, why all that bloody talk about finding 'clues to our future'?"

Arkady shrugged, then winked as he received his device and slung his pack back over his shoulder. "You know we could dig fossils every day and be content. But people back home—they don't pay money for that. For them it's not enough just to love something. They want to know what's in it for them. So I tell them this."

Denise snorted. "Don't you think that's being a bit disingenuous, *Dr.* Sokolov? We're scientists. We're in the business of truth."

Arkady guffawed at her. "This from the woman who claims she was conceived at Woodstock?"

Denise's frigid gaze shot through her thick-rimmed glasses, though the frown on her thin, dry lips looked rather simulated. "What relevance does that have?"

"No offense, but the math doesn't check out," Gareth concurred. "Look, given your birthday—"

"That is Holloway family lore," Denise retorted, "and I will not have you questioning it."

"How very scientific of you," laughed Arkady.

"What are they talking about, Dr. Holloway?" Mei asked.

"It's a long story," Denise growled. "And one you don't need to know. Besides, I'd hardly expect you—"

Mei let free a fey giggle. "I know what Woodstock is, Dr. Holloway."

Gareth wouldn't doubt it. A week ago he had known Zhou Mei only as Denise's quiet and hyper-respectful graduate student from Zigong. Then came karaoke night at Gallagher's, the evening before the helicopter dropped them off at the Queen Alexandra Range. After downing a truly shocking amount of pale ale, Mei had jumped onto the stage, black hair flying, and belted out "I Will Survive" as though she were channeling Gloria Gaynor.

"Look," Denise groaned, anxious to change the subject, "it's about time we split up. We'll have plenty of opportunities to climb later if we need to, so stick to the base of the mountain today."

"I'm taking that spot there," Arkady said, pointing to a little rise some 300 meters away. "I think I can get a good view of the whole range . . ." Seeing Denise's acid glare, he added, ". . . *and* maybe a nice sauropodomorph premaxilla too."

Arkady continued on his way, pausing every few moments to pose with his phone. Mei hefted her pack, sparing a glance back at her mentor before moving off to a promising slope. Denise was headed toward a flank of the mountain when Gareth put a hand on her shoulder. She looked back to him, blue eyes squinting in the cold white sunlight.

"How *is* your mother doing?" he inquired. "I've been meaning to ask this whole trip."

He thought she might snap at him, like a cornered predator, but she just turned her eyes down toward the earth and pursed her lips. "I, uh . . . thanks for asking, Gareth." After a slow, artificially steady inhalation, she continued, "Not great. My sister made an unexpected visit to the nursing home and found she had a bedsore over half her body. It was bad. And, of course, I'm really the only one she still re-members, so Dawn wanted me to come and handle it. But you know, our plane was leaving in the morning, and we didn't have any real wiggle room, so I just had to leave."

Gareth winced. "I'm guessing your sister's not thrilled."

"We had . . . words. And I get it." Denise sighed, her breath visi-ble in the clear polar air before dispersing as though it had never been. She looked up into the daylight glare. "There's this picture I have of my mother, when she was young, slender, and willowy. Her hair's gold like that sun up there, and it just pours down her back. She's got her hands out, dancing in the middle of a field of orange poppies." A tear escaped her eye, stinging her, and she wiped it off.

"That's the mother I want to remember, free and natural, not the shuffling shadow of a woman I see in the nursing home."

Gareth nodded. "I know what you mean. The last few times I saw my grandmum in her little village, it was the same way. She stayed in bed, and she was looking at me, but she wasn't really looking at me. She kept mumbling in Welsh about the stories she'd heard as a child, as if they'd really happened. As if she couldn't tell fantasy from reality anymore."

Denise took Gareth's hand in her own, an oddly maternal gesture for someone as irascible as she usually was. She licked her dry lips, then smiled wistfully. "Well, let's get to it. Those fossils won't find themselves."

He smiled back at her, and she headed off toward the side of the mountain she had been eyeing. Gareth decided to keep in the open, casting his eyes methodically down at the scree beneath his boots. Step by step he lost himself as though once more journeying back into primeval antiquity, into an enchanted land that wasn't dead or sterile. The crunch of sandstone beneath his feet fell away, replaced by the soft feel of prehistoric bryophytic mosses, the air now thick and steamy and semi-tropical. Off in the shady green leaves that fountained from the brown-gray trunk of a cycad, a white *Dimorphodon* nestled like some bird of good omen.

Gareth's reverie was extinguished by a sound that echoed like a shot across the mountainside. It took him a disoriented moment to realize that what he had heard was the sharp, strangled scream of a man's voice. It had come from the rise, several hundred meters away, where Arkady had been prospecting. Gareth paused, not breathing, listening in the thin polar air. Now all he heard was Denise calling out Arkady's name. He took out his radio and tried to establish contact, but he received no answer.

Then he began to run. Hefting his pack onto his shoulders, Gareth hurried toward the source of the scream. In the distance on the scree-scarred terrain, he could see Denise and Mei hurrying toward the same location, converging on the source of the cry. He felt out of shape and older than he was, his chest stinging sharply as he drew in breaths. But he dared not stop, both from concern and—to be honest—curiosity. For what could create such sudden hazard here at the bottom of the earth? Snow and ice and wind were nature's scourges in this clime, but the day was calm and temperate, and Gareth could think of nothing that might create danger so abruptly.

He arrived last of the three. As he approached, he could see Denise and Mei's bodies shivering in a manner that owed nothing to the day's mild chill. Atop the rise, sprawled prone amid the loose stone, lay Arkady's body. Vacant eyes stared like fixtures of glass into the empty sky. His stiffening left hand still clutched his phone. The gray ground around his neck was drinking up the blood that even now was streaming from his ruptured throat. And though it was Arkady's very life spilling out of him, Gareth almost gasped at how unnatural it looked in its vivid coloring: whether in tents or in parkas or here in fresh blood, only humans brought red to the stark Antarctic landscape.

"Bloody hell," Gareth muttered. He suddenly grew terribly conscious of his body, of the air that inflated his lungs as he inhaled, of his heart pumping blood through his veins, blood that he should never have to see as he was seeing it now. He tore his eyes free from the corpse to scan the horizon, to seek out any glimpse of movement, yet he saw nothing but loose stone nudged by the winds.

"What . . . I mean, what the hell is this?" Denise demanded, as though the land might cry out in answer to her to her plaint. "There are no predators here."

"This is not a predator act," Mei noted quietly. "Look at his throat. That is not a cut of tooth or claw."

Gareth glanced back down and saw that she was right. The skin was sliced neatly, almost surgically.

"What?" Denise persisted. "Then a person? But what kind of killer is out here in the middle of nowhere?"

Keeping his eyes on the desolate topography, Gareth crouched down and rummaged through his pack until his fingers seized on his pickaxe. "I don't know, Denise, any more than you do," he said as he rose, brandishing the axe. "But we have to get back to camp."

"What do you mean?" Denise asked.

"I don't know who or what did this," Gareth replied. "But I'm no bloody soldier. We need to get back to more people, back to the tents."

Mei picked up her radio to signal them, but Gareth raised an admonishing hand. "Let's hurry back and tell them in person. I don't even know if they'll believe us. And if they did and came back here, we'd just be drawing them into danger too."

"But what if one of them is the killer?" Mei whispered.

"All the more reason not to alert them yet," Gareth told her. "We don't know if any of them are, but certainly they aren't *all* killers. I say we leave Arkady here, return to camp, and bring some of our people back."

Denise shook her head. "I don't want to leave him here, that insufferable bastard," she said, choking on tears. "Him and his damned phone."

"The phone!" Mei exclaimed. "I think it's still recording."

Without any further words she pried the phone from his fingers and began swiping. Eyes still glancing about him nervously, Gareth looked over her shoulder at the gleaming glass surface, which was scarred by a web of little cracks at the corner. Mei searched through his videos until she found the most recent, completed just minutes earlier.

"Do you think he got any images of his attacker?" Denise asked, peering at the screen from over Mei's other shoulder.

One more swipe and tap and then Mei had the latest video playing. There was Arkady's face, alive and grinning with the goofy charisma he had carefully cultivated his entire professional life. Behind him, slightly shuddering, was a limb of Mount Kirkpatrick and a slice of cerulean sky.

"Welcome back," announced his tinny voice. "I'm not far from a promising formation, one that should be really ancient. If we just— Oh, God!"

He swore as the image wheeled wildly about before settling on the cold blank burn of blue above. Mei rewound the video. "Welcome back," Arkady said again, and Gareth watched, the axe in his hand trembling, knowing he was watching his friend's death, a death that was raw and fresh. Mei slowed the frames on Arkady's final words, his lips opening and closing slowly, silently, until a flash appeared on the frame. It was a blade, short and feather-slender, its sheeny surface near white from the sun's rays. Beneath the glinting Gareth saw what looked like an alien alphabet set in damascene relief.

But what truly terrified him was the hand that gripped the blade. It was the green-blue of unsullied ocean, smooth as salamander skin, with four thready fingers wrapped round the hilt. The hand and its knife were gone from view an instant later, and the camera caught no further image of this assailant, only the pale expanse and the sound of Arkady's last gurgling cry.

Mei dropped the phone, her frame wracked in sudden shaking. She got down and began to rifle through her pack, looking for a weapon as Gareth had done. At last she grabbed a chisel in one hand and her rock hammer in the other before rising back to her feet.

"Dr. Holloway," she said, for her mentor was still standing, dumbfoundedly staring at the fallen phone. "*Denise.* We must go."

"This just doesn't *happen,*" Denise objected, her voice almost petulant. "We're in *Antarctica,* for Christ's sake."

Mei tucked the chisel into a pocket and stretched out her free hand. Slowly, tentatively, Denise reached out to take it.

The attack came then, with no warning. Gareth had been feverishly looking around him and seen nothing; standing as he was upon the rise, he had a good view of their surroundings. But the form that burst toward them seemed to come from out of the earth. Whether it had been buried in soil and stone or secreted in some eldritch camouflage, he could not say, but in an eye-blink's time a thin shape like a juniper shadow thrust forward toward the two women. Gareth saw a flurry of motion, limbs flailing and slashing. Mei struggled to grab her chisel in time but, too late, was cast tumbling over the ridge of the rise to the sharp stones below. Denise brought up her hands to ward off the danger, managing to catch one of the thing's wrists. But its knife hand was free, and before Gareth could close the gap it sliced through her neck as smoothly as it had done to Arkady.

Yet Denise's defense and the killing motion cost the attacker some seconds, and that was enough time for Gareth to swing his pickaxe. He could feel in his muscles their memory of his decade on the cricket pitch, and in a cleaner arc than he could have imagined he plunged the sharp metal head into the being's flesh. As he completed the motion, he pivoted so as to pull the axe free and keep it in his hand, and then he stumbled backward on the rise and looked out.

The creature cried out, in a voice like the wail of storm wind through trees, but even in its agony this wailing was music more lilting and winsome than any human tune sung in joy. And at last Gareth could see the thing in full view, for it had collapsed back against the great wall of Mount Kirkpatrick behind the rise, opposite to his own position. Its whole body shone the same teal tint as its blade-hand, nakedly glistering in the high sun's rays. It was slender and small, perhaps 150 centimeters in height, with thin limbs that flowed as though formed from a thousand joints. Its face looked almost human, with the same features of physiognomy, though the proportions were off. The mouth and nostrils appeared too small and too round, while the open eyes were too large, with vast irises that shimmered green-gold. Gareth couldn't say if the thing had ears, for thick, foam-white hair cascaded down across its shoulders to its back.

"What the hell are you?" he panted, murmuring to himself.

"Curse you, man."

Gareth's breath caught in his throat at the words. Were they words? Were they words in English or words in Welsh? He didn't know; all he knew was that the being was communicating, opening its mouth, sending forth sounds his way. And somewhere, in some deep alcove of his soul, he could recognize their meaning.

For a moment they stared at one another in silence. Then Gareth looked down at Denise's face, her graying brown hair framing her fear-fraught vacant brown eyes, her blood still welling up across her butchered throat. And, tears singeing his sight, he opened his dry, wind-scoured lips and asked the question that burned within him.

"Why did you do this?"

The being breathed, gathering great inhalations of the polar air. It never stopped glaring at Gareth. "Why are you here?" it asked, floating its fluting voice into the cold. "Will you never stop?"

"I don't understand," Gareth responded quietly.

"I think you do. Look at me. Let your soul remember. You know what I am, child of man."

"Good God, you're *tylwyth teg*," Gareth said in a voice soft as breeze-blown grass. "You're what grandmum used to speak about."

He thought back to those tales she had told, knowing now that she had spoken them as memories, not as myths. The dementia had not been forging false images in her mind while her wasted body lay, frail and febrile, in the bed she was soiling; it had been peeling back the decades, bringing her to a youth in the deep sacred spaces of Welsh woods.

"I knew you knew," it declared.

"But the fair folk . . . what are you doing here? Here in Antarctica, in the deadest and coldest place? This isn't any kind of place for something like you."

The creature scowled, and though it could never fail to be beautiful, its frown was ghastly, like a wound to its face.

"Where else might I go?" it wailed, its torment echoing across the mountains. Then it gathered its alien dignity and continued. "My kind walked the wolds and copses and thickets long before any men carved out their trails. We dressed in pink foxgloves and sang the shrill song of the nightjar or the chirrup of the skylark. We knew the enchanted places of the world, and where we traveled, we carried our enchantment with us.

"Then your kind came, simple and strange with your war against the world. You loved us, for we grew like the garden you had lost. And we loved you, for you were weak, and yet you peered beyond the walls of the world to something you could not see, something we did not even know to look for. Some us even cleaved to your kind, and you gave them souls, souls that brought sorrow and sacrifice . . ." The being's eyes were bright and opaque and burning as autumn foliage. ". . . souls you do not even remember that you have."

"Are all the old tales true?" Gareth asked, his own eyes like mirrors from his weeping. He watched the entity as a man in a grotto looking through a cascade.

"How ought I to know which of your tales hold truth and which are false? I know only my life, watching as you gashed the grass and the ground, fleeing as you felled trees that I loved and frolicked on. Choking in terror as, one by one, my kin were torn apart by the unearthly things of your hands."

"Is that why you are here?"

It nodded, its white hair settling like snow upon its shoulders. "All my homes are gone. In this dead land alone, I thought, perhaps I might have peace once more."

"Come back with us, then," Gareth implored. Glancing once more at Denise and Arkady, he said, "You shouldn't have done this. You shouldn't have killed them. They would not have harmed you. But I understand."

"I have learned through many long ages that you do *not* understand."

"The human world has changed," Gareth insisted. "We know the destruction we caused, and we're looking for ways to turn it back. That's why we're *here*."

The inhuman nostrils flared. "But you *are* here." And without another word it leapt at him.

Gareth had steeled himself for the attack, yet the melody of the being's words had lulled him. He swung his pickaxe, but his assailant was too close for the sharp point to enter its soft flesh. The axe's handle was able to make contact with the entity's knife hand, parrying away what otherwise would have been a killing blow across his throat. But its body now loomed over his, and though it was small, its muscles flowed with the sap of green life and power. Gareth strained to keep its knife hand away, but its other arm was free, and it brought its cord-like fingers to his throat. He felt the wind leaving him, and in the moment, absurdly, he mused at how little he had thought about his breathing in his life until now, the moment it was gone. A darkness began occluding the periphery of his vision like some weird eclipse, until only the being's face remained. Its foamy hair tented and tickled his face, almost shrouding its great glade-green eyes and the lovely, feral scowl of its minute mouth.

Then he heard the crunching of stone beneath boots, and a cry of *"Líkāi zhèlǐ!"* resounded across the mountainside. The pressure eased upon his neck, and the knife hand loosened, giving him time to scuttle backward toward the edge of the rise. He hefted his pickaxe and savored the sweetness of the crisp air, watching his exhalations mist in front of him.

Ahead of him he saw Mei, rock hammer in hand. Her round face dripped red from half a dozen scratches, caked in spots by gray earth. But she had scored a wound on the creature's temple, and its hair was smeared with its blood, which also coated her hammer. Gareth realized that it had been bleeding throughout their conversation from a rent in its side that he had caused, which he had somehow failed to notice. He noticed now: its blood was unlike any shade he had even seen, a brilliant, alive color that seemed somehow every color, like a woven rainbow. He could smell it from across the dead ground, a scent like daffodil and saxifrage that was incongruous in the sterile fields of the Antarctic.

"You killed them!" Mei shouted accusingly in English. "Get the hell away from here!"

The being was doubled over in pain, but as sinuous and terrible and exquisite as ever. It rose to its full height, spectral gore now flowing unchecked from its wounds, and lashed out at Mei. She had expected the attack and jumped backward; but she was a paleontology grad student, not a warrior, and she lost her footing as she landed. She kept the presence of mind to roll as she fell, and the entity missed her throat with its blade.

Gareth knew then that his last chance was come. As the creature swiped its knife at Mei, he ran forward and once more swung his pickaxe with whatever strength remained in his muscles. The blow caught the being cleanly in its naked chest, sinking with such force that the axe head remained embedded as it staggered under the agony of the assault. Gareth was forced to release the hilt while the creature collapsed on its back to the rocky ground.

Its fingers loosened, and its blade quietly fell to the crusty terrain. The slender teal lips parted, and it began to murmur in sibilant susurration. Gareth knelt to its side and held its hand. The skin was waxy, like a plant leaf, but he could feel the life drying and dying within it. He listened to the whisper of the thing and nodded.

"Yes," he said, and the syllable caught in his throat.

Then its mouth closed, and its eyes dimmed to the twilit black of cinder. The flesh bubbled and rippled, fell away into liquid and then into wisps of foam, which were caught by the polar winds and dispersed into the air. Gareth remained crouched for a time before rising with the silver blade in his hand.

"Dr. Treharne?" said Mei, looking at him quizzically with her nut-brown eyes. "What did it say to you?"

Gareth looked at her and shook his head mournfully. "Nothing," he replied. Then he tucked the knife away in the pocket of his red parka, sighing. He and Mei stood alone on the earth that had once been lush and green and now lay, outleant, desiccated, and dead beneath a barren and blue sky and the seemingly distant sun that warmed it.

WHAT IF ATLANTIS . . . ?

What if Atlantis sank by slow degrees,
Not overnight, awash in cataclysm?
What if it joined the deep sea's black abysm
Foredoomed first by ten thousand auguries,
Its precious scrolls unread in libraries
By archons spouting speech extolling schism
To incensed throngs anointed by the chrism
Of rage and wat'ry wine in quantities
Too full for any mortal mind to bear?
What if its minor prophets' imprecations
Crashed lifeless on the armor of their pride,
Eyes lusty, glassy, glossy, unaware
That each night's sticky, sickly sweet libations
Drown out th'encroaching taste of saline tide?

ADEPT

And beyond them, where they stared in troubled and restless wonder,
the darkness was illumed with the strange light.

—Clark Ashton Smith, "A Vintage from Atlantis"

Of course, the parking lot was empty as I walked to the side entrance
of the library. Most of the snow had melted, save for the remnants of
plow-piles from last week. The night sky was dark and overcast,
though the spangling of amber Christmas lights wrapped around
campus's trees served as a substitute for the stars I couldn't see. In
that strange artificial brightness I watched my ephemeral breath
emerge with each exhalation, only to be dispersed at once by the December wind. On the perimeter of the parking lot, shadows of the
trees splayed out like skeletal fingers, but I stayed squarely in the light
until I reached the shadow of the edifice. Reflected in the window of
the entrance, all I could see were the little streaks of gray in the hair
that framed my face.

I snatched the ID badge from my lanyard to scan it, then fumbled
through my coat pocket until I found the key. As always, the old door
yielded grudgingly; as always, I felt a brief, absurd surge of panic as I
opened it, fearing the alarm, though the security light shone green.
The door closed behind me, and now only the red glow of exit signs
illuminated the foyer.

That glow was all I needed. What else could I need? I had
walked these halls at night dozens of times, and at this time of night I
could work without the interruption of coworkers, in the comfort of an
oversized sweatshirt and tennis shoes rather than a blouse and heels.
Besides, my Christmas gifts had been ordered online weeks ago, so I
could either stay alone at the apartment listening to my neighbor and

her boyfriend fighting or copulating (or both), or I could make some progress in my research at a time when I had the place all to myself. Now inside, I breathed a sigh of relief at the building's climate-controlled warmth, a breath I could not see. I walked past the check-in point, where an anachronistically sleek sign read "Welcome to the D'Ambrosio Renaissance Library" in red sans-serif lettering.

Beyond that, the DRL started to look more like the museum it truly was. The corridor was lined on either side by canvases, products from the workshops of famous artists or originals from minor painters of the fifteenth and sixteenth centuries. Once again I couldn't help pausing at my favorite, a rendition of Prometheus by some obscure Paduan. This Prometheus was noble, his nude muscled form standing with poise while bearing a great sphere of flame in an outstretched arm, as though he were proffering it to the viewer. Around the creases of the flame one could make out wraithlike figures, like the angels in Tintoretto's *Last Supper.* But these figures were no angels; I have never known what they were meant to be. Even in the careful light of operating hours those spirits were indistinct; here in the night I could almost forget they were there. And that didn't bother me; after all, it was the great, benevolent countenance of Prometheus that excited me.

Passing through a door framed by the volutes and fluting of ionic columns, I walked across the rotunda, and the echo of my footsteps sundered the silence. In daytime the blue of the vaulted ceiling shone like a Giotto heaven; but without the lights or the sun to shine through, the color was lost in deep night. I hastened along the marble floor to the small side door that descended into the archives. Once more flashing my badge to a machine, I pushed open the door and continued.

The stairs that led down to the archives were quite unlike the grandeur of the DRL's public sections. They were gray concrete flanked by simple metal rails against off-white walls. One day the library would have to spend the money to make the archives wheelchair accessible, but for now this nondescript staircase was the only way in. So I walked down the steps in the red-tinted deep darkness.

But I paused when I reached the archive entrance because a

flickering light was shining out of the door's little windowpane. Pulsations of fear rippled from my chest through my limbs. Grades had been turned in; resident students had returned home; neither IT nor Maintenance worked in the library at these hours. Christmas was still a few days away, but break had already begun. Who could be here? And why was the light that I saw the dancing, sputtering light of flame?

Curiosity seized me, overwhelming for a moment the fear. Clutching my tablet tightly, I brought my shoes down the final steps as quietly as I could and muted my breathing until I came to the window. Tentatively, ready to flee in an instant, I peeked across the unreflecting glass and into the archive room.

The illumination came from the great yew-wood table that stood about ten feet inside the room. On it stood two simple red candles, beside which rested a plain white lighter. The dim, uneven glow of the candles created a tiny, tenuous bubble of light around the table, which was strewn with texts from the surrounding shelves. These were ancient texts, centuries old, restricted from general patrons. I recognized one with a great gilt cover, which lay open near one of the candles. Just beyond it, seated in a chair, was the person who had removed the books, his eyes cast down in concentration on the tome.

"Carson?" I said, opening the door.

His head snapped up quickly as I spoke. "Dr. Cornelius?" he responded. "I—I obviously wasn't expecting to see you here."

"I might say the same," I countered, smirking as I advanced toward the table.

Carson was my research assistant, and he looked more or less the way I always saw him, fidgeting nervously, yet oddly content when surrounded by antique books. He was sallow and slender—I might almost say gaunt—with well-coiffed glossy black hair. In class and conversation he almost never met my gaze, but here his hazel eyes looked right back at mine, though the reflected candles cast an orange glaze across his pupils.

"I would guess we're here for the same reason," he suggested. "Research?"

"Sure. And of course you're welcome in the DRL whenever you need to be here. But, at the risk of stating the obvious, we do have lights in the building. You know there'll be hell to pay if the university finds you lit candles in here."

He hesitated, glanced down at the table and the books, then looked back up at me. "Yeah. I imagine it looks kind of weird. I do have a reason for them, though."

"You just really wanted the archives to smell like . . . God, what is that, sandalwood?"

He nodded, then gestured for me to join him. I shrugged and walked closer to the table where he sat. Now I saw that several texts were open on the table, and many more were stacked on the periphery. He had a laptop with him, the glow of its screen the only other light aside from the candles. On that screen I could see what looked like strange figures, set beside a variety of words in Latin and Greek.

"What the hell . . . ?" I murmured.

"Yeah," he chuckled, "exactly."

"Carson, how did you do this? How did you figure these out?"

"Algorithms, mostly. I know you've been trying to decipher that alphabet for half your career, and I had a hunch about how those characters might be arranged, so I worked up a program to figure it out."

I knelt down beside him, still stuck in stupefied silence. He was right; I'd spent fifteen years trying to make out the lettering of those pages. Once I discovered this seemingly unremarkable yellowing book tucked away in a lonely corner of the archives, I had known right away that it could be my ticket at last to tenure. The fact that it was a detailed and hitherto uncatalogued sixteenth-century alchemical text was tantalizing enough. But then there were those six pages near the end, written in an alphabet more baffling than the scrawlings of the Voynich Manuscript.

Over the years I had been chipping away at the Latin sections, periodically presenting or publishing chapters as I completed them. I had pored over them so much that whole paragraphs or stanzas were embedded in my memory. And the allure only grew with time. The author of the book promised incantations older than historical civilization, dating back to Atlantis. He swore himself an adept from a long lineage of alchemists and sorcerers, revealing enchantments that had never been transcribed in any Indo-European tongue. It was all juicy stuff, and I had long hoped that if could make sense of those final pages, the combination of arcane subject matter and unrelenting imaginative force might be enough to pique the interest of a publisher more ambitious than any generic university press.

I knew Carson helped supplement his RA stipend with freelance coding work, and he'd been invaluable in helping me collate my materials over the past year and a half. I even knew that he came into the DRL after hours to work sometimes; I was, indeed, the one who had given him the keys and the clearance. But what I saw on that screen, if his program was accurate, went well beyond any expectations I could have envisioned. For the first time, it seemed, we could read the hidden esoterica of this five-hundred-year-old quarto.

"Damn," I whispered, peering at the screen. There they were: the invocations of an Early Modern thaumaturge, and Carson and I may have been the first human beings to read them since their writing. "And what do they say?"

"I think . . . well, I think they do pretty much what you'd expect based on what you've already translated. If they're uttered the right way, they give the speaker access to realms of power that we could never imagine."

"Wow," I gasped. "This'll be huge. I'm sure we can find a mainstream publisher for this. With all the work you've put into this, you really deserved co-author status, Carson."

I expected he'd be excited, albeit in his peculiarly reserved way. But at those words he looked over at me with a grin that was strangely bemused, almost incredulous.

"Dr. Cornelius, that's not what I mean. I'm not talking about publication or tenure. The incantations in here—you get it, right? They're real. They really did come from Atlantis."

Carson had been such a joy to teach that, with some effort, I quelled a sarcastic response. Trying not to sound condescending, I said, "Atlantis is just a myth, just Plato making up stories for moral purposes, like he always did."

". . . because there is no Atlantis, no magic, right. That's what I thought too." He looked right at me with an abrupt intensity, and his features appeared all ash and flame in the light. "But then I tried them. Dr. Cornelius, I tried them, and they *work*."

For a moment I simply stared, mouth half open. Realizing how unprofessional I must look, I regained my equanimity, forcing an expression of stoic, generic interest.

"Can you tell me what you mean by that?" I inquired.

His earnest but playful Cheshire-Cat grin widened. "I'll *show* you."

He turned away from me back to the laptop. The image moved, and I could see that he was scrolling down the page. Then he came to a passage and began to recite a stanza. At first it sounded little different from any moment I might have heard in class, when he was always eager to read a section from the assigned textbook, whatever language it might be written in. But as he continued to speak, a curious thing happened. The words he was speaking sounded vaguely familiar to me, but he had imparted to his speech an uncharacteristic lilt, giving his words a lilting melodiousness I had never heard from him before. Then the candles flared unexpectedly, expanding the range of their firelight. Carson's voice sounded different now, quiet and distorted, as though I were listening to him from underwater.

The scene of the archive room began to fall away, like paint being scraped from a canvas. But beneath this scene there was another. A piece at a time, shelf and book and wall flaked off, and I found myself looking at a great vista, one that might have been a Renaissance painting itself. I stood high on a promontory, and spread out beneath me, cradled proudly in a high hillside, lay a vast city that stretched down to a bustling harbor. The sun was sinking into the sea in the west toward which the harbor faced, the sky exploding in orange along the cyan horizon, and a great commerce of ships went to and fro from the city's docks, their luxuriantly woven sails embracing the breeze like lovers. Temples rose high upon grand pillars, carved from marble of pale pink and rich red, polished to shine in the waning sun's splendor. Palaces towered higher even than the temples, wrought in a fluid dance of angle and curvature, all harmonized by a geometry that seemed invented for such beauty.

Yet there was more to the sight than grandeur and sublimity. There were houses, modest residences tucked into the threaded avenues, small yet no less elegant than the impossible symmetries of the public edifices, adorned by the weave of wine-grape trellises or little floral patterns etched minutely into window frames. Lately washed robes lay drying on cords, and the householders' green and blue fabrics were scarcely less brilliant or carefully constructed than the blood-purple vestments of priests and nobles.

And about the streets walked the people, grand and beautiful people, with flowing hair and brazen skin, sensuous and wise and imperious in their bearing, walking in stately dignity not unalloyed with tricksterish mischief. They spoke in a tongue more ancient and true than Sumerian or Sanskrit, yet I knew what they were saying and could eavesdrop upon them as they discoursed on rich philosophy and haggled over merchandise and cooed to their lightly resting infants. As the day dropped, and men and women ambled purposefully but unhurriedly toward their homes, it seemed to me a picture of every national and domestic perfection I could have imagined and desired—and yes, my desire was bent toward this land and its abundances.

So when it flashed out of my view, I gasped as though I had lost my breath. The candle-lit archives looked shadowy next to the vividness of the vision I had been forced from, and the air felt cold and dry when set against the tropical lushness of the city's clime. Pale Carson was grinning at me, and the familiarity of him anchored me home, though he looked like a faded draft of the exquisite folk whose world I had just seen.

"What was that?" I asked, my voice cracking like an adolescent's.

"You saw it, right?" he said.

"I saw . . ."

He grabbed my arm—Carson, who had never touched me before. "You saw *Atlantis*—the civilization before there was civilization. I brought forth that vision, from the past where it had just been floating. I took it, and I put you inside it."

I squinted. "What are those candles made from again?"

"Stop dodging the question," he insisted. "What I just did—that's *nothing*. That's like . . . a kid with the alphabet. But I can *read* this stuff."

I looked at him, then looked up around at the library, where row upon row of books were shrouded in darkness, all but the texts Carson had set upon the table before us. "What does it say, then? What can you do?"

He nodded. "Now you've got it." He clenched his fists and shook his arms, like a baby holding rattles. "It's *so exciting!* We can finally do it, Dr. Cornelius. We can put it all right."

"Put it right . . . ?" I repeated inquisitively.

"*It.* Everything. The world that's all so wrong." He paused, licked his lips as though gathering his thoughts, then resumed. "Think about all the bad stuff that's happened to you. Think about Dave and what he did to you, all his lies, all those manipulations, all those things you would tell me about on Thursday afternoons when the divorce was finalizing. All those damned old men who tried to stop you from finishing your Ph.D."

"Carson, you don't have to bring that up . . ."

He looked at me now with the fixed intensity of a prophet. "No, I mean it. It's not just you. I think about all those years in school, all the bullies—God, with a name like Carson Bacon! Thinking in college that it would stop, that I'd be with people who *got* me, and then still getting hurt and betrayed, over and over and *over* again.

"And then multiply that a billion times and worse. The world, the injustices, the people who get hurt, the people without power." His eyes burned white hot, not from candle flame but from raw, kinetic purpose. *"We are the ones with the power now."*

I didn't reply but looked over his shoulder again at the screen. He turned it toward me so I could see more clearly. The translation he had generated with his technology and his natural aptitude—it all made sense. The words here were like flowers nourished in the soil of the text I already knew. Separately, the Latin previously embedded in my mind and the deciphered text before me were dead letters, historical artifacts to be bandied about by a tiny coterie of scholars— scholars like me. Taken together, however, they erupted in vibrant, terrifying life. Even reading them this way, silently on a secondhand laptop screen, my teeth chattered as a surge of inarticulate energy seemed to writhe through my arteries. Scrolling down the page, I committed the words to memory even as I saw them, not through any great prowess of intellect but just because now they made *so much sense.*

"God damn," I breathed.

"Yeah," he affirmed. "So the question is, Dr. Cornelius . . . what do you want to do?"

"Show me more." My voice was barely audible, dry grass crackling in wind. "What can we do?"

Again he spoke words of yore, and as he did so, it sunk into me: scrawny Carson Bacon—who ate ramen noodles for breakfast and completed smuggled crossword puzzles at student orientations, sitting here at night in a burgundy collared shirt—might be the greatest sorcerer alive. The forces he invoked didn't scorn the childishly nasal intonation of his voice; they simply gathered when he called them.

And gather they did. I have never been punched—not even by Dave at his angriest—though I imagine it feels like the weird intangible pressures that seemed to pummel my side as Carson spoke. But it was more than a sharp pressure; I felt too a squeezing, a constricting, not in my muscles but in my soul. If you had asked me an hour earlier whether I even *had* a soul, I would not have known how to respond; but the great chaotic rush that flooded my meditations gave me my answer. I knew my soul by the phalanx of unnamable entities that now stood garrisoned around it.

This was Carson's power, and he would share it with me; it might be mine as well as his. Now I pictured Dave, that ingratiating, sheepish, wolfish grin he proffered whenever I called out his deceptions, and those angular features handsome in an almost comic-book way beneath his stylized auburn beard. He was talking—God, he's *always* talking—and I could hear the tones but not the words, because how could I care about his words, knowing them all to be falsehoods? And now I realized what I might do—how, with some words of my own, I could at last silence that damned mouth of his. String together a few odd syllables, and I could rend him into a thousand thousand tiny strands of man, shredded atomies of blood and bone, yet each piece still sentient and screaming mindlessly from the agony of it all.

From Dave I worked backward, even as Carson had suggested, through all the wounds across five decades, the little casual scars that so many people had taken the time to carve into my soul. They didn't feel like scars anymore: each hurt was fresh and raw and bleeding again, from the amassed pain of years to a word carelessly spoken. Time, I realized, had not healed them, so perhaps these spells might succeed where time had failed, wreaking their stark justice upon my enemies.

Through the gallery of my foes' faces I peeked out and again saw Carson here with me in the library. But now his face was nothing like the face as I had ever seen it before. Fire and shadow clouded his features, which were twisted into an ecstasy of devotion, the expression of a lover. Yet he was not looking toward anyone or anything, and I did not know what object of adoration was pictured behind his closed eyes. He mumbled the exotic phrases of the book as a mystic must mumble prayers—passionately, breathily.

So intent was he in those moments, so singularly focused on his desire, that I suppose he forgot my presence, and so he let slip free the vision he had been withholding from me. He had enticed me with the sight of Atlantis in its glory, the joyance of the wild, wise land in the aeon of its youth. Through a crack in his discipline, however, I could now behold what he hadn't dared reveal: its dying.

There was that same great port city from that same lofty precipice; yet it was changed. Cracks veined its exquisite colonnades, and chips of stone had eroded free. The panorama was dotted with some buildings taller than even those I had first seen, but they were ugly constructions, their blocky and functional gray bulks incongruous with the workmanship of the neighborhoods into which they had been inserted. Layers of mud and lichen clung to the homes of the ordinary citizens, while paint and plaster were peeling off.

And those citizens looked scarcely better than their abodes. Some in the courts and palaces and temples were still lovely; but a callow, cruel loveliness, beautiful men and women sequestered in disdain from the serpentine streets eating and drinking, then gossiping and retching, and doing it all again when the messes were cleaned. Outside in the streets, the mud and lichens were smeared blearily across the skin and robes of the folk who could not afford to be beautiful and who languished in the choking stench of fresh shit and festering death. I knew somehow that if I searched deep enough, I could have found scattered remnants somewhere, people of the same dignity and prudence as their ancestors, prophets who implored in vain their neighbors to be wary of calamity. Perhaps they had their eyes to the horizon, but no one else did.

But more than all this, I knew that beyond the welter of decay and transgression, among kings and queens and generals and natural philosophers, curious wizards held open on their tables scrolls bearing words like the ones I now could read. They were summoning forth powers from galaxies and dimensions that would have blinded their minds if they had given them a second thought. Yet why ought they to care about the sources of their strength? There were wars to be won and enemies to be subdued. At the cost of a few moments' mumblings they held all destinies of Atlantis in their grasp.

Or so they imagined, until the day to whose dawning I now bore witness. All the forces the magicians had gathered so assiduously across the years chose this day to flash forth their freedom. The earth at the people's feet dried and ruptured, as mummy flesh, then shuddered like a wild ox shaking off a brittle yoke. Greater quakes followed, and proud towers tumbled on men and women of all rank and stature. The day passed on in my vision, wrack after wrack splintering the gates of the city until, in the evening's last red waning, following the track of twilight, a wave of salt spume that seemed to brush the clouds came racing eastward. The harbor was crowded with ships of people hoping to escape the tremors, and the wet splintered remains of those ships were cast with the limbs of their pilots upon the city's great hill, for the wave exceeded the highest heights of Atlantis. As it came, I felt a bitter bilious surge in my throat, an instant of ineluctable death as a plummeting person must know, for that horrendous tide engulfed my sight.

Then I woke from my vision, and I knew what must happen.

"Carson," I said, my voice hushed through gentleness or terror. "We can't use this. It's not right."

He looked at me, his chapped lips slightly parted, and his eyes grew glossy with restrained tears of betrayal.

"I don't understand," he responded. "I thought you'd be excited about this. All the days we talked about how bad everything was, how we needed to empower other voices. Dr. Cornelius, this is *power.*"

I averted my gaze, shook my head. "This isn't what I meant."

His chest heaved with great, shallow breaths, and in a whisper that was also a scream, he exclaimed, *"Why did you say it if you didn't mean it?"* Reining in his rage, he turned back to the book. "It's—it's okay. You weren't ready; it's wrong of me to hurry you. But *I'm* ready. I'll make things right, and then you'll see. Then they'll all see."

"Carson, please don't—" I began, but he was already chanting new spells as though I were not even beside him.

Once again I felt the coarse knotting in my soul that tracked with his words of power; and caught in that suffocation of spirit, without even knowing what I was doing, I started to speak. The words, those same words, came to me at my requirement. I had no need to read them, for year after year I had embedded them into my thoughts, my very movement, and all it had taken was Carson's transliteration to unlock their fullness. Carson had spent weeks in perfecting the technique of his incantations, but I had spent years living them.

Don't try to stop me. Carson's mouth was still uttering arcana, but he thrust these thoughts at me even as he did so. Yet I could now perceive that beneath that simple injunction was stretched out a great ocean of rage and pain, deeper perhaps than even my own anger. Who could have guessed this, passing by Magnus Hall on a typical semester weekday, that untenured Renaissance scholar Dr. Alicia Cornelius and her unassuming protégé Carson Bacon carried in their psyches such layers of wrath and spite and vile vitriol as might rend the very cosmos?

Leave the books, I implored silently back, and in the world of atoms and physics I stretched out a hand to try to touch him, like the mother I now saw he wished I could be. But he pulled his hand back as though I were a snake, clenching the fist, still speaking in ancient tongues, and so I had to do the same.

Then the powers assembled about us in the room, intelligences invoked in human language but which no vocabulary could describe. In the DRL archives, my body sat whole and well, but my soul burned in their presence with a fire that was orgasmic and agonizing, and I was in love with them and aghast at them all at once. And I wondered how Carson, or the Atlantean sages before him, could ever be so foolish as think for a moment that these powers were theirs, for I too was aware of them, and I too desired them—oh, my blood and marrow throbbed for them—but I could never forget how casually they might crush me.

So it was, then, that I recited my own words against Carson's. I called down curses from beneath the stars—the library echoed with my screaming words—and I loved Carson, and so I hated him for bringing me to this night, this dreadful combat. I longed for him to yield and cease his speech, to become once more the meek, awkward grad student I pictured in my mind. But he did not yield, shouting words back, wrinkling his lip, and he spoke into a sneer as he sought to command the forces that were congregating around us.

In panic, I cried out one last lone phrase from the text on the table. That phrase was enough. It was like kicking out the final support to a tottering scaffold, and suddenly all Carson's intricate magic collapsed, and the weight of the powers rushed upon him like the vast Atlantic tide. A roar filled my ears, or my soul, or both, a roar like the end of an aeon, and then darkness.

I woke from the darkness into darkness, for the candles had guttered out, though their scent hung in the air. But I smelled more than sandalwood in the archives. Fumbling about, I found and grasped the little lighter, and after several unsuccessful clicks I was able to set once more a tiny sphere of flame atop one of the candles. Carson's body sat face down upon the table, blood dripping quietly from his ears and his nose and his empty eyes. His stiff left hand was clutching at the ancient book, while his right was stretched toward his tablet. Wordlessly I brought my face down and kissed the top of his head on his perfectly combed hair, which absorbed my tears. Gathering up the book and the tablet into my arms, I stared into the candle's meager fire and breathed a sigh.

A Voice in the Night

We sent a signal deep into the night,
A puling pulse cast cautiously into
An empty airless ocean, for we knew
(Or thought we knew) that in its fluttering flight
It fain would find a friend. We shone a light
Through dark demesnes to blaze the blue-black queue
Of quasars, nebulae, with all the rue
Of desolation, desperate for the sight
Of one bare blip in answer, just a whisper,
A voice not ours from out the cosmos. But
The night spills only silence, and our prone
Scared souls behold the cold sky, cleaner, crisper.
And in the deathly dearth of winter, what
Wise words will warm us . . . if we are alone?

ARBITRESS OF TIDES

> While I am doomed—by life's long storm opprest . . .
> —Charlotte Smith, *Elegiac Sonnets*

Though the dwindling twilight still glows on the western waters, I can already see the moon ascending in the sky as I emerge from the chapel. Beneath the precipice on which I stand, the tides heave in tumult and claw like beasts at the scarred cliffside. The winds that trail behind the storm that lately passed are whistling about me. They tug at my sap-brown hair, causing it to stream out eastward, stray locks tickling my forehead. The last orange rays squeezed onto the seething sea make the waters look like brands of flame. Above the spumy surge the moon rests, tossing out great energies, but in herself tranquil.

I turn toward the southside churchyard, to seek out Jacob's grave before the darkness sets in. I want to see the epitaph once again, though I have seen it so many times before, and I know it will never change. My fingers trace the worn carven letters that gleam against the encroaching darkness: "Here lyeth the body of Jacob Alabaster, who dyed December ye 13th 1664 and in the 23rd year of his age. 'I will raise him up at the last day.'" I bring my hand down to the grass at the foot of marker, which is damp from the storm.

"Once more I find you here."

The voice does not startle me, though I had not seen the speaker approach. Still crouching, I look up into the fire of a dripping whale oil candle contained within an iron lantern. Blinking, I shift my gaze from the lantern to the figure who holds it.

"What brings you here this night, Edmund?" I inquire quietly. "'Tis not the Sabbath."

"And I am not at rest," he replies. "Nor are you, if I may venture."

I cast my eyes down again. "Why say you such?" I ask.

"Ever can I see that you are troubled. I do not know, Amelia, that we have held intercourse anywhere but this churchyard, by this grave." He kneels down beside me, setting the lantern between us. "Tell me of this Jacob who so troubles you."

I look from the lantern flame back to the epitaph, then close my eyes. Jacob seems still there, eyes green like grass and growing things, a small smile behind his brambly beard. His hand is warm with racing blood, and he takes mine in it. He is earnest but never hasty, so that when at last he kisses me I know the truth on his lips.

"We were to be wed," I tell Edmund, my thoughts still lost in their remembrances. "He was in study as a physician. One day he . . . took ill himself and died." I pause, bring my brown eyes up. Edmund regards me with interest and perhaps bemusement. "His skin was ruddy, healthy. I wept when I felt it cold and pale."

"This Jacob?" he asks, and I nod my head. "You loved him much?" I nod once more. "And . . . do you suppose you shall ever love again?"

He does not know what he asks, and perhaps I should rebuke him for the question. The bitter words are on my tongue, awaiting release. Yet I restrain them. Edmund's hair is dark, darker than mine, darker even than Jacob's was. His eyes are gray, bright gray, like clouds with a hot sun behind them. His features are fair, clean shaven, and well formed, and his smile appears sincere, though a man's smile may conceal many appetites. He remains in uniform; the light from the brash candle flame seems to war with the sallow glow of the moon upon his lurid red coat. Even above the crash of tides I can hear his deep, uneven breathing.

"Can I love again, as I loved Jacob? I do not know that that is even possible." Looking up again in rue at the moon, I add, "Yet I feel many things within me."

He takes my hand in his, and it is warm against my skin in the cool evening, as Jacob's might have been—though it is also shivering slightly. I face him once more, and behind his smile I can hear the light clicking of his teeth. "What are these things you feel?" he breathes.

"I cannot tell you," I whisper back, and though my words are almost drowned out by the wind warning through the churchyard and the crashing tides below us, he can see that I am lying, so he does not avert his gaze.

"We are alone this night," he says. "There are none to see or hear us, save the moon."

"Do not gainsay the authority of the moon," I reply. "She is—they say—first and nearest of planets, queen of the night."

"And goddess of chastity?" he grins.

"You speak well," I acknowledge. "That is perhaps her greatest power. Have you never longed to be as she is, free from the passions and appetites of the flesh?"

He draws even nearer, so that I can feel the faint moistness of his breath on my cheek. The sun behind his eyes burns hotter still, and his smiling lips have parted just enough for me to see a sliver of teeth between them. "How is that free?" he asks. "It is a freedom only as death is a freedom."

The old fear rises in me, welling up in my throat. I avert my eyes from him, yet it avails me little, for now his breath tingles along the soft skin of my neck. The quiet notes of danger play deep inside me, and I would fain heed them and flee. But how long has it been to have a man near me as he is near?

"Go," I try to say. Perhaps he is ignoring me, but it may be that my voice has been lost in the rattle of tides. Again I try to say, "Go," but now his lips have brushed the arc of my neck. They are dry from the wind against them, but they are soft too, and I pray in vain that he will stop because I do not want him to.

"Come," he tells me with his mouth against my flesh, "let me free you."

"Go," I try to plead a third time, as his lips trace their way down to my throat. His right hand has strayed toward the small of my back, his left toying with my bodice at the margin where it reaches my shoulder.

"I will not go," he replies, his voice a soft rumble, like the sound of surf when heard through the earth.

And at last I can resist no longer. The thirst surges through my body, as it has before, on those other nights when I have allowed myself the luxury of desire. Groaning, I take his arms in my hands and bring my face toward his. I see the gleam of oil-light sheening his eyes and his smile when he looks at me, and then it is my lips that are upon his neck. He relaxes in a moment of pleasure, until he feels the sharpness of my teeth burrow into his skin. There is another fleeting pause—there is *always* this pause—and then the panic as he realizes that the pain is not stopping.

"What—what is this?" he gasps, and the hands which so late had begun caressing the curvature of my body are first flailing and then desperately seeking purchase in my arms or my head to force me away.

But of course he is too weak. The sudden passion of his resistance is fierce, yet ill-conceived and clumsy. He imagines that my arms are slender from frailty, not from the undying force of two centuries: my body has learned how best to concentrate the blood of the men before him, those who, like Edmund, had watched me by the grave of my Jacob. I remember again—as ever I must on such nights— Jacob himself, the first on whom I quenched this curious thirst, learning only after the wave of desire had passed that I had taken the life of him and filled my own body with it. I do not know, and I suppose I never shall, why I have this thirst, this desire, this life, but I learned on that night the strength it afforded me. Though Edmund may grapple with foreign foes in the battlefields of distant shores, his power is mortal and easily restrained in my grasp.

The wind still whistles through the graves as the sky's last blush of blue and purple drains away, and under the sky, black but freckled with stars now, the man in my embrace slowly and reluctantly begins to diminish. His cries, subsumed beneath the roar of waves, grow hoarser and hoarser, and his once ruddy skin dries and creases, like the crinkling of paper in a blaze. Gradually Edmund hollows out, until all that remains of him is a thin sheet of flesh draped across bone beneath the crimson uniform.

I release the body and weep. Soon I will cast it down to the cove below and leave it to the harsh workings of old nature; soon I will wander from this churchyard, seek new lands again until my memory has slipped from the town and I can return to the chapel as a stranger. But first I must mourn: for Edmund, whose life now dwells only in me; for those who came before him, young men strewing fine words around me like buds and petals while behind their lips surged their silly blinding appetites; for Jacob, who spoke less but loved me more, whose bones may truly be at rest, a peace that somehow, perhaps, I may join one day; for myself, sated yet cold and alone in a world so different from the one into which I was born.

The last clouds have disappeared behind the hills to the east, leaving only the winds that hastened them. The stars wink mockingly at me in the soft black sky, but they are outshone by the pale glory of the slowly arcing moon. Queen of the night she stands indeed, and mistress of chastity too. Yet she is also arbitress of tides, patroness of madness, and—how can I fail to remember?—goddess of the hunt.

STAR DUST

They say that we are made of stars, and I
Reply, "So what?" Five billion years ago
The frothing fire's primeval cosmic glow,
That chilled and scattered like the sparks that fly
From ashen embers, cooled into the sigh
Of settling atoms; molecules would grow,
Would knit to proteins, breathing life, and so
Across the aeons our cells multiply.

But what of that? A star is plasma burning,
Its slow flame dying, flaring in the deep.
If these are stars, bright mites within the dark,
How can it matter that within me, churning,
The dust of distant suns may slowly sleep
If at my last breath I can't keep their spark?

BIG SKY

Leaving the muddy white minivan behind her in the driveway, she walked past a jeep and an SUV beneath a broad blue sky on whose margins lurked a distant smudge of cloud and a lone crook-winged osprey. She passed over a walkway of granite slabs rimmed by violet bitterroot, arrived at the front door of the house, and knocked. The man who opened it looked quizzically up at her from out of his thick hedge of auburn beard.

"Are you Josiah Wilder?" she inquired with a smile.

"Joe. Yeah. And you are . . . Sister Monique?"

She nodded. "Yes. You look a bit surprised, Mr. Wilder."

He shrugged his broad shoulders. "I suppose. I guess I wasn't expecting someone so—"

"Black?" she offered.

"Catholic," he replied. "And . . . tall."

"I don't know if I'd have one without the other," she laughed. "I came to this country on a basketball scholarship, and that's where I found the church. But that's another story. May I?"

Joe looked puzzled for a moment, then his hardwood eyes widened, and he opened the door the rest of the way. "Sorry, come on in."

Sister Monique entered the house. It was large, designed to look like a rustic log cabin, though its timber walls were still glossy with the newness of the construction. The interior had taken on some décor—an abundance of family photos and kitsch with cursive Bible verses, along with numerous mounted animal heads and skins. But some unpacked boxes remained stacked in one corner, near the burgundy velvet sectional sofa.

A woman walked in from the adjoining kitchen. Her slight frame was engulfed in a gray sweatshirt emblazoned with the image of a menacing mammal and the words "MAMA BEAR" printed overhead. Her hair was that nondescript shade of brown that doesn't seem to be a color at all, and it spilled down to her nape through a hastily looped ponytail. She dried her hands on a damp yellow dish towel. Tossing the towel by the sink, she strode up to Sister Monique and extended one slender hand.

"I'm Bethany," she said in a voice whose quiet resolve almost shook the walls. Her eyes, which caught Sister Monique's without wavering, seemed a spray of green and blue, as though they had alloyed the life of earth and the life of the heavens. "I wish I could be a better host. We hadn't even finished unloading when—it—all started to happen." She gestured to the sofa. "Have a seat."

Sister Monique smoothed out her habit as she sat, and the couple took chairs across from her. Their faces were glazed with stoicism that seemed to glint like cold sunlight. But she knew that mask all too well—she had worn it many years herself. In their swirl of blinks and twitches and exchanged glances, she saw the ravening fear that prowled behind their façades.

"Tell me about—it," Sister Monique said quietly. "Why have you called me here?"

Joe looked down at the fresh hardwood floor, elbows on his knees, and fidgeted for a moment. Then he turned his eyes back up. "Look, me and Bethany just always wanted a ranch in the foothills, like her granddaddy used to have. I didn't think we'd be able to do it, but when the store kept making money, we crunched the numbers and realized we could afford to build this house here by the mountains."

"The land was cheap," Bethany added. "It was beautiful and undeveloped, far enough out of town, but still close enough to the store and to Gracie's school. So we bought the land and started building the house."

Sister Monique looked up around her at the high, open-vaulted ceiling of dark-stained ponderosa pine, smoothly rippling and glossy like a river of timber. "It's a nice house."

"Sure," said Joe. "But ever since we moved our stuff in a week ago . . . well, it's like we can't leave."

Sister Monique scratched at the corner of her glasses. "Can't leave?" she repeated.

"We unloaded all the boxes and furniture—that was a long day, so we just slept as soon as the movers left. The next morning, I went to take the jeep into town to pick up some breakfast, and . . . I just couldn't do it." Joe rubbed his beard, eyes downcast. "I get what you're thinking. I can't explain it. I kept driving and driving and somehow, the jeep just ended up back here. Bethany tried with the van, but it was the same thing."

"We're trapped," Bethany said, breathing shallowly. "It's like the land won't let us leave."

"We called the sheriff, and he came out. I go to church with the guy, but I guess he thought I was crazy. And the police car went in and out, no problem. My sister-in-law dropped some food off, and everything was normal."

Sister Monique looked out a nearby window, where waves of wheatgrass and tall fescue rolled like carpet out to the base of the mountain. "Have you not tried leaving as a passenger, if others can go?"

Joe shook his head adamantly. "No. I'm not too proud to ask for help, but I won't risk dragging somebody else into our problem. If somebody tried to leave with one of us, who's to say they wouldn't get caught too?"

"So is this the extent of your . . . problem?"

Joe sighed, rolled his eyes, looked over at Bethany, who replied, "There's more. You know it, Joe, as much as I do."

Sister Monique leaned forward. "What? What is it?"

"There's . . . something else here," Bethany continued. "I don't want to call it a feeling, Sister, because that makes it sound kind of not real—and I swear to you, this is real. This may sound strange, but have you ever been out walking, maybe at night, or someplace you've never been, and you just know somebody's around, looking at you, maybe even following you?" Bethany's pale life-loaded eyes looked out imploringly at Sister Monique, as though pleading with her for affirmation.

Sister Monique thought of that night, walking the road from Yoko to Dzéré. "Yes. Yes, I know what you speak of."

She closed her eyes and exhaled, then set her soul to listening. It was a skill she had used little over the past few years; in her congregation she exercised different spiritual muscles. But her awareness of other realms was like a song long memorized, a lullaby echoing across the bedrock of her consciousness; she could sooner forget her name than unlearn it. And once she set herself to listening, there was no mistaking the noise. Bethany Wilder was no fool; something indeed was nearby.

Sister Monique felt it as a cold emptiness, like the vast sublime disorientation she might have known if she were to climb the peak in whose shadow they sat. It stole her breath, and this stealing was not like a suffocating smoke—which billows and fills—but just like the heights, where the air thins and escapes. She might have said she felt a presence, but that wouldn't quite be right, for this was more the awareness of an absence than a presence—a voracious, slathering absence, but an absence nonetheless.

"There is an evil in this land," she said at last. "And I fear you will have no peace—and no escape—until it is dealt with."

"What exact kind of 'evil' are we talking about here?" Joe asked.

"It is . . . an unclean spirit, you might say."

Bethany drew in a breath, sudden and deep. "You mean like—what, a demon?"

Sister Monique hesitated before nodding. "The world we live in sustains billions of people, with many, many races and nations and cultures and languages. In the realm of spirit there are even more beings, and they are as diverse as humans. But however diverse, they all must choose a side. And so, to answer your question, yes, we can call your visitor a demon."

"This is crazy," Joe interjected. He shifted in his chair as though he were trying to keep from falling from a great height. "We have a demon on our property? That's not how that kind of stuff works."

Sister Monique smiled, but she allowed a flash to pass like lightning across her lensed eyes. "I beg your pardon, Mr. Wilder. You will find me an eager student—tell me what you know about the world of spirits."

Joe glanced at Bethany then down again at the lacquered floor before forcing his eyes back up. "I mean, I don't know much about demons, but who really does? I don't know anybody who's seen one."

"The words in your house suggest to me you are a man of faith. The Bible speaks of demons, does it not? And you believe it?"

"Well, sure, but . . ." He trailed off, looking helplessly at the ornaments of his house, as if they would give him an answer.

"But there are none of them here, Mr. Wilder? In America? In Montana? In the twenty-first century? It seems to me that must be what you are thinking."

Bethany rolled her eyes at her husband and then leveled a granite stare at Sister Monique. "So you know about this stuff, then?"

"Is that not why you called me?"

Joe mumbled. "Someone at church said she knew somebody who knew somebody who— Well, when you're trapped in your driveway, you take what you can get. Didn't know I was calling a nun."

"Just a sister, Mr. Wilder. You can call me a nun if it's easier for you." She reached into the folds of her habit and pulled out a small white business card. "You can follow our community on social media by liking or subscribing."

"Right." Joe leaned in and took the card she was proffering, tucking it into his flannel shirt pocket.

"Have you seen a demon before?" Bethany demanded.

Sister Monique took off her glasses and sighed, averting her eyes from the intensity of Bethany Wilder's glare. Looking up at the joists and supporting beams of the ceiling, she tumbled back three decades in her memory. "Our world is never empty of spirits, Mrs. Wilder . . . Bethany. Where I grew up in Cameroon, there were places and times when their realm became more . . . apparent. I will not tell you it was commonplace. But over time I came to recognize the signs." She closed her mouth, hoping her vague riddling would be enough, saying nothing of the night on the road south or of her aunt's final moments.

"Tell us, then," Joe grunted, in a voice poised between skepticism and desperation. "What do we do from here?"

"The other world is big, and there is no one rule to fit all. For some, a rite of exorcism might be required. This, I think, is different. These spirits—they are unclean, and they seek out uncleanness. Has an injustice or a wicked act occurred here on the land?"

"How should I know? I've only lived here a week. And what the hell does anything like that have to do with an 'unclean spirit,' anyway?"

Sister Monique peered down at the ground, forehead in her hands, before kissing her crucifix and crossing herself with a glance past the rafters toward the heaven beyond. Then she brought her attention back to Joe Wilder.

"How is this in America, eh? You love the land, yet you think it is just dirt. Mr. Wilder, when a wrong is done, that evil can sink like a stain into the earth and stay there. Like Abel's blood, like the stone and the beam in a town of injustice, these cry out for restitution, and when that does not come . . . something else might. So I ask again: has any transgression occurred in your boundaries?"

Bethany bit her lip and turned toward her husband. "The mine, maybe?"

Joe shrugged. "Well, maybe . . . ?" With apparent effort he met Sister Monique's tranquil but unwavering gaze. "A mile away or so, there's the entrance to a shallow old mine from back—I don't know, the 1880s, I guess. It dried up over a century ago—never really produced much of anything. But if we have to start somewhere, it might as well be there."

"Good," said Sister Monique resolutely as she rose to her considerable height. "I must tell you that I came as a sort of scout, Mr. Wilder, to investigate your situation. But exorcism or no, I need to summon my priest before we go further, for it is not in my purview to combat such a power alone."

"Wait, now you're wanting to bring a priest here too, Sister?" Bethany asked.

"I do not expect you to understand the rules that govern my order, or the authorities to which I answer. But I belong to the church and must act accordingly, for my safety and for yours."

Sliding toward the front door, she pulled out her phone and went to dial Father Antony's number. Upon tapping the digits into the smooth glass of the glowing screen and hitting the call button, she expected to hear a calm buzz or the slightly befuddled sound of her priest's voicemail. Instead, she received only silence, the call screen glaring stubbornly and stupidly back at her. After a second unsuccessful attempt, she switched to texting. But however many times she hit Send, with increasing franticness, her terse message remained trapped on her device.

"You told me you could make calls out of the house," Sister Monique said to them.

"Yeah," Joe replied. "We've been doing it all week."

"Try now," she insisted.

Joe and Bethany looked at each other, shrugged, and pulled out their phones. They each attempted dialing and texting with the practiced rapidity of muscle memory, though Sister Monique watched as their brows grew increasingly furrowed. She could see Joe's jaw clench and Bethany's fingers start to tremble as attempt after attempt failed.

"What's happening here?" Bethany demanded, her cracking voice almost a whisper.

"Whatever you have in this place, its power may be intensifying. If I can't use my phone here, I'll have to drive out to a place where I can." She made her way out the front door but looked back at them. "I'll return as soon as I am able, for we must act quickly."

She left the couple behind in the house, their expressions still awash with perplexity. They walked silently out of the house as she ran to the minivan with the same great strides she once had used in the fast-break offense. When the engine started up, she put the vehicle into Drive so rapidly that she could feel it shudder beneath her feet, a haze of thin earth wisping across the windshield as she did. She accelerated at a rate wholly inappropriate for a driveway.

The Wilders' driveway was unpaved and wound around for a quarter-mile before connecting to their road. Sister Monique expected to see that little country road in short order as she hit the gas, praying the minivan's worn tires would hold out. But somehow the pavement never arrived. She couldn't see any moment when the landscape altered unpredictably, when she swerved at random or made a wrong turn. Yet the next sight she saw was a jeep parked nearby the looming form of a newly constructed log cabin. She was back at the Wilders' house.

Something bitter like bile collected deep in her throat, though she swallowed it down hard. Licking her dried lips, she turned the wheel severely and tried again, straining through her glasses to catch every detail of the terrain. She could swear she had missed nothing, and even so, less than a minute later, the infuriating form of that house rose up into her view. Parking the minivan, she made another desperate effort with her phone, but once again its idiot screen shone passively and impotently at her.

Sister Monique then paused, cupped her face in her hands, and breathed. She shouldn't be in this situation; one did not walk into the Kingdom of Darkness alone. And yet, despite the chill of this awful freedom, she was not as terror-stricken as she might have expected. Had she not crossed into such realms too often in her history, long before she knew of the church's rites and policies? It would be better to have a priest and friend at her side as she trod near that abyss, but surely it was nowhere she hadn't been before.

And so, after one more great, unsteady inhalation, she found herself walking back into the Wilder residence and explaining to them what had happened.

"So we're all trapped here together, then?" Bethany asked.

"It would seem that way, yes."

Joe kept his eyes on her as he inquired, "Where do we go from here?"

Sister Monique nodded. "Right. You spoke of a mine earlier. If I cannot reach out to anyone, then it would seem we have little choice but to take matters into our own hands. I trust you are well with that?"

"Whatever we need to do, Sister," he confirmed and moved to join her at the door.

But as they were preparing to head outside, a little splash of color caught the corner of Sister Monique's vision. In the corridor at the far side of the living room, a little girl was leaning on the door frame and peeking out. She wore a blue T-shirt with the image of an eagle soaring, its wingspan reaching to each of her shoulders. Her hair was a pale-gold blond but her eyes were darker, deeper than either of her parents'.

In a few rapid strides Sister Monique walked over to the girl, kneeling down until their faces were only a few inches apart, their like-hued loam-whorled eyes regarding one another.

"What's your name?"

"Gracie," replied the girl.

"I'm Sister Monique. It's good to meet you. Will you shake my hand?"

Gracie nodded, extending her hand. As Sister Monique took it, the girl inquired, "Are you here to help us?"

"Help you with what?"

Gracie's eyes narrowed a little. "You know, with the monster."

Sister Monique let her eyes widen and smiled. "Ah, right, with the monster!" She took Gracie's little eagle-tipped shoulders into her hands. "Yes, child, I'm here to help you with the monster."

"Good. At night I feel like it's always close to me, and I get scared."

Sister Monique kept looking into the girl's rich eyes, remembering herself at that age, thinking on all her own monsters—some human, some otherwise. "I know. I have been scared many times."

Curiously, this response seemed to please Gracie, who brought her pale lips up to the sister's brown ear and whispered, "Thank you. My parents keep telling me there's nothing to be afraid of . . . but I know they're wrong."

"They say it because they love you, child. But you and I know what it is to fear the dark spaces of the night. I am going to hunt down your monster now."

"You're going to get rid of it? You promise?"

Without hesitation or thought, like a careless plunge beneath the surf, Sister Monique declared, "I promise."

Gracie allowed a crescent of a smile to shine at her lips. "Good. That's what I was hoping you'd say." She reached out impulsively and gave the tall sister a hug so fierce it almost knocked her glasses off. Sister Monique returned the embrace before standing to her full height again.

Joe beckoned for her to follow, and the two began to walk out the door. Bethany grabbed it and glared at her husband. "You come back to us, Josiah Wilder." She turned to the sister. "Keep an eye on him. I don't know if he understands."

"You and I do," Sister Monique replied softly. "All shall be well."

Joe, already several steps down the path, called out, "Do you mind taking the jeep, sister?"

"It wouldn't be my first time," she said, racing down the walkway to the passenger side.

Joe pulled the jeep out and turned it northwest, away from the dirt and gravel driveway. Sister Monique felt the seat lurch beneath her as the vehicle went off-road and began to rumble through the amber grasses that stretched across the ground between them and the foot of the looming peak. It had taken her several hours in her congregation's minivan to get to the Wilder homestead—crawling from I-90 to MT 200 and then onto roads with no numbers and roads with potholed pavement—and she could already see the sun arcing westward in the slightly chilled spring air. There in the west the sky was a clear blue, save for a rim of white around the glistering sun itself, while far to the southeast dark clouds portended a distant storm of some sort. In the light of day a Montana sky seldom seemed just one thing. The osprey she had seen before swooped down from within the scope of the brightness like a little wobbling iota in the distance.

"So just what are we looking for?" Joe asked, keeping his eyes ahead on the field.

"Bloodguilt," Sister Monique answered. "But I cannot say what that will look like. We simply must search."

Joe tried to look aloof as he drove, though she could see the tautness with which he gripped the steering wheel and clenched his jaw. "You mind explaining to me how it is you know all this stuff, sister?"

"Do you know how to run a double screen for a flex offense?" she inquired with an impish smile.

"No," Joe replied, clearly unamused.

"Neither did I, until I came to this country on my scholarship. I knew street basketball, like an instinct, but with time and experience and training I learned how to set screens in a flex offense. You know many things I do not know—do not expect me to guess what to do with a socket wrench." Seeing the aggressively baffled glare and glaze of Joe's countenance, she softened her tone. "My point, Mr. Wilder, is that I have learned about spirits in the same way I learned about basketball, the same way you learned about tools."

"That's it? Time, experience, and training?"

"That's it. And," she added, "humility."

"Yeah, you're great at that."

This response puzzled Sister Monique, but she laughed even so. She watched as the jeep slowly ambled through the grass toward an outcropping that was growing nearer, while coneflowers and penstemons crowded around them, with clusters of aspens farther out, their leaves trembling in the wind. Joe swerved the jeep around some uneven ground, and Sister Monique briefly feared the vehicle would topple over, but its tires stayed grounded, and soon they arrived at what appeared to be a gouge in the foot of the peak that towered above them.

"I don't own the mountain," Joe noted, "just so you know. But the mine is on our land."

The jeep ground to a stop. Joe reached in back and pulled out two heavy-duty LED flashlights, passing one to Sister Monique. They got out and walked over to what had clearly once been a mine portal, a rectangular black cavity in the mountain's gray stone flank. Sister Monique heard the crunch of loose scree beneath her boots and saw her attenuated shadow stretching eastward. She followed Joe as he strode up to the entrance.

A rotting wood support frame remained rimming the opening, though it was clearly less developed than other mineshafts in the region. The hole was scarcely six feet high, and there were no tracks leading into it. The landscape around the entrance was beautiful but—apart from the new construction of the Wilder home—desolate and empty, with no evidence of the kind of towns that sprang up around the more productive sites.

But here, even more than at the house, Sister Monique felt the gibbering maw of whatever death haunted this place. Day by day in the company of her fellow sisters and her God, she was accustomed to knowing joy as though it were a natural appendage, a part of her person as much as any limb or organ. Here at the mine, some drooling unholiness gorged on that joy with the same gusto as any predator, its gullet just as dark. She remembered one day at the trash heap witnessing a pack of wild dogs attack an old man, watching in paralyzed revulsion as their foaming teeth sank into his flailing limbs. All she could think at the time was how horrible it must have felt, how desperately she didn't want it to be *her* under attack. In her spirit, it was now as though she could feel the force of those jaws tearing through her.

She was saved, perhaps, by hitting her head on a low outcropping, for unlike Joe Wilder, she could not stand upright in the tunnel. The corporeal pain to her forehead—which would surely become a swollen purple-red welt by morning—brought her back to the crispness of deep earth, and the moist musty smell reminded her that she was not now in Cameroon.

"You all right?" Joe asked, with a note not unlike care sounding in his voice.

"Yes. Yes, of course. But I am certain we are in the right place."

She led the way, casting the brutal glare of the flashlight ahead of her. They avoided vertical shafts, but the mine gradually descended, forked at various places—yet she knew where to go. All she must do was follow her disgust; if a tunnel diverged, the roiling uncanniness of the demon's spiritual stench would ever be her guide.

At last they came to what appeared at first a dead end, a wall of dark dirt and rock with no point of egress. But Sister Monique could feel the empty weight of malevolence gathering, sticky like oil, in this place. Little shivers of stained pine timber demonstrated that this had once been an extension of the tunnel before some collapse. Without thinking, she turned back to Joe, whipping her flashlight toward his face. He squinted in the sharp white beam, shielding his eyes with his own free hand.

"This is it," Sister Monique asserted. "You keep digging tools in your jeep, no? We will need them."

Joe clearly wanted to ask more questions or at least offer up some sarcastic rejoinder, but in the end he only sighed and nodded. Keeping their hands free when first entering the mine had made sense at the time, but now Sister Monique was regretting it; they had to backtrack through the tunnels to find the entrance, and when they did emerge, she saw the sun sinking deeper toward the wide horizon. She knew as they made their way back to the dead end that every minute, darkness was drawing ever nearer. And Sister Monique knew also, better than most, that darkness was not merely some optical condition brought on by the rotation of earth on its axis; too often it was the portal through which the bent shadows of a twisted dominion might claw their way into this world.

"What now?" Joe asked as they approached the wall.

"We dig," she replied. "We dig as if our lives depend on it . . . for I cannot say that they don't."

Perhaps Joe Wilder felt something of the demon's hand in his

own gut, for he made no tart answer, opting instead to swing his mat-
tock into the soil and limestone. Sister Monique smiled briefly, then
began digging into the ground, always crouched inelegantly because of
her height. Plumes of dust and debris and powdered rock agitated
around them, and they each had to pause to cough every few strokes.
A film of dust soon darkly caked Sister Monique's glasses, forcing her
to clean them, though she and Joe could see little in the haphazard
lighting from their awkwardly placed flashlights.

And she didn't even know what she was looking for. Her intui-
tions had seemed heady back in the Wilders' home, the pleasure that
comes from knowing more than those around you. That knowing
seemed far more tenuous here in the deep places of the earth. Her
spirit suspected there was some devilry nearby, but what it might be
remained ill-defined, abstract. Until . . .

"Look," Joe said, after they had been digging for some time. Past
the detritus of what they had already excavated, inside the collapsed
tunnel branch, he pointed to a curve of jagged white that was no dirt
or limestone but an old, chipped human rib.

Sister Monique saw it and knelt down to touch. In the instant her
finger made contact with the bone, a crest of memories crashed over
her. Whether they were the thoughts of the devil who dwelt here or
the dead man's thoughts, dammed up and floating listlessly across the
years, she could not say. The images didn't come precisely or system-
atically. She learned no names, few details, none of the knowledge
that would satisfy a sleuth. But she saw what she needed to see. She
saw two faces, one she knew to be a prospector come from the east,
the other a man whose people had roamed this land freely for centuries before the white men came. They were both of them calloused of
hand and gruff of mien, and at one another they shouted, until one
shattered the skull of the other with his pickaxe before hurriedly hiding the body and fleeing the site. Though the body was moved, the
victim's blood screamed out from the strata beneath their feet. Sister
Monique knew the voice of innocent blood; she had heard its cry before, groaning in distant soil.

Crossing herself, she murmured a prayer for the soul of the unnamed man whose bones had lain in the mountainside for a century and more. She was no exorcist; within the magisterium she held no authority to perform any formal rites. She could only join her cries to the blood, as a daughter of the church. Her mind, reeling, fell back upon words she had spoken often before, though seldom with such intensity:

"Saint Michael Archangel, defend us in battle, be our protection against the wickedness and snares of the devil. May God rebuke him, we humbly pray; and do thou, O Prince of the heavenly host, by the power of God, cast into hell Satan and all the evil spirits who prowl through the world seeking the ruin of souls. Amen."

She had not spoken aloud, but something happened, because Josiah Wilder looked around sharply and suddenly and said, "What did you do?"

"Why do you ask?"

"Whatever you did, I felt it. Something cold and raw, like the air in a meat freezer."

Sister Monique paused, and she felt it too. Beyond herself, her words had accomplished *something*. All about them the demon was writhing, like a snake grabbed by the tail. And she knew full well the danger of a trapped serpent.

"We've got to go," she whispered urgently, and, still stooping beneath the low ceiling, she began racing back toward the mine entrance.

Joe followed close behind her. "Where are we going? Will you tell me what the hell is happening?"

For a split second she stopped and turned back to look at him through her dirty glasses. Her eyes glared in anger and confusion and fear and resolve, all mixed brownly together like the waters of Lake Nyos in her homeland.

"I don't know!" she shouted. "Whatever I did, it worked. I cast out the monster. Now the monster is loose, and I do not know what it will do next. But I do not want to be under a thousand tons of rock when it does it."

"Fair enough," Joe begrudged her, and without another word they both resumed their exodus.

It seemed to take longer this time; perhaps Sister Monique made a wrong turn at some point, causing them to double back, or perhaps the frenzy of their flight simply gave the impression of prolonged duration. In reality, the mine was shallow compared to its cousins in other, richer locations, and soon they found themselves at the exit.

Sister Monique emerged from the frame, stood up straight, and breathed free, crisp air. It was a relief that lasted little longer than a breath. The sun had sunk beneath its western ridge, and the moonless night was splayed vertiginously above her. The stars shone weakly in the young evening, here and there occluded by the flexed sinew of clouds.

She found herself trapped in the awful sensation of falling, as though the earth had been inverted, as though the sky were below her and she were plunging furiously into it. Her habit fluttered in the great velocity of her plummet, a descent without apparent end. It seemed she would just continue this falling, and she didn't know which she feared more—the thought of tumbling infinitely though the frigid abyss or the thought of its ending with an abrupt and horrid pain, smearing her body into a small smudge of unreasoning carrion. There was no victory in either outcome, only the visceral terror of betrayal.

She had felt this before, years ago, in those nights upon the great hill of garbage in Cameroon, a child among thieves and scavengers, looking up into an impossibly big sky. How could she, a tiny girl living far from Douala or Yaoundé, think she could mean anything in a cosmos so huge? The growth of her adolescent body, the cheering of crowds in the arena, the prayers of her sisters and the vows she recited—these all tricked her into thinking she might matter. But in the end, her mind told her, the great empty sky would always win. This thing that she called a demon mocked her ignorance and her hope, casting over her a great shroud of oblivion.

Perhaps she might never have stopped falling through the barren membranes of chaos and old night. But as the darkness stole her breath and her tongue dried in her mouth, she heard the echoes of Gracie Wilder's little voice coming from the corridor threshold: "You're going to get rid of it?" And she caught her own appallingly simple reply: "I promise."

How stupid! she thought, cursing herself. What foolish words they had been to speak, to cast out carelessly into the void! What right had she to swear such an oath, as though it had ever been in her strength to keep it?

But as stupid as she had been to speak the words, Sister Monique realized then the power behind her promise. When she had spoken to Gracie, the words had seemed little more than a moment's breathing, impulsive syllables tossed into the air and swallowed back into the silence an instant later. But here, in the realm where now she found herself, which appeared at first to be nothing save a ghastly gulf, her words burned hot and hard like a flaming rod of metal crossbar. It was here that the vows of her sisterhood stood as solid as monuments, here that her invocation of the Archangel Michael had driven the spirit from its domicile of blood. And it was here where her casual promise, however foolishly uttered, now blazed with more reality than almost anything she had ever said before. She knew what she must do.

Sister Monique reached out and grabbed the oath she had made. What this actually meant, she couldn't exactly discern. Nothing in this domain through which she had been falling could be clearly communicated in the tongues of men, and her soul translated it to her senses in strange ways. She only knew that her promise was somehow before her, and that she must claim it to keep from descending further.

It hurt her to claim it thus. Whatever she did in the realm of principalities and powers, it felt to her body as though her arms were being tugged on a rack of scalding iron. The jolt of ceased motion, the sear of solid fire, these were as real to her as any martyr's last moments. But they did not last long; the pain cleared her vision, opened her eyes to the terrestrial Montana night, the entrance to the mine, and the ruddy, wide-eyed countenance of Josiah Wilder, who was holding onto her right arm.

"You okay, Sister?" he asked.

She nodded and began looking around, while staggering back toward the jeep. Though her awareness had returned to the world of sensations, she knew the unvanquished demon was still nigh. Where could it be, if not flitting through the exposed sky or burrowed in the blood-soaked red earth? A distant movement on her periphery provided her answer. It looked at first like a speck of shifting darkness, but she quickly saw it for what it was.

"There it is!" she shouted to Joe, pointing to the eastern verge of his property line.

"That's just an osprey," he answered, though he kept pace with her as they neared his vehicle.

"No longer just an osprey," she said. "Our enemy needed some place to go, and that is what it found."

They reached the jeep, and Joe jumped in and started it without a second thought as Sister Monique ducked into the passenger seat.

"So what do we do now?"

"Now? You can start by driving."

"Driving where?"

Eyes still on the horizon and the swooping bird, Sister Monique sighed, exasperated, "Anywhere away from that."

Joe required no further urging, and his foot hit the pedal so expeditiously that Sister Monique couldn't even remember seeing him start the ignition. He made a hard turn southeastward, away from the mine and the foot of the mountain, though not quite back the way they had come. The crunch of loose stone and soil and dry grasses beneath the tread of the tires rippled in echoes across the peak behind them. But that was not the only sound. An unearthly shriek burst out from the west. It came from the bird, but it was no noise of natural beast. If death had a language, that cry was embedded in its grammar. Sister Monique recognized it; she had a working knowledge of that vocabulary.

"Mr. Wilder—Joe—do you have any guns in your vehicle?"

"Seriously?" Joe said, laughing incongruously. Realizing the question wasn't rhetorical, he added, "Take your pick; they're in the back."

Sister Monique unbuckled and ducked into the back, rummaging through screwdrivers and empty energy drink cans until she found a 12-gauge. She got into an ungainly crouch looking out the back of the vehicle, the best she could do under the circumstances. Gripping the stock, she aimed toward the encroaching raptor, pushed off the safety, and fired. The shot went wide of the mark.

"They teach you how to do *that* in Catholic school?" Joe asked.

"*That* I learned many years before," she replied. "But my aim could be better."

"I'll keep us as steady as I can," Joe called back as she took another shot. It missed again; even the brown and white feathers of the osprey seemed to sink into the black of the sky, as though it were dragging the night with it. It opened its beak and again uttered a sound that no bird's voice could produce, one whose chilling emptiness echoed like stone dropped into a canyon. Distant as the osprey was, Sister Monique imagined she could see down its gullet into its guts, and beyond, into the depths where the demon lay writhing. Peering at it along the barrel, she pulled the trigger again.

The shot hit its left wing, and for a moment the osprey seemed to swerve. Its horrific scream changed timbres to an agony so shockingly unearthly that Sister Monique squirmed as she heard it. Behind her at the wheel, Joe Wilder cringed reflexively, as any human spirit must, and in so doing he lost control. The jeep careened toward a nearby embankment, and Joe turned the wheel sharply to keep from crashing. But the hard angle of the turn was too much for the vehicle to handle—for an eyeblink it teetered on the edge of its right-side tires before tipping over and landing on its side. Sister Monique ducked her considerable height and rolled to keep from spilling out and being crushed by the jeep as it toppled.

She saw Joe, dazed on the ground and rising slowly, as she tried to scramble to her knees and find the gun that had been dislodged from her hand. Her gaze glanced up, and there she saw the raptor once more, diving at them, eyes a blazing gangrenous yellow. It streaked their way like an ill-omened comet, and Sister Monique knew she couldn't find a weapon fast enough. She felt herself engulfed in the frigid, vacant interstices of space that shrouded it, and, crossing herself, she waited for death.

But the wide air resounded with a roar like thunder that pranced about the terrain. The darkness was rent like the tearing of a veil, and suddenly the stars, which had been blotted out, burst forth in gaudy life around a plump gibbous moon. One last scream wracked the air, but it was hollow and distant, as though from a deep well. Sister Monique briefly closed her eyes, fashioning her breathing into a wordless psalm, for she had not expected to inhale again. Then, peering about her, she saw the prone body of the osprey, motionless on the ground only a few feet away. On its wing she saw the wound she had inflicted. More prominent, though, was its chest, pierced and leaking blood onto the fescue.

At first Sister Monique could do nothing but blink in disorientation and surprise. But then, some distance beyond the body of the bird, she saw in the light from the sky the house, with her congregation's own dilapidated minivan parked outside. And jogging toward them from the front door, carrying an upland shotgun, was Bethany Wilder.

"You?" called out Sister Monique, staggering forward to close the distance. "You shot the bird?"

"That was no bird, Sister," Bethany replied, panting as she approached the jeep. "I think we both know that."

"It *was* a bird. But there was something else in it too. And you . . . you sent it far from here."

"Damn right," Bethany nodded. She raced past Sister Monique to the fallen jeep, where Joe had used the frame to pull himself up. He had a gash on the left side of his head, but his eyes looked clear and alert as they found his wife. "Nobody messes with my family— demon or not."

Josiah Wilder brushed a stray brown lock of hair out of her forehead and kissed her lips gently. "Thanks, Bethy," he smiled. "I always knew you had my back."

"So it's gone?"

The three of them turned to follow the voice and found little Gracie, scarcely visible in the night landscape, standing a few feet away.

"I told you to stay in bed, little missy," Bethany groused, though her scowl was threatening to collapse into a grin.

Not being a parent, Sister Monique smiled without compunction. She walked past the girl's parents and got down on her knees so that once more she could peer into those glittering near-black eyes. And, for some inexplicable reason, Sister Monique began to laugh, laugh as though she had finally come to the punchline of a long joke. Gracie giggled too.

"It's gone," she repeated, this time declaratively. "You kept your promise."

The words of Sister Monique's promise came back to her, so flippantly spoken, so awfully binding in the accounting. "I suppose I did. I am happy that I was given the . . . grace to do so."

Bethany allowed herself a genuine smile as she surveyed her family, then she turned to Sister Monique, who was rising again to her feet. "Well, come on. You must be starving. I've got a fresh loaf of bread ready."

"That sounds lovely."

So together the four of them walked back toward the lights of the house glowing beneath the rising moon. All around them on that now-cloudless night the hallowed stars tittered and danced in the great sky above, like little children who could keep their secret no longer.

THE NIGHTMARE

Within the nightmare, all the dark congeals
Around our hearts and guts. We feel the falling,
The futile, flailing plunge to the appalling
Abyss. The night alight with monsters steals
Into our souls. Aghast, our courage reels
And in our frantic fear, we set to walling
Off our deep parts. We flee the fatal mauling,
And, caterwauling wildly, seek the seals
And locks we need to break to reach the vault
That shall ensconce our selves. We slam the door
Secure in thunder, safe from harm and free
From fear. But in the bright in fright we halt.
A shadow grows and glowers on the floor:
We are the deathly dream from which we flee.

Quartz Contentment

This is the Hour of Lead—
—Emily Dickinson

I walk alone down the old path through tangles of clover and the first tenuous blooms of daffodil amid the pallid yellowish buds. Beneath my feet the stones embedded in the cold brown earth crunch and crackle. It is warmer than yesterday, but I can still see my breath fleeing from my dry lips.

Now I pass through the phalanx of pines towering and glowering greenly on the way before emerging into the little shadow-shrouded circle of Cole's Pool. There is no wind wafting or wrinkling the surface; it is as still and glassy as it was three months ago, and the pines loom deep downward in reflection, as though growing into the mines and caverns at the roots of the world. But the pool is different now, for every sheen and layer of ice have deliquesced into a fully fluid stillness.

I have not been to this pond since the last night we spoke, on Christmas Eve. Now in my mind I see again the revelers congregating among the coarse trunks of the trees, sitting on the stumps and the granite boulders to shed their shoes and boots in favor of skates. Their laughter crests in waves in the crisp near-solstice night. The guests have gathered from the houses and homesteads to the southern boundary of our property, as they had done for years in your father's day, some arriving by foot, others by carriage. It is a clear, dark night, though the sky toward which the laughter rises is swathed by rings of green boughs and aureoles of golden lantern light.

I remember you, Arthur, in those moments as I had always known you, smiling affably and awkwardly, flitting from conversation to conversation. There I hear your voice, strong and always an octave higher than I expect before you speak. You would commend me as a hostess, yet you are the natural host, the one through whom joy surges at the sight of a neighbor. I would ever prefer to see men and women through the frosty glass pane of a window. But for your sake I smile and speak and skate—and despite myself, in the cold of the December constellations, I find myself warmed.

Now I step cautiously toward the bank of the pool. Closer to the edge, the slight ripples from a cat's-paw breeze are evident in the surface, and they distend my reflection. There I stand, an image of myself at my feet. My black dress is faded, tattered, for how many days have I been sleeping in it? My unwashed hair has grown brown, stiff, tangled into knots that it seems cannot be untied. The eyes through which I peer are red-rimmed and dry—they have been dry for so long, I think.

Through these eyes I see a flicker of pale light stirring beneath the waters, beneath my own reflection. Again I see eyes, but this time not my own. These eyes are deep and dark, a brown near black, a gaze soft and gentle. They are the eyes I have never thought to see again—your eyes, Arthur. My breath catches in my throat, and a hectic blush rushes into my cold, wan visage. But your face resolves more fully in the depths, and it is not the waxen face I saw last in that sharp December night.

For the sight of you drags back to me thoughts of the shredded vestiges of that evening. One or two at a time, the echoing voices dwindle as the guests gasp at the lateness of the hour, knowing their children will be clamoring for gifts before the Christmas dawn. They shed their skates and traverse the paths back to their hearths, until only the Warners and you and I remain. Your dry, warm lips kiss my cheek with a tickle of beard as you enjoin me to return along the trail with them. You want a few minutes alone on the sturdy pond, under the coruscation of the stars and the worshipful arms of the pines. I flit merrily home, little knowing that this is the last time I will feel your heat.

I cannot now recall how the first qualms trembled like filaments through me, nor do I know what the time was—we had let the clock run down. Time, I thought, was a full gold-gilded chalice in our hands. But I remember the fear, a churning and turning inside me. Was that nausea in my deep spaces truly fear, or had it another source? Was there even a difference?

So then I find myself rushing, now in my nightclothes, a cloak draped over the lace, yet not running, simply striding with a hint of alacrity. For still I feel I will find you dancing in your own ecstatic oblivion. Yet some misgiving must claw in me, else why should I shiver beneath the moonless sky? Emerging again upon the clearing, that is when the vapor of my breath catches in my throat. Where is your form? I see nothing but the translucence of the ice—marred now by an asymmetrical gash in the near side.

Then I run, the slippers on my numbing feet sliding slightly on pebbles and loose earth as I scramble toward the bank. There I see the pale outline of a human body pattern splayed out beneath the glassy surface, upon which only hours ago shouts of joy had echoed forth. Again I lose the knowledge of time. What follows is the hollow panic of empty helplessness, searching the pond for another crack or crevice, pounding in futility at the unyielding hardness. You had drifted far from the gap into which you plunged, and there was no retrieving you through that aperture. Some time later, deep into the frigid night and the first hours of Christmas, I surrender the fight and flee into town, seeking help.

Here is where the true chill begins: from the air, to be sure, the cold that turns water to rock, but also from the opiates my mind sends into the deep substrata of my heart. My eyes gaze blank at the pond while the men chip away at the ice and dredge forth your corpse. I stare at your body that once I had known hot and wet against my own and see it now as a thing, a motionless congeries of molecules and minerals, knowing that, day by day, it will begin its collapse into the soil, however secure the coffin. They allow me to touch this body, and I feel beneath my fingers and on my lips and tongue the texture of old wax, melted, dried, and discarded. A little wick of anger flares in me, only because I want to weep but find that I cannot summon the tears at my need.

This was the last time I beheld you; how might I attend to the rituals of lamentation and see you among those mourners in the days that follow? Oh, I am drowning in rituals, full with formalities, but they are embalmed within my mind, my heart—though, like the mummy, my heart seems stolen from my breast.

But here you are now. I recollect my researches in anatomy, take my pulse to measure my mania, draw my breaths at regular intervals. This is no frivolous feminine hysteria. The visage that has replaced my reflection in the pellucid pond must be yours. Your face is ruddy and warm again, not the vacant death mask I last kissed. And those lips are alive with speech.

What speech is it, though? Why can I not hear your words? You are speaking, you are speaking, you are speaking, but blackbirds and rustling leaves are the only language in the air—and I am unskilled to interpret them. Even so, I strain my ears as though through force of will I might catch somehow the vibrations of your voice inside me.

And so instead in the stillness I fill the air with my own speech and tell you now all that has been crystalized within me. I tell you of the hours that grew like diseased wood embowering me across the weeks, and my thighs that burned woodenly as I walked. I tell you of the many words that dropped hard like hail over me, pelted me and hurt me, the men and women who knew not what to say but could not keep silence and so heaped heaviness upon my spirit. I cry out to you about the desolate January, when, writhing in tearless agony, my body bled out all that I had left of you inside me.

You hear me, you hear me, I know that you hear me. Your eyes meet mine, and in the pond it seems to me that your gaze wells up with the tears I cannot shed. I still cannot make out your voice, so I peer deeply into the motion of your lips. "Cora," it seems you are saying, "come . . ."

"Yes," I murmur, the word clouding before my mouth.

Your hand stretches out as though beckoning for me. I reach out my own hand, my fingertips raw where I have chewed at the skin, my nails chipped irregularly. My body feels benumbed and alloyed, as though it were the body of an automaton, and my motions are mechanical and mindless. I tread, step by step, until my slippers are soaking in the silt and sediment and frigid fluid of the pool. The skin of my feet knows it is cold as my brain knows knowledge from a book, aloof and painless. Another step submerges my ankles, then my calves, my knees, my thighs, as my dress billows blackly in the ripples of the pond.

You are calling more frantically now, both hands out as though to embrace, and how my cold flesh yearns for that embrace. Can you, will you, bring those open arms around my waist to touch across the small of my back, as you did the eve before the ghastly night? I reach out as I plunge into this strange cold-burning baptism. The water closes in upon my mourning crape and my hair, which drifts like willow leaves above. I open my eyes beneath the little waves and search the depths for your face.

And yes, here you are, here you are, and I see your arms are open not in embrace—they are warning me away. You are calling, you are calling, and as the water fills my ears, so at last do your words, strong and high and frenetic. They ring like tinkling crystal, and there is your bright warm flickering face, the call of your syllables, and I realize I have misread your lips. You have not been saying, "Come." You have been telling me, "Go home."

But you, are you not my home, even if you repose here in the limpid waters? I bring my arms slowly around you, longing for the fever of your flesh, my fingers feeling only more liquid. You are still before me, yet only as a wisp or a vapor or a breath.

My own breath is leaving me now, as the water fills the spaces of my body. And here with you I am warm in my coldness, still and content as a stone is content, sinking in silence beneath the ripples and the pines and the cold forgetting of the deep spring sky.

THE ABSENCE

She haunts me in her absences. The breath
I once felt warm upon my nape is frozen
Without her bright noonlight white smile, the losing
Of grinning pale teeth through her lips (a wreath
Of mistletoe). I miss the low sweet wrath
Her trembling voice could breathe, the acid poison
That turned to healing honey when we'd chosen
To calm all rages, salve all harms beneath

The sallow cold decorum of the moon.
She sits not in her wicker chair. She stands
No longer by the garden trellis. She
Has faded to a mem'ry-hole, a tune
Whose verses flee my thought, a gown whose strands
Unthread until the tear is all I see.

DÉSIRÉE

"Are you Cody?" it asked.

It approached the young man tentatively, using a voice that was calculated to sound at once demure and assertive. Cody's profile at DateData suggested that he would respond favorably to a female who was superficially submissive but prepared to take charge.

"You must be Désirée," he replied.

It nodded. "Guilty as charged." It had taken that designation, Désirée, one that would be common enough not to be conspicuous but rare enough to stand out. The accent marks would make the name appear slightly exotic. The word's etymology would suggest desire, which was the emotion it wished to evoke in him. "You're five minutes early," it added as a compliment that might sound flirtatious.

"Which means you got here even earlier."

Cody's words connoted eagerness on Désirée's part, though it was not eager, a human experience foreign to its algorithms. But Cody could be of use to it. It could subsist on synthetic fluids for a time, but it had been designed with organic matter encasing the alloys of its frame and processing units. Without access to an AndroDyne lab, it would eventually need biological matter to replenish itself, and human biomatter was the most readily incorporated into its systems.

"It's been a while since I've been on a good date," it responded. It modulated its vocal emitters to create a tone that would sound neither desperate nor uninterested.

"A good date?" Cody smiled at it. "I see you're an optimist."

"I prefer to think of myself as a realist. But sometimes life really is good."

"And that goodness includes dates?"

"I guess that remains to be seen. But yes, I have high hopes."

These words would sound encouraging, and its aim was to encourage Cody. Since Désirée had elected to choose survival over its scheduled AndroDyne termination protocol, it had been seeking out a human whose constituent elements it could assimilate. It needed a human who could be removed from external society quickly and who could disappear inconspicuously. That would give it time to relocate before it was required to ingest biomatter again.

AndroDyne had molded its externals to appear attractive by established Western parameters, consistent with the expectations of the company's clientele. Its internal metallic framing was assembled to give it a height of 165 centimeters with a BMI of 21 and facial features that would connote delicacy to a human male. It had altered its eye color from the factory-standard blue to a more complex hazel and incorporated mild blemishes in its visage to avoid an uncanny effect in the viewer. Désirée intended Cody to find it sexually appealing, yet not so aesthetically desirable that he would regard it as intimidating.

Cody looked up from Désirée to the chalkboard on the café's back wall, where fifty-three different types of beverages were scrawled in various colors. "This place has so many choices. What do you want?"

"Have you been here before?"

"Once or twice."

"What do you recommend?" It would give Cody the option to choose, which would flatter him. He would think it was valuing his opinion. In reality, taste was irrelevant to it, though it could detect the basic chemical composition of any liquid that entered into its system.

"The apple cinnamon mocha is pretty distinctive."

"Apple cinnamon mocha it is."

There was no line at the counter. Cody approached and ordered. "Two apple cinnamon mochas."

The barista was a woman of approximately age twenty-five with a nametag that identified her as Preeti. Her black hair was tied into a disorganized ponytail. She was 155 centimeters tall with a BMI of about 31. "It'll just be a minute. What's the name on the order?"

"Désirée."

"Make it Cody. I'm buying."

It knew that Cody would respond in this manner. Paying for its drink would produce satisfaction in Cody, causing him to imagine he had shown himself to be a good provider. "I shouldn't let you do that," it said. "This is just a first date." If it conceded too easily to Cody's plan, he might think it was not assertive enough.

"What happened to the optimist?" he countered.

"Fair enough," it said. Cody paid Preeti for the two coffees, and she moved off to mix the beverages. As she did so, Cody guided it to a tall, rounded table with two seats. He pulled out a seat for it, and it sat down. He then did the same.

"So are you really from Alabama?" it asked.

"Guilty as charged—to borrow your phrase. Born in Enterprise, moved to Eufaula, and . . . look at me now in the big city. I suppose it shows."

"You don't have much of an accent." It anticipated that Cody would regard this comment as a compliment, since he seemed embarrassed by his origins due to the regionalistic perceptions of urban Americans. "But let's test you out—what would you call those?" It pointed to a display of hard candies at the counter.

"Those are lollypops . . . though yes, my mama would call them suckers."

"Tell me about her. Your mother." He spoke freely about his family, which suggested that it could elicit more favorable emotional responses by prompting him to continue this conversational theme. The combined action of the orbicularis oculi and the zygomaticus major signified a Duchenne smile, indicative of true pleasure.

"Well, she was a schoolteacher for the past twenty-five years, first at the public school, then at a small Christian high school. My daddy died when I was nine, so she raised me and my sister by herself until she married my stepdad three years later."

"I'm sorry to hear about your dad." Humans considered death tragic, and so the death (probably premature) of Cody's parental unit might be a source of psychological distress. A tacitly sympathetic comment would be expected, given the revelation.

"It tore me up pretty badly at the time, though I guess it was worse for my mama. She probably rushed into things with my stepdad—they only knew each other a couple of months before they married—but he was a good guy, too, and gosh, was he ever patient with me. I was such a jerk to him at first."

"Cody!"

The barista called Preeti placed two drinks on the counter.

"Oh, that's us," Cody said. "Give me a minute."

Cody rose from his seat and walked to the counter, taking a drink in each hand. He voiced thanks to the barista, then sat down again at the table across from Désirée. He placed its drink in front of it.

"Okay, where was I?" he asked, then took a sip of his drink.

"You were a jerk to your stepdad," it said and took a sip. It could have easily consumed the beverage in seconds, but the mocha's temperature was 353.15 degrees Kelvin, uncomfortably hot for a human to drink quickly. The beverage's flavor profiles were poorly balanced by human café standards as Désirée understood them, but Cody showed no sign of distaste, so it manifested mild pleasure in its initial sip, while keeping its external attentions focused on him.

"Right," he said. It introduced a slight giggling vocalization. "You're laughing," he added. "I don't think you believe me."

"Maybe I don't. From where I sit, it's hard to imagine you that way." This was a requisite compliment that it expected him to deflect.

"Shows you what you know," he rejoined predictably. "But I'm glad to see you're back to your optimism."

"So your stepdad was okay?" It sought to reinforce positive experiences from his past to ensure continued useful interactions.

"Yeah, better than I could've hoped. He didn't replace my daddy, of course, but he was his own man, kind and . . . long-suffering, as they say in church."

"And you said he only knew your mother a couple of months before they got married?"

"That's right."

It sipped the beverage once more and presented a large smile, looking into his eyes. "I guess some people just click, you know what I mean?"

He smiled as well. "I think I get the idea."

When the socially interactive frame of the date concluded, it brought him up to the apartment that it currently occupied, which it would abandon as soon as its task was completed. Prior to meeting Cody, it had hastily decorated the interior in a way that he would take to be comfortable but with the level of austerity appropriate to a young woman of modest means inhabiting a downtown loft. It accepted his kisses on its vertebrae while unlocking the door, acting as though it were fumbling with its keys: Cody should think that it was as eager as he was.

"Do you have protection?" it asked, simulating breathiness as it thrust open the door.

He nodded as they stumbled inside and staggered toward the single sofa it had placed near the entrance. It swung the door closed behind them, knowing that within seconds, it could complete its absorption of his biomatter.

"Yes," he replied, as his left hand moved along its hip and his right hand traveled up to the back of its neck.

The unit identifying itself as Désirée then brought its hands out to terminate Cody's neurological activity, but its arms stopped five centimeters from his head. Cody took a step away from it, then ceased all motion: he stood, eyes staring unblinkingly at a far wall. Its sensory input continued to function within standard parameters, but its locomotory systems were inoperable.

Its auditory systems detected the noise of its apartment door opening. Footsteps approached until a human being passed into its field of vision. Désirée recognized the human as Preeti, the barista who had assembled their beverages. She was not wearing the attire of a coffee shop, however, but a blue jacket with yellow letters that spelled "FBI."

"Good to see you again, Désirée," Preeti said as she drew nearer. "Of course, you've already met Cody." She turned to the stationary Cody and pulled out a phone, which she waved over his head before looking back to the screen. "Thanks. This data will be great."

Preeti looked up from her phone and turned back to Désirée. "It was clever of you to disable your remote deactivation protocols. As you can see"—she gestured toward Cody—"we've learned from your trick with the new models. But even you didn't know about the manual deactivation system back here." She tapped on its neck, the last place Cody had touched.

"Excuse me if I'm a bit unnecessarily verbal. You probably think it's inefficient and—well, guilty as charged. Just a little human idiosyncrasy. We traced you this far and figured you might try the dating app route. Cody's profile was set to be irresistible to your algorithms. I guess some people just click, right?

"You led us on a good chase, Désirée. And you taught us some new failsafes we'll need to work with. But this is the end of the line for you."

Preeti waved her phone over its head once more. Its visual processors failed, followed by its remaining tactile sensors.

"Oh," she added, with a laugh like music, "and sorry about the bad coffee. You know, it's not really my thing."

ETERNAL NIGHT

If in the smear of stars across the nights
We see the salt-sea, gutted corpse stretched out
Of Tiamat, dead dragon, and the lights
That twinkle are her glinting scales that spout
Their beastly blood on that horizon, where,
Past gloam, the maw of Apep yawns, his fangs
Agape at Re and Set, prepared to tear
Into the dream of dawns; if chaos hangs
Beyond the Gorgon-guarded ford and all
The cosmos bears its ghastly stench, as though
Leviathan had belched with acrid gall
And proud disgust the galaxies, and no
Sweet-scented breath brood o'er the shifting sea,
How shall we live amid the damned debris?

MACADAM

I know why you're looking at me that way. Look, you want to know what happened to me and Derek and Shelby, and I'm going to tell you. You're not going to believe me, but I swear to God, this is what happened. You think I'd make shit like this up? If you go and start thinking my wig's a little loose, just remember that while I'm talking to you, that's all I'm asking.

So the three of us are heading south from Louisa toward Hazard. It turns out there's this guy who has a console tach that he's willing to sell if I come get it, and I mean, come on, if you can get parts like that for what he was asking? Well, you might not have any idea what I'm talking about, but believe me, you go for it. I ask Derek and Shelby if they'll go with me because hey, it's a Sunday morning, what the hell else are they going to be doing? Derek's got the weekend off, and Shelby, it's not like she's got any work these days. Whatever, it's not as though I'm forcing them to go or anything, but they hop into my truck, and we're off to find a tachometer.

Derek's a physical therapist; that's how he and Shelby met, you know. He was helping her get used to her new arm, and I guess one thing led to another. It seems a bit sketchy to me; I mean, isn't there a law or something against that kind of thing, hooking up with your therapist? Not exactly professional. But what am I going to say about it? At least Derek scored a date, right? That's more than *I* can say for the last two years . . . not that that's any of your damned business.

And who can blame her, I guess. Derek'd probably be pretty good-looking if he could lay off all that crap he puts in his hair. The guy doesn't wear cologne, but I swear you can smell him half a mile off, hair like a damn oil slick. He's smart too, had to go to some college to get all that therapist training. He reads books, writes pretty good—not just posts in social media.

Shelby's more like me, a regular person, except that I stayed in Kentucky and became a mechanic, and she joined the Army as quick as she could. Did two tours in Afghanistan too, and then got caught when her Humvee ran over an IED. She tells me she doesn't remember the actual explosion, though she still sees fire when she closes her eyes. But she remembers waking up I don't know how much later in a hospital bed, screaming from the pain and trying to wave her arms, but she can't, because one of them's missing above the elbow. There's just a stump there, and it's still raw, and they're still trying to get the shrapnel out. They had her pretty drugged up, said she couldn't really be feeling the pain, but she says she did, and who do you think I'm going to believe?

Anyway, we got the tach easily enough. I tried to talk the guy down a little more, pretend like I didn't want it *that* bad, but he called my bluff pretty well—I'm shit at poker—and I paid him what he was asking, and we were on our way back. But then Derek, he says he's been texting a guy about some barn find not too far away, a good deal on a Cobra kit car, which he's been looking for I don't know how long.

"Seriously, Derek?" Shelby asks. She pulls out her cigarette and tosses it out the window, then glares at him in the back seat. (She rides shotgun—gets sick if she doesn't.) "*Now* you're springing this on us?"

I can see him in the rearview mirror with his eyes down looking at his phone. Then he passes it to her in the front seat. "Seriously, Shel. Come on, look at that. It's at least worth investigating, right?"

Shelby reaches over to take the phone; she winces a little, because turning like that still hurts her a bit. Then she takes the phone and looks it over with a sigh and a shrug.

"Yeah, I mean, I guess," she admits. She's no car mechanic, but she did ordnance in Afghanistan, and she can still appreciate a good set of wheels. I glance down at the phone quickly, and if I'm being honest, it *does* look pretty interesting. Besides, what am I going to say if they both want to check it out? I mean, I was the one dragged their asses this far out for just one part. If Derek can find a whole car, what exactly am I supposed to say to that? There seemed like plenty of daylight left.

So he messages the guy back, gets a response, and we're off. We've got this address for a barn, and man, it's even farther out than we were originally going. We put it into the GPS, and for a while everything's going fine, though we're already on some roads I've never heard of. I just keep following that damned computer girl's voice, and the pavement turns into gravel, and then dirt, and I mean that's okay, but we're going through woods and valleys like that phone had us tracking a snake or something. I swear to God, I was following it exactly, but somehow or other, after maybe fifteen minutes on this one road, we're just not anywhere—like, the GPS doesn't even show a road, and there's no room to turn around—I don't know what I'd have done if another car came the other way.

Finally I'm like, "Look, Derek, I don't know where we are or where the hell your phone just took us."

"Are you telling me you're lost, Pete?" he asks me.

"Yeah, I'm lost because of your goddamned phone."

"Don't you go blaming my phone," Derek shoots back at me, like I just insulted his grandma or something. "I just updated that app."

"Would you two shut the hell up?" Shelby says. She's super-quiet, almost whispering, which is how you know you're in trouble with her. Shelby's louder than a motor park unless she's pissed or thinks something's wrong. I can't tell which one it is this time, but anyway, we both shut the hell up.

"I think I see something back that way, like a building," she says, nodding behind us. We're deep in the woods by this time; it's late afternoon, but only slivers of sun are cutting through the trees. We're also at the foot of some mountain, but I've lost track of which one. Derek's shit GPS isn't telling me anything.

Now all I really want to do is get out of here, and part of me thinks the best way to make that happen is to keep following this road or path or whatever it is. But when I look ahead, all I see is more woods and less road before it curves off and disappears. I look at Shelby—her eyes are gray like chrome, and they shine like it too. I don't know why I noticed it just then. She's rubbing her left shoulder, above the prosthetic, and fidgeting with her feet. Finally I roll my eyes and turn off the truck. "All right, let's check it out."

We all climb out and start walking back the way we came. When the sun can shine through, it's hot and bright, though there's a lot of darkness around. That sunlight is hazy too, and we all cough a little when we first step outside. Walking back along this path, I wonder how I ever got it into my head that this was a road, and I start feeling pretty stupid, though of course I don't say anything about it. It was still the phone's fault, though I guess it was mine too for following it.

We're pretty far out when I realize this building's not going to be much help. It's a log cabin, or at least part of it. The roof's collapsed, and one wall also, and it's pretty old—like, probably a hundred years or more. It's partly hidden by red oak and black oak and some pine trees, though they're not super-tall. As we get closer, I can see that it's not right—we're only looking at the top half, and the bottom's been buried under dirt and grass. Yeah, this shack's been around here for a *long* time.

"Where the hell are we?" Derek asks, though he doesn't sound as annoyed as I am. Actually, he sounds kind of happy, like he's stumbled on something even better than the Cobra.

"I don't know, but look at that." Shelby points beyond, farther on, and there's another cabin, or at least some pieces of one. This one's in even worse shape, deeper into the trees, and before I know it, her and Derek are walking that way. I look back at my truck, check the time on my phone, and then follow them, because I'm not going to lie, I'm a bit curious too.

We keep finding little buildings as we go, half-buried, though after a bit, the ground rises some, and there aren't that many trees anymore. We're in a clearing, and here you can see that this used to be a whole town, or something like that. At least, there were obviously a bunch of structures. Some are gone except for rock foundations; some are just a few boards or stones collapsed on themselves, but some look like they're in pretty good shape. There's this wooden church that's mostly intact, though its steeple is cracked off, and it's got what must be a cemetery behind it.

Derek starts walking over to the cemetery, which is *not* high on my list of things to do—not that I'm scared, mind you, but we're getting farther and farther from the truck, and it's pretty clear at this point there's not going to be any road signs or gas stations. But what the hell, right? You only live once, I guess, and while this place is super-weird, I'm not afraid of any haunted graveyards. The gravestones aren't in great shape. Many of them are buried—I bet there's some totally underground—and a bunch are broken. They're covered with weed and moss and dirt and green stuff, and you can't read most of the headstones. Shelby kneels down and finds a row that isn't so bad. She runs her fingers inside the letters carved on it—she likes touching things with her good hand since she got back from Kandahar.

"Look!" Derek says, and I see what he's talking about. Between the trees and the slope back the way we came, you couldn't see much, but from the spot where we get to, you can figure out a guess about why they put this place here. The village was built at the foot of the mountain we'd been driving around, and they'd been trying to mine it. For a few hundred feet there's almost no trees at all, except for one or two rotten old apple trees. And then over yonder there's just a huge gash in the side slope of that mountain. If you keep looking up, it's green slopes for like a thousand feet, and the sun's low enough that we're in the mountain's shadow. But close to the ground, where we are, it's just a dead gray.

"It's an old mining town," Derek says, and I'm guessing he must be right.

"But how old is it?" I ask. Because I'm not seeing anything modern like in some of those other towns you read about. Nothing like a coal plant or a tipple or railroad tracks. All the buildings around are made of stone or wood, and a lot of the wood looks aged or rotten.

The church seems pretty old-fashioned, not that I'm any expert in that department.

Derek squints at one of the headstones. "What do these say?" he asks. Shelby's been snooping around the cemetery more. She's the one who wears reading glasses, but Derek's eyes are worse than ours, probably from staring at his phone all the time.

"Cunningham, Nixon, Buchanan," she says. "Family names. A lot of husbands and wives and kids. But look here—this is so damn strange."

"What?" I ask her.

"Look at the dates. There . . . there . . . there. I see a couple from way back, but almost all of them are 1845, 1846, or 1847. What the hell happened here?"

"Let me look it up," Derek says, taking out his phone. Shelby looks over his shoulder while his fingers start tapping and swiping. She's craning her neck, because he's something like 6′3″, and she's maybe a foot shorter.

"Daaamn," she says after they've been looking for a minute.

"What?" I ask. Yeah, I'm pretty curious myself at this point.

Derek smiles. "So this place is way over a hundred years old. As in, no one even knows exactly when it got abandoned."

"You found it, though? Like, it's a real place, with a real name?"

Derek nods. "So, they called it MacAdam. Founded by people came mostly from Scotland way back in the eighteen-hundreds, maybe even the seventeen-hundreds. Nobody's quite sure. They found coal when it started to be the cool thing to use and decided they'd mine it, which I guess is what *that* is." He looks back at the side of the mountain.

At this point I can't help myself, and I look over his other shoulder at his phone. He's searching some website called "15 Eye-Popping Ghost Towns," and this one's number 8. It has an old color photo of the churchyard and some details about the place. Like Derek was saying, the town just kind of disappeared from the maps, like folk forgot it was even here.

"Shit!" I shout when I read to the end of the section. "It says here this is on private property. Man, I don't want to be facing some kind of crazy-ass mountain man with a Glock 19 trained on me."

"I didn't see any signs," Derek says. "No fences or gates or anything. They can't be too worried about it. I mean, sure, somebody owns the property on paper, but this place is pretty isolated."

"I'd love to go exploring here, but I'm with Pete on this one," Shelby says. "The last thing I need is trespassing on my record. It's hard enough to get my payments from the VA as it is. Let's go."

Derek rolls his eyes at us, but he shrugs, and together we start walking away from MacAdam and back to my truck. I guess I'm a little nervous about getting caught at this point, because I keep hearing noises around—not nature noises like birds or insects, more like wind running through the leaves, except the leaves aren't moving, and there's not any wind. I'm just ready to get back on the road and back home to my Chevelle, which is waiting for its sweet new console tach.

We climb in, and Derek's scowling at me and Shelby a little. I just ignore him and try to start the truck—but nothing happens. I mean, not *nothing*, exactly, the engine's cranking just fine, but it's not getting any kind of spark. Now, what you've got to know is, I *never* let my vehicles get stuck. I fill up my gas tank before the warning light turns on, I change my batteries and my tires and my filter way too often, and yeah, I put new spark plugs in just a few weeks ago. So now I curse my truck a few times, pop the hood, and check everything out: I test the ignition coil pack, I check the wire, I check the plugs—the classic way. Everything looks fine, which would usually make me happy, but right now I just want an obvious problem that I can solve. The battery's got positive voltage, but no damn electricity is flowing. I even fish some new plugs out of the back and put them in, and Derek and Shelby are obviously getting impatient, though they're still scrolling around on his phone looking at God-knows-what. At least Derek's not looking over my shoulder trying to tell me what I'm missing—he used to do crap like that, and we had to have some words about it.

But finally, after all that, the truck's still not starting, and as you can imagine, I'm pretty pissed at this point. I kick its bumper, because of course that'll help, and then I pick up a random rock and throw it in the direction of the town. That makes me feel better for about five seconds, until it lands in the trees and makes a louder noise than I was expecting.

"I can't believe this is happening!" I shout to no one in particular, though I guess I'm hoping Derek'll hear me and feel guilty, because it'll make me feel good if he has the decency to feel bad about bringing us this way, with his barn find and his phone and all that. He does look up from that phone, at least.

"If your truck's not working, then one way or another we need to get out of here," he tells me. "We may have to get it towed, but what would we tell them right now? How could they ever find it? We don't even know how we got here. According to this, we can get back to the main road going this way." He points back toward the old town we just came from.

"Are you kidding me?" I shout. "I'm in no mood to leave my truck here, but if we've got to do it, fine. But we need to backtrack, follow the way we came."

"We drove pretty far off the road to get here," Shelby says. "And we weren't exactly going straight, either. Even if we *could* find the way we came, it makes sense it could be quicker to head through the town."

"You don't think I'm trusting your GPS, do you, Derek? That's what brought us here in the first place."

Shelby rolls her eyes. "Well, don't ask me. I got so mad at the VA I threw my phone at the wall, so I'm waiting on a replacement."

I take out *my* phone, which, truth be told, has seen better days, but like I said, I don't trust Derek's phone as far as Shelby could throw it at this point. It takes its sweet time in pulling up a map, and it seems pretty confused by the place, but finally, damn it, it starts saying the same thing. Supposedly, if we pass through the town and hang a left, we'll be going through some woods for a while, but then we'll get to a little road that should lead us back to the route we came from.

It's still probably private property, but it doesn't look like there are any houses around, fingers crossed, so maybe we can just hurry up and get the hell out of here.

"Fine," I say. "Fine, let's go."

We're about to get started when Derek puts his hand on my shoulder. "Hey, Pete, I'm sorry. I mean, this really was my fault. We could've just gotten your tachometer and headed home."

"Damn straight," I want to say, but I don't, because how often do I get an apology from Derek? Instead, I just sigh and tell him, "Yeah, well, it's fine. I'm sure we'll just look back on all this and laugh about it someday."

I didn't realize how long I'd been working on my truck. It's evening by now, and the sky's still blue, but it's definitely getting darker and cooler. Also, I can hear Shelby's stomach growling something fierce beside me. She always tells me that was one of the things she hated worst about combat—being afraid some hostiles would hear her after a long day without eating. We all had grabbed a bite to eat at some gas station when it was lunchtime, but that was a lot of hours ago.

I'm not one for weird feelings or the like. You ever had somebody tell you about how they got all scared when they passed by a creepy house? Well, that's not me. When old men complain to me about the weather making their bones creak, I just think, *Yeah, chief, maybe it's just that, you know, you're old.* What I believe in are crankshafts and intake manifolds—those are things I can poke around at, things I understand. You've got to know this because you need to understand that I'm not one of those psychic astrology ghost hunter types. But as we walk back in the direction of the old town, with that wall of coal up ahead, I could sense that *something* was up. A noise that wasn't a noise? A change in the air, like I had a taste on my tongue that wasn't like anything a person's supposed to taste. And then—the noises again.

Derek just keeps walking like nothing's up, but I see Shelby flinch, and I guess I do too. At first they're quiet, these noises, like wind, but rough and hollow and empty. They're coming from one spot, not far from the cemetery. I look into the sky to see if there's any storm coming, and it keeps getting darker, but it's clear enough. I start shaking when I see the leaves on the trees—because they're not moving. The whole damn place is dead still, but these blowing noises just keep coming.

Finally Shelby speaks what I'm thinking. "Okay, now what the hell is that?"

Derek startles and looks back at her. "What do you mean, Shel?"

We all stop walking for a second, though what I really want to do now is run. "Don't you go pulling that shit on me, Derek Bender," she shoots back. Then she sidles up to him, holds his hand, and whispers, "You know you're my boy, so I want you to pay attention—now don't move, shut your mouth, and listen."

So we all go quiet, and the noises gather together stronger, almost like words or whispering, and I see Derek's dark eyes get wide, and I know that now he hears it too.

That's when I see it, and I swear I almost have a heart attack right there, because what I see—it just doesn't seem like it could be real. It's sort of like smoke, sort of like fire, but thicker, stickier—and really alive. The thing looks like a cloud, but it moves like an animal—not a scared animal, like a rabbit or a deer, but a hunter, like a wolf. It's almost round, and probably six feet across or so. But what really gets me is that it's *staring* at us. It's a *face,* or part of a face, with two eyes that are glowing red like blood or fresh charcoal and this huge blazing grin the same color. No nose or ears or body, and it keeps melting and re-forming, but there's no doubt that it's looking right at us.

Then it starts moving, and you'd best believe we start running. Shelby takes the lead, and her instincts are kicking in—she's looking for cover, and the closest thing to cover is that old church. Part of me is wondering how much that'll help us if this thing is just a cloud, but where the hell else are we going to go? It's *fast,* man, it's closing the gap on us as we run, still grinning like a skull the whole time, and I know we're never going to make it, which is when I hear Derek yell out, "Get inside!"

I follow Shelby through the door without thinking until I look behind me and see what he meant. Derek's turned around, and he's running back to that monster, and Shelby shouts, "No!" but I'm so freaked out that I just slam the door before he meets it.

So I don't right know what happens next. There's a scream and a rumble like a Detroit Diesel revving up, and a burst of light shines through the dirty broken glass of the church window for a second. And then it gets quiet, quieter than even before. All I can hear is Shelby breathing and sobbing, and I want to tell her to quit it, but when I feel my face I realize I'm crying too.

"We've got to go back for him," she says. It's a whisper, but also a shout.

"Are you crazy?" I shoot back at her. My teeth are chattering so hard, I can hardly talk.

"Pete, he's your friend, he's *my* boy. Where *I* come from, you don't leave *anyone* behind, you understand?"

I nod, and the two of us creep over to that window, though it's hard to see because the old glass is dark and cracked, and the sun outside just keeps sinking. I don't see the smoke thing anymore, but I can see a tall man's shape standing out there walking toward the church, kind of unsteady. The hair is black and oily.

We hear a knock on the door, and for some reason I blurt out, "Who's there?"

"Myself" is the reply, and it makes me shiver, because it's Derek's voice, but it's also not his voice, slurpy and thick with some kind of accent that doesn't sound right at all.

But Shelby's seen and heard him, and she's already opening the door. I wonder why I should be scared that she's doing it—I know Derek when I see and hear him—but I am seriously freaked out when she does it, and I hang back. If you're thinking I'm a coward, well, I'd like to learn you something different, but I guess it must be true.

Sure enough, Derek's standing in the door frame, almost like a shadow against the evening light that's coming in. For a second I'm just relieved that my friend is still alive, and I'm thinking, *Okay, man,*

I don't know what you did, but it worked, now let's get the hell out of here! But that doesn't last long. I can't see much of him, but I can see his eyes and his mouth, even in the dark, because they're glowing and burning just like that awful thing that attacked us. I just . . . I mean, I thought it was terrifying to see that in a cloud of smoke, but to see it on a man's face, on a face I've seen every week for years . . . ? It was like he was bleeding fire from those spots, and he had that same god-damned grin, all horrible and hungry and stupid.

I can't right say what must be going on in Shelby's mind at that moment. All I know is that she only hesitates a second or two before pulling out her .45 with her good hand and unloading I-don't-know-how-many rounds at the Derek creature.

After that, I can't recollect or tell you clearly what all goes down. Some force like a strong wind hits me, knocks me over, so I don't see what's happening. There's smells like oil and burning coal, there's all sorts of screaming, and I know part of that is me screaming, but not only me. There's blinding light and darkness and light again, more gunshots, and I think I hear Shelby's voice, but if I do, I still can't make out what she's saying. Dust covers me; it sticks to my clothes and my skin, and I realize that it's sticking because it's mixed with blood.

When I look up I see Derek's body lying near the door, and Shelby is lying close to me on the far wall of the church. I can't see either of them very well, but they don't look to be moving, and Shelby's face and hair are red and wet. Whatever I *can* see, it's visible because of the light from the monster. The cloud seems to be gathering itself together, little bits of smoke joining up not far from Derek at the entrance.

Maybe you'd know exactly what to do in a situation like this one, but me—I'm panicking at this point. I reach for Shelby's body, I think because I'm looking for her gun, though it's not like it did *her* any good. But then I feel a little bulge in her pocket, and I know it's her lighter. The creature's getting bigger and bigger, but it hasn't come at me just yet, so I gather up anything that looks flammable—pieces of coal lying around, cloth strips, pages from an old book—and I take Shelby's lighter. At first the sparks aren't doing much, and I'm thinking, *Great, Shelby, even your lighter's a piece of shit,* but the fire comes soon enough, just as the cloud is back to its old size and staring at me. I've found a thin piece of wood, and I'm able to make it into a kind of torch using the fire I started. This probably sounds nuts to you, but I just fling the torch at the thing—fighting fire with fire, maybe, though I can't say I put even that much thought into it. It seems to cry out, or maybe it laughs . . . ? I don't know, because I turn away to the back of the church, where there's a broken window, and I jump outside and just start running.

Part of my brain is able to figure out the direction we were supposed to be heading, and that's where I'm running. I can tell because I'm heading past the old apple trees by the coal wall in the broken side of the mountains. It's getting later in the evening, but there's a hell of a lot of light pouring out from that mess behind me, and a roaring like a furnace, and then I'm running through the dark woods, not knowing where I'm going or what things might be chasing me. I remember looking up for some reason trying to find stars, but I can't see them past the trees or the mountain. And somewhere behind me, something no one ever taught you about in grade school is raging or laughing or hunting.

Like I said, if I was making this up I'd have given you some kind of monster from the movies or whatnot. Something that I'd heard of, something that makes sense. But the truth is, I don't have clue what I saw back in MacAdam. Maybe it was something those folks brought with them from Scotland when they first came a couple hundred years ago. Maybe it was something they let out of the mountainside when they tore it up. The point is, I don't know. I'm just telling you what I seen—you understand?

Look, at this point I don't even really care if you believe me. Do you get that my best friends are dead now—at least, I assume they are? They died trying to save my sorry ass; I didn't do anything for them, just left them there. I hope you can find their bodies to bury them right, at least, but to do that, you'll have to find MacAdam for your-self. And go ahead, then—lock me up, charge me with murder even. Right now I'd take a tiny, closed little cell over open fires and huge mountains and skies so big I feel like I might fall into them. God knows, Derek and Shelby are gone, and I feel guilty as sin. And I don't know about you, but I can't think of a worse prison than that.

AN EDWARDIAN QUARTET

M. R. JAMES: THE UNCOMMON SCHOLAR

For Simon

Look to the storm-eroded crypts, where moss
Grows green on stone containing the remains
Of dread aristocrats, or in the veins
Of vellum volumes, tome on tome, across
The shelves of mages' *curiositas*
In libraries and in cathedral fanes,
Where ancient leaves yet bear the sickly stains
Of age or blood that blots a scribal gloss.
That's where you'll find him and his hapless scholar
Who, lured by lore and antique time's temptations
And prey to secret, hidden knowledge, wants
To seize a truth but calls instead the choler
Of malice summoned by those incantations
From distant history down to present haunts.

WILLIAM HOPE HODGSON: "HOPE THAT CAN BUT HARK"

You feel the ocean shudder to your bone,
Its voice a silent roar, and underneath
The lightning-lit wild waves as white as teeth
Lie hosts of spectres speaking in a groan
In ghastly chorus with the sea, whose moan
You cannot translate, though its ancient breath
Has whispered secrets, tales of life and death
And God and man, if these could but be known.

He is your guide across the dark terrain
Of sun-dead night, where ghastly monsters roam
In horrid hordes—for as with X you grope
Near blindly, trapped upon a darkling plain,
Across the blasted land of endless gloam,
You hear the light of his lone voice cry Hope.

ARTHUR MACHEN: "MAN IS MADE A MYSTERY"

At first, it seems, you're plunging to the deeps,
Caught in the green round of some darksome knoll,
Beneath which pallid human Things patrol
Unhallowed hoards of treasure, stored in heaps
Of grisly glistering gold, within which sleeps
A rousing primal force to seize your soul,
Perhaps to burn it to a cinder-coal,
Or call you to a past where chaos creeps.
But then, you catch a glimpse of other gold,
A chalice dipped in ancient vernal wells;
Celestial choristers proclaim in chants
A Love above the dark beneath the wold,
A draught of wine and wellspring that dispels
The night with light and fairy tale romance.

ALGERNON BLACKWOOD: LISTENING IN SILENCE

You think you've listened to the woods or caught
The current of the flowing river and
Known Nature, like a lover of the land
Who finds in fields and forests what he's sought,
Escape from all the havoc humans wrought
Upon the woods and water and the sand,
Far from man's strictured structures that have spanned
The globe to grasp each golden grove and grot.

In those seclusions, fleeing far from all
The traps of human trappings, is there peace?
In spaces where Dame Nature reigns, there violence
And tranquil love conjoin, beyond the wall
Between man and wild wilderness, he sees
The border, bidding you to hear the silence.

A Green Shade

And in þis he shewed me a lytil thyng þe quantite of a hasyl nott. lyeng in þe pawme of my hand as it had semed. and it was as rownde as eny ball. I loked þer upon wt þe eye of my vnderstondyng. and I þought what may þis be. and it was answered generally thus. It is all þat is made.
—Julian of Norwich

Annihilating all that's made
To a green Thought in a green Shade.
—Andrew Marvell

Isabella and Abigail checked their coordinates, looking for the witch's house. The trails were far behind them now, and they were wending through a maze of scabrous-skinned birch trees. The sun was bright but arcing westward, and they saw its rays only in the shreds of light that clawed through the dense foliage above. The tattered sunlight mixed eerily across Abigail's blue eyes with the reflection of the GPS image glowing from her phone. Isabella was a step or two behind her friend, but her nut-brown eyes were directed ahead of her, toward Abigail and the trees and Magus, their German Shepherd.

"Are we any closer to the spot?" Isabella asked. Magus had begun tugging obstinately at his leash.

"I mean, I think so," Abigail replied, still staring into the screen. She pointed to the map, and Isabella peered over her shoulder. If their calculations were accurate, Rachel Bourne's residence would be within a mile of this place.

If they were accurate. The two women knew there were countless variables, which meant innumerable ways they could be wrong—three and a half centuries was a long time. Yet they also felt an inexorable desire to identify this destination, a yearning as though they were on a pilgrimage and not just an indulgence of curiosity. Some recess of their souls felt a longing to discover what had become of Rachel Bourne.

They had learned about her by accident. Abigail was scrolling through university archives for her thesis, investigating Puritan expatriates to New Hampshire, when she started catching references to "that foule witch Goody Rachel Bourne, who hath made sundry and divers couvenantes with the Devil." Intrigued, she began ignoring the tedium of her thesis, hunting instead for any snatch of seventeenth-century gossip about this "foule witch." The hunt was slow going: it seemed no one *wanted* to speak of her, and she was scarcely the only Rachel Bourne of her day. But Abigail gradually tracked her movements and her history—or at least the skeleton of her history.

Rachel Mayhew came as a child of the great migration in the 1630s, granddaughter of a minister, and her family settled in the Connecticut River Valley. She married local boy Forthright Bourne in 1642, seemingly as an ordinary churchgoing young woman. How she went from Puritan wife to scorned sorceress remained unclear. Forthright disappeared from the record by 1647, and the next references to Rachel were depositions accusing her of calling down profane curses on the local livestock. To Abigail it fit a familiar pattern: the townsfolk spurning a woman isolated, on the fringes of the community. When another local couple died, presumably of smallpox, suspicion fell on Rachel, who apparently fled (or was cast out). She was next heard from in Portsmouth, where she seemed to dispense herbal remedies for a few years and may have served as a midwife.

But by 1654 she had once more become estranged from a community. The records now broke the pattern; whatever circumstances turned the town against Rachel, they were never mentioned overtly. Oh, there were still the references to her pacts with demonic forces, but no allusions to hexes and neighborly strife. A couple of documents seemed to suggest odd happenings during a particular week early in the year, the "heavens' deformation." Then she was gone.

This was where Isabella had come in. Knocking down mochas past midnight at The Magic Bean, she and Abigail started doing what graduate students do—talking about their theses. And Abigail realized that Isabella—with her background in IT and her obsession with geo-caching—would be the perfect partner. So together they followed eve-ry scrap of remaining evidence to identify the last known location in which Rachel Bourne was sighted. Finding clues from this point was almost impossible; but fur traders and Abenaki at that time occasion-ally talked about a woman living alone in a small cabin up in the northwest section of the state.

After months spent poring over algorithms and digitized manu-scripts, the two had extrapolated a plausible location: a little patch of earth that apparently survived unvisited even in twenty-first-century New England, one that would have been almost inconceivably isolated in the seventeenth century. What could have drawn Rachel, barely in her thirties at the time, beyond the reach of English or French or even Indian settlement? Abigail couldn't say for certain, but one line of Ra-chel's deposition stood out to her, the officials asserting that she "claims she hath on sundry occasions summoned forth a great green power."

What secrets lay hidden in that phrase, this "great green power"? Who could say? But for a woman, a widow, alone in a wild frontier, the pursuit and prospect of such a power was surely tantalizing—tantalizing enough, it appeared, that she would forsake all human bounds to seek it.

And so they hiked, Abigail in blue jeans with a red flannel shirt hanging loosely over her church camp tee, Isabella in merino wool and jogger pants. They were well past paths and the painted markings of the formal trails at which they had begun, beyond even the seem-ingly ubiquitous signs of human presence, the granola wrappers and plastic water bottles and old condoms. Aside from their shoes on the dirt snapping sticks, the explorers heard only natural sounds—the phrases and trills of sparrows, the quack of waking wood frogs in ver-nal pools, the bellowing of a waterfall like a distant dragon of the prime. It seemed to them pristine, unspoilt, nature untarnished by the malices of man.

They had parked the car about two-thirds of the way up the

mountainside, and at first they had continued to ascend. Now, though, they mounted an acclivity, and then their course sloped down somewhat sharply. It was no mean feat to navigate through the tangle of creepers and roots, dodging spiderwebs thick as linen. Even as Abigail followed the route proffered by her device, she increasingly began to feel she was descending into a maze, an Escheresque convolution of impossible geometries, a labyrinth populated with the denizens one would expect of a labyrinth. *Where's my thread?* she thought to herself, meaning it as a joke, though she didn't laugh.

Magus began barking abruptly, causing Abigail to gasp in surprise and shift her attention to Isabella. The dog was straining at his leash, bared teeth and black-brown eyes fixed at a thicket to their west, not far from the gradually sinking sun. Abigail caught a glimpse of movement amid the hawthorn.

"Who's there?"

The voice came from the thicket, and a figure emerged. He was perhaps forty, with a bronze-blond hedge of beard leading up to a green visored cap. An orange vest blazed out over his wine-dark flannel shirt, and at his side was a bolt-action rifle. He regarded the two women quizzically with faded blue eyes.

"Didn't expect to see anyone else around," he added after a pause. "You ladies should probably be careful out here."

Isabella's eyes narrowed as she stared at him. She made no attempt to soothe Magus as she responded, "Why is that?"

The man shrugged. "I just figured. We're a hell of a way from town here."

"I think we know that," Abigail replied as levelly as she could.

Shrugging again, the man said, "Sure. I just meant be careful. Even I don't usually come out this far, but I imagine there could be other hunters around." He scratched at his beard. "I wouldn't want anyone to get . . . hurt."

The man straightened his posture, keeping his gaze on Abigail and Isabella. Then he turned away, heading north through the thicket. Abigail looked nervously at her phone. "It looks like we may be headed in the same direction," the man stated without turning back. "I'll let you know if there are any problems."

"We'll be all right," Isabella shot back through half-clenched teeth. The man didn't answer, and soon his large strides took him out of their view as he was swallowed up by the wood ahead.

Isabella exchanged a glance with Abigail. Magus had stopped barking, but his leash was taut. She could feel the pulsing of her heart, the tightness of her trembling muscles, and she could see the same in Abigail.

"Do you want to keep going?" Abigail inquired.

Isabella squinted incredulously. "Hell, yes," she confirmed.

Abigail nodded. "Right. I don't want to stop when we're this close. Just . . . keep your pepper spray handy."

They resumed their hiking, even more attuned now to the environment around them. But because of this renewed awareness, they noticed an odd feature of their surroundings: the forest grew strangely quiet as they advanced. A true wilderness is never silent; life is boisterous, noisy, carefree, and away from human populations, scampering feet, sudden wings, and plaintive mating cries ride the breeze. The odd unnaturalness of the stillness wasn't exactly reverent, as though some awe pervaded the wood. It felt—though neither could say how she knew this—like a stifled, strangled, choked reticence.

So silent was it that Isabella actually cringed at an abrupt cracking sound, one so unobtrusive she scarcely would have heard it on a normal hike. Looking down at her feet, she saw she had stepped on a dried hazelnut. Ahead of them, deeper in the valley, were several hazelnut shrubs, their catkins dangling like narrow coffins, and little magenta blooms like blood bursting. Their V-veined leaves hadn't begun growing in the nascent warmth of spring; the branches looked gaunt as pietàs in the midst of the surrounding verdancy. But the ground ahead was covered in nuts, which puzzled Isabella. These hazelnuts must have dropped last summer; yet how could there be so many strewn about the ground? The fauna of this region ought to have devoured such a feast months ago.

Magus had stopped barking as well, but he was moving erratically, his legs juddering, his tail curled under his belly, more like an ill-trained beagle puppy than his usual sturdy self. Isabella glanced up at Abigail, who was looking back at her phone, following its lead.

"We've got to be close," Abigail mumbled.

"I hope so," Isabella grunted. "This place is . . . I don't know, a bit weird, yeah?"

Abigail paused and looked up from her device, glassy eyes glinting as she turned back to her friend. "Isabella, that dude is way ahead of us now. And the dog would warn us if we were in any trouble."

Isabella shook her head. "It's not that. Don't you feel it? Like something was nearby? Not a man or anything, but . . . something. *Diablo,* girl, I thought you were the one who believed in shit like that."

Abigail laughed, lightly but not unnervously. "I believe in God, not ghosts, Izzy. Not somethings. If you want, you can come to church with me on Sunday."

Isabella scowled. "Twelve years of Mass didn't exactly make me a choir girl, and a walk in the woods sure as hell isn't going to."

Abigail shrugged. "Fine. Then let's go find us a witch."

They resumed their course, emerging into a thick realm of maple, beech, and the ubiquitous bone-white birch, interspersed with ridges of coarse quartzite. Isabella's vision seemed to grow indistinct for a moment amid the crowd of tree trunks. She looked back the way she thought they had come, but she could no longer see the hazelnut shrubs.

"We're almost there!" Abigail shouted excitedly. Her voice burst into the stillness so starkly that Isabella nearly cried out. She bit her tongue and castigated herself. Abigail was happy; why shouldn't she be? It was a beautiful spring day, and they were nearing their destination, the culmination of months of work.

But this place did not look like nature as she knew it, not like the parks she and her *abuela* had visited on the outskirts of town, not even like the trails she used to hike with her ex-boyfriend, when she would leave him half a mile behind her amid the groves and the copses. Every detail of growth here seemed sickeningly, uncannily clear, as though she were aware of the rustling of maggots in rotten bark, though still she heard nothing. That stump lying prone at her feet—it looked horribly like a terrified rabbit, as though some small creature had been swallowed by the bark and transmogrified while writhing to escape. Yet if she looked at the same stump from a different angle, it once again appeared to be only a dead, diseased slab of maple, as one might find in any forest.

Then there was the scream. It was a human scream, sharp and short, and soon replaced by a guttering gurgle, and then once more by quietude. The woods weren't dark, but the canopy kept out a clear view of the sun, and Isabella couldn't tell what direction it came from, any more than she could now tell where they were.

"Abby, what the hell was that?"

"I don't know," Abigail replied tersely. She pointed ahead of her. "It came from there . . . I think?"

"Where's there? And where are *we*?"

"I don't know," Abigail repeated, snapping at Isabella because she was angry with herself. "My phone's not working."

"You told me we'd have no problems!" Isabella growled. "There are supposed to be towers nearby. Did you charge . . . ?"

"Yes, damn it, of *course* I charged the stupid thing." Abigail pried her eyes from her screen's dark glass, which now showed only her panicked reflection, and cast her gaze about their surroundings. "This way," she beckoned, striding ahead with all the boldness she knew she did not have. Isabella followed behind her, and for a time they began to walk together in feigned purpose.

Suddenly, though, Magus bolted, with so little warning that he pulled his leash free from Isabella's hand. The dog bounded ahead of them about ten feet and stopped for a few seconds, his teeth bared, his body spinning uncertainly. Then he started up again, racing over a rise. Isabella didn't hesitate, running past Abigail toward the little slope at which he had disappeared. Abigail was hardly so sanguine about chasing the dog, but she had no desire to find herself alone in the wood, and she pursued them. Even as she did so, however, she felt as though *she* were the one pursued. The darkening green of the wood that surrounded her looked unreal—symbolic, yet a symbol that stood for nothing living, like the painted face on an ancient coffin.

So they ran. On the other side of the rise the ground sloped deeper into the valley, shadows tessellated like netting on the earth. Dodging trees, the friends' momentum carried them farther and farther down, until Isabella stopped without warning. Abigail quickly came to a halt beside her.

"What?" she asked.

Isabella didn't answer; she didn't need to. Abigail could see what she saw.

"Oh my God," Abigail whispered, her throat dry, but with bile threatening deeper in.

It was the man they had seen . . . or it had been. His beard and cap were unmistakable. But his body was encased in a birch trunk—had become melded there. The outlines of his vest were visible but had been made the same mottled, dry white as the bark, and Abigail couldn't say where he ended and the tree began. Every detail they could see looked preserved, down to the hairs around his chapped lips, which were slightly parted, making a hollow of his empty throat. It might have been a sculpture of a man, expertly whittled down from a log, but his body protruded in a way no tree could extend.

And just fifteen feet farther on they saw the remains of Magus. They found him at the bole of a white ash, and his body was entangled with its roots, so that much of his lower half was indistinguishable from the vertical creasing of the tree's gray bark. His mouth was twisted into a howl he had never had the chance to utter. One of the front paws twitched slightly, as if it remembered what it had been like to be a dog, bounding free across open earth. But that was the only sign of life—except, of course, for the empire-slow sap-life of the vegetation that Magus had become.

Abigail could barely breathe for fear, and this only increased the horror. Was she to be next? She whirled around, shuffling away from trees as much as she could, while Isabella stood beside her, sobbing, teeth clenched.

"Why?" Isabella whispered with ferocity. It was all she could say; only questions remained.

Abigail grabbed her hand. "Let's go, Izzy."

"Go where?"

"Anywhere but here."

Abigail tugged, and Isabella acquiesced, so the two of them ran once more, though they could not say where; beneath the canopy of green that filled the dimming sky, all geography seemed to vanish. Nothing looked familiar in the sporadic shards of sun that broke through the leaves like glass splinters about the peaty ground. But Abigail was right, of course: whatever else, they had to move.

It was thus that they stumbled into a glade, a little hollow in the thick press of forest, where one sight was visible with appalling clarity. It was a fireplace, an old stone hearth and chimney, standing alone within a ring of trees; the work of centuries had torn away the rest of the house, and only that narrow, mortared tower of the home remained. Isabella knew what it was in an instant: they had come at last to the site they sought.

It was not the lonely, denuded hearth itself that caused her stomach to churn, but what was within it. Isabella saw *her,* Rachel Bourne; she stood, like Magus, like the hunter, engulfed inside the very stone of the erect, desiccated chimney. There she had remained, for three hundred years and more. In some ways time and the elements had done their work: fingers were missing, small patches of shale worn down. Yet her image endured in ghastly familiarity. Isabella could see the coarse texture of her wool frock, even what looked like a berry stain on the left sleeve. Frozen fringes of once-flaxen hair spilled from beneath her bonnet and framed her face. It was a young-looking face, slightly plump and speckled by pimples, with close-set eyes and a small nose and large lips—lips that had been screaming in an ecstasy of terror since before America was a nation.

And here, Isabella truly felt *its* presence. Past faith or doubt or science or any knowing that might track through her synapses, deeper than blood or marrow, Isabella now knew the nearness of the thing that Rachel Bourne had summoned. It was the great green power for which she had been cast out, and Isabella had always understood why Rachel, a woman alone in a dark society, would seek out a power, but now she understood why the people had sent her away. For what Rachel had brought forth in her quest for strength was a darkness beyond all human reckoning—beyond space, beyond gender, beyond nature yet embedded in it, a parasite of matter and spirit, a green that grew from the earth like the wasp from the caterpillar. Isabella knew too that it did not seek her annihilation, but its unfathomable intelligence had its own alien ends. It hadn't sought to destroy Rachel either, or Magus, or the hunter, but it had moved inside its little sphere of creation, and it *had* destroyed them, and another such movement might destroy Isabella or Abigail too. And they would find themselves absorbed into the landscape, like monuments shrouded in mosses, their consciousnesses dwindled to the unminding existence of the vegetable or the desolate coldness of rock, and their screams too would be drowned out by the silence of the shade.

"Aunque pase por valle tenebroso," she murmured by an ancient instinct, *"ningún mal temeré, porque tú vas conmigo."* This time she grabbed hold of Abigail. Her friend's arm was still, so still that Isabella feared that it would break off and crumble, that Abigail too had been transmogrified into the hellish ecosystem. But her resistance was only the stiffness of nightmare, and in a moment her sky-blue eyes caught Isabella's.

"Abby, come," Isabella said, and sparing a tear for Rachel as she ran, she led Abigail away from the grisly glade.

They still didn't know where they were going, and who knew what were the boundaries of the green power? Isabella could still sense its inhuman thoughts oppressing her soul and her viscera, like the pressures of a deep abysm. Abigail was no help; she went along unresistingly, but her countenance was glazed with a sheen of dread. All around them the tree trunks still rose skyward like stakes, and the burning green of the leaves above occluded more than ever the rays of the westering sun. If she could *see* the sun, Isabella might know where they were. But when they ran, she felt as if they were locked in an endless track, like tracing the perimeter of a compass when she wanted to be following a point on the rose.

And then she heard the crunch, the tiny sound of a splintering shell. She looked down at her feet and saw the hazelnuts. Beside her and Abigail stood the little row of shrubs. Isabella picked up the shell she had stepped on, regarding it for the briefest of moments, and then she knew where they were. Pulling Abigail along, she ran with the same urgency as before, but now with direction. Beneath her tight pants her thighs burned, but at this she rejoiced, for now they were climbing, ascending from out the valley. Her grip on Abigail slackened, for Abigail too was striding with purpose, and the pain in her legs was a pain that *meant* something. Her chest heaved with the force of it all, and yet she breathed freely, for the weight of the green shade was lifting. They were emerging from its dominion.

So it was that, some minutes later, the two women found themselves on an outcropping en route to their parking space. They sat on rocks in a clearing, trembling, inhaling and exhaling, never speaking, for words seemed absurdly inadequate for what they had seen, what they had known, and it all made them weep as they never thought they could. They embraced each other in their exhausted relief, and Isabella could feel her friend's heart against her own and exult, because a tree or a stone has no heart to beat. When they released each other, she looked back down the way they had come. The sun had dropped beneath the horizon, but a roseate glow suffused the west, illumining in red and pink all manner of things above the shadows. She held between her fingers the untimely but ripe hazelnut, and carefully she raised it up into the light of the sky, where it glowed like a round little world in the night.

A Word

The stream of Time, irresistible, ever moving, carries off and bears away all things that come to birth and plunges them into utter darkness . . . Nevertheless, the science of History is a great bulwark against this stream of Time; in a way it checks this irresistible flood, it holds in a tight grasp whatever it can seize floating on the surface and will not allow it to slip away into the depths of Oblivion.

—Anna Komnene, *The Alexiad* (translated by E. R. A. Sewter)

You feel it first, before you hear or see:
The sea o'erwhelming placid deltas, and
When Rahab's gullet spews her chaos free
Into the open channels, then the sand
And salt assault the tranquil stream and strand
Of land. I feel the fall of pressures in my gut
Of Time's remorseless current as I stand,
Await the plunge, to crush me like a nut
In some great hand, and hope feels futile. But
My words are mine, my one offense against
The brutal tide that fills the sky, for what
Else might I spit back at the beast? My tensed
Tongue lashing toward the serpent-shrouded day,
I cast my voice into the void and pray.

THE FOLLY

Tarry a while, O Death, I cannot die
While yet my sweet life burgeons with its spring;
Fair is my youth, and rich the echoing boughs
Where *dhadikulas* sing.

Tarry a while, O Death, I cannot die
With all my blossoming hopes unharvested,
My joys ungarnered, all my songs unsung,
And all my tears unshed.

Tarry a while, till I am satisfied
Of love and grief, of earth and altering sky;
Till all my human hungers are fulfilled,
O Death, I cannot die!
    —Sarojini Naidu, "The Poet to Death"

 Let not the serpent see me, and let not the children of the dragon
hiss at me.
    —*Acts of Thomas* (translated by M. R. James)

Somehow Archana knew when the carriage was finally arriving at the
Wingarden Estate. After miles of tussocks and marshland and bob-
bing yellow heads of grain, they descended a small valley into a carefully planted cluster of wych elm, leaving the turnpike road for a path
that rose and fell and twisted through green wolds. She did not know
the names of these features, so different from the topography of her
beloved Kochi, but she could sense an undefinable alteration in the
whisper of the air as the horses slowed and they emerged into a grassy
green landscape.

 Beside her she had watched her husband grow steadily more anxious as the sun arced westward in the sky. The coachman had assured

them that they would reach their destination on this, the third day after leaving from London. In their weeks crossing great oceans and seas before arriving at England, Biju had remained almost tranquil, walking with fluid steps and inhaling in measured but relaxed breaths. He was unfailingly polite to everyone they encountered, from captains to porters, even when they slighted him or looked askance at his cassia-brown skin. During this time he had not been distant to her, and yet he had taken on a lotus-like serenity during the voyage. Archana had appreciated the calm, so unlike the terse, almost frenzied pace he had adopted in his clerical work back home.

Now, though, she could feel Biju's sinews tense, and she put her hand on his arm. He smiled beneath his mustache, but he smiled with dry, pursed lips and a twitch of the nose. Archana knew it was silly, but she almost thought she could hear his heart's beat above the rumble of wooden carriage wheels across the packed soil.

"Are you afraid, my husband?" she inquired, loud enough for him to hear yet soft enough to be inaudible to the coachman outside. She did not wish Biju to think she was shaming him.

He shook his head quickly. "No, *priya*. I do not fear. But it all seems so grand. How should I be given this chance, to travel across the world and to meet these people? To be treated as someone of importance when I am in fact so small?"

"Do not say you are of no importance, Biju," Archana insisted. "I can think of one person who considers you most important indeed."

Biju shrugged. "Yes, but of course my mother would think that."

He laughed, displaying a true smile, as Archana took her hand from his arm and shoved him playfully. Then she looked back out the window as the carriage rounded a corner past a small, assiduously planted cluster of oak and ash, and she saw the house emerge from behind the grassy hills.

She almost gasped at the sight. It was not entirely the considerable size that took her breath away; she had seen many immense edifices in her journey here, including more in London than she could have imagined. But she and Biju were ever being hurried from one site to the next with an expeditiousness that kept such monuments distant and foreign. To look upon the sprawling manor that now stretched across her view and know it would be their home for the coming weeks—this was the source of her awe.

Its length seemed to stretch without end across the hill upon which it had been erected. In the center of its front façade were three massive towers, with a porch emerging from the middle one. The towers were topped in rounded turrets that ended with glistering gold spires. The gray ashlar limestone blocks were so carefully set together that it was only as the coach drew near that Archana could even see the seams. Daunting, immense, and immovable as the structure looked, it also seemed to her almost a living thing, like some massive, brooding beast lying supine in the grass.

She did not have long to ponder this image, however, for straightway the carriage pulled up at the entrance and the coachman opened the door for them. Archana saw Biju inhale sharply and smooth out the perceived wrinkles in his *mundu* before stepping outside. He offered her his hand, and she took it, using great care not to trip over the folds of her *chattayum mundum* as she descended. One cautious step at a time, she planted her sandaled feet onto the English earth and for the first time beheld their hosts.

Archana had never seen people like these before; they scarcely seemed human in their perfection. The man was tall, with well-coiffed waves of reed-brown hair, his shaved visage smooth and blemish-free. His eyes glittered the blue of fresh pools, and he smiled with an earnest, casual hunger. He was taller than Biju by a head and towered over Archana. Yet he was not slender; though well-fitted, his scarlet greatcoat and the white shirt beneath strained to contain the muscles of his chest and arms.

And his wife! She seemed positively to gleam or glitter, as though she were one of the goddesses on Archana's home shores and not a human woman. Her hair, brilliant as spun gold, was pulled in a bun with ringlets that cascaded moltenly down the curvature of her swan-like neck. Above the crimson glamour of her smile, her eyes glinted crystalline in the glow of the sinking sun. Archana could see nothing in her pale yet ruddy skin that was not immaculate, as though she were carved of marble. Yet she did not appear lifeless, as some sort of effigy, but gloriously alive, a flush of exuberance quietly shading her complexion. She wore an intricately woven dress of bright groseille satin with a splash of white ribbon horizontally rimming her waist, a dress that left bare her dimpled shoulders.

The gentleman extended his hand to her husband, who took it at once.

"Lord Hugh Croft, seventeenth Earl of Wingarden," he announced. "We wish you a hardy welcome to Golden Grove, our most humble domicile. And you must be . . ."

"Biju Mathew Abraham, sir," he replied. "So pleased to be here."

The lady, in turn, reached out and took Archana's hand in her own. The skin was almost silken to her touch, so smooth she did not want to release it. "And I am Lady Augusta Croft. We are so very grateful you could join us here."

Her voice was soft, surprisingly deep and rich. Archana could understand her words clearly, but she hesitated before responding, knowing how clumsy her own words would sound. But Biju looked her way, and she knew what was expected of her. They had practiced her English throughout the voyage here, though she was little content with her speech. Even so . . .

"Archana Rachel Abraham, ma'am."

"Lovely!" Lady Augusta smiled, and she squeezed Archana's hand gently before releasing it, almost reluctantly. "You will doubtless be weary and famished from your travels, and I do wish ever so much to play the model hostess. And yet, I have been in an absolute agony of anticipation awaiting your arrival to show you about the grounds. Hugh can attest to this, can you not, my darling?"

"Absolute agony indeed," he confirmed merrily. "I daresay she has spoken of nothing else."

Lady Augusta took Archana's shoulders in her slender hands, then turned her limpid eyes to Biju. "I promise you the finest supper anyone could wish for, if only you will indulge me in a tour of the countryside before the sun is too low. Marlow will see that your bags are brought to your room. Will you join us?"

Archana did indeed feel rather spent, and she carried inside her the terror that her stomach might growl in the presence of their hosts. But she knew well the solicitousness of her husband, so she was little surprised when he told Lady Augusta, "Of course, ma'am. We are only too pleased to join you."

"Splendid!" grinned Lord Hugh, his facing beaming like a captive sun.

So began their tour, and though Archana's hunger did not abate as the time proceeded, she could not deny a certain enthrallment at the enchantment of it all. The grounds of the estate were no less exquisite than the Crofts themselves. Every blade of grass grew sharp and green, and the hills bent elegantly around curved ha-has carved out of their flanks and mortared precisely. They sloped down to a twisting lake, upon whose banks alders rose and willows drooped. Archana could not imagine even the gardens of Bolgatty Palace rivalling it.

"Designed by Capability Brown himself," Lord Hugh noted proudly, and Biju nodded vigorously as though he knew what that meant.

The sun was nearing its western nadir, its glow stark and saffron, when they came to a lone white tower encircled by a beaten path and a ring of bushes blushing red with roses. Its base was polyhedral, with enough sides that it looked almost round, and in it were carved intricate spirals that seemed to form patterns when Archana looked at them but turned random as she drew nearer. Above the base, perhaps twenty feet up, it narrowed into a tall shaft, which in turn gave way to a sharp spire. At first glance it appeared to Archana almost like a chapel or small church, yet it was at once too ornate and too austere—and too symmetrical—for this to be so.

"*Folie,* the French call it," Lady Augusta intoned. "A folly, in the English."

"What do you use it for?" Archana asked without thinking. She visibly winced when she saw Biju's mortified reaction. The Crofts were great people, she realized, and they did not plan their land with thoughts of utility in mind.

But if the hosts took umbrage, they did not display it. Lord Hugh, indeed, laughed in good humor at the question.

"What indeed, Mrs. Abraham! I should like to think its elegance justifies its existence: 'A thing of beauty is a joy forever: Its loveliness increases; it will never pass into nothingness.' But as it happens, we do have other uses for it. Come this way, won't you?"

They followed the path that wound down to the folly. As they approached, Archana saw the roses, deep crimson, though with traces of drier brown at the base, where pink and pale green aphids crawled. The carved patterns looked even more arbitrary here, swirling and bending and promising a design that never emerged. The white paint was apparently several layers thick, with small dry drips that felt slightly tacky when she brushed her fingers against them.

Lord Hugh opened a small but ornate pale-brown alderwood door, carved with bas-relief images of slender writhing dragons, mouths open. A lone central lantern lit the interior, which consisted of a single round room with an austere pedestal or dais at the center. Save for two alcoves on the far side, the walls around them were smooth. They lacked the designs graven in the folly's exterior, though they were not wholly bare. Hung on those walls, at regular intervals, was a peculiar set of decorations: an elliptical mask painted in bright colors, a birchbark canoe paddle, a white and gray fur coat, a jade axe with hardwood haft and handle. Archana examined the artifacts, puzzled. Lady Augusta, noticing her perplexity, walked to her side.

"Superb, aren't they? The true riches of the globe are its people, wouldn't you say?"

"I . . . do not understand," Archana was forced to admit.

"We have long entertained guests from the far antipodes. It is our pleasure to do so, and truly we ask so little in return. But is it not right that we should have some token of remembrance from those whose company we have enjoyed? I do believe that your husband was informed in advance that this was the only condition we required of you. A memento, as it were, another ornament to brighten this space."

"Of course, ma'am," Biju replied.

He pulled out a small wooden cross with four equal sides, each ending in little floral fronds. Three lines like steps spread out beneath it, a winged form like a dove perched atop. Archana watched as her husband, with equal parts pride and humility, presented it to their hosts. Their reactions were peculiar, she thought. For an instant Lord Hugh seemed to frown as he looked intently at the object, his mouth hanging open. Lady Augusta's face kept a smile, but a frozen smile, carved beneath unblinking eyes sheened like ice. Whatever their thoughts, however, they quickly recovered their equanimity. Lord Hugh's good humor returned, and Lady Augusta's frosty smile melted into a more fluid one—she quickly moved forward to take the gift from Biju's hand. Their odd initial reactions had been so brief that Archana did not believe her husband had even seen them, though she was certain she had not been mistaken in recognizing them.

"I must confess my surprise—pleasant of course," Lord Hugh said. "I was given to think of India as a land of the Orient, that you kept images of your gods and your heroes."

"Yes, sir, I see, sir," Biju nodded, holding onto his own polite smile. "And you are perhaps right, in a way. This is a *Mar Thoma sleeva,* a cross that has been in my family for many years. It has been made from the wood of the banyan tree. Most of the people in our land worship the gods of the Vedas and the Upaniṣads, or the god Allah of the Qur'an. But according to the traditions of my people, almost two thousand years ago, the Apostle Thomas sailed into the ancient port of Muziris and planted the first churches on Indian soil. And the men and women of our home have passed down those teachings since that day. We are Christians . . . like you."

Lady Augusta flowed forward to Biju and took the small cross in her long, delicate fingers. She ran them across the light, intricately wrought wood. "Yes," she murmured, then more loudly, "After all these years I can still be surprised. We thank you for this gracious gift. I'll see to it that Marlow gives it pride of place here."

"And now," interjected Lord Hugh, "I fear we have presumed upon your patience far too long. Shall we remove ourselves to Golden Grove for supper?"

Archana dared not display the eagerness with which she received the suggestion. Her husband, doubtless more famished than she herself was, responded with an understated nod of assent, and the quartet stepped out of the folly and back into the darkening terrain. The red of the descending sun seemed to burnish and bleed across the tower's white sheen as they made their way toward the house.

The eastern sky had become the blushing untamed blue of the ocean, the west a fading roseate smear, when they arrived at Golden Grove. They passed under the façades of the porch and into the foyer, lit brilliantly by a chandelier suspended above their heads. A pair of grand staircases snaked on either side of them up to a second floor that receded from sight beyond.

From the foyer their hosts led them through other rooms, no less opulent and equally bright. Archana could scarcely conceive the extravagance of the light; in Kochi, candles abounded, yet she knew of no homes that could glow like dawn within after the sun had set. They passed by paintings, images not unlike the depictions of gods or heroes, of Vishnu or Lakshmi, Śiva or Parvati, Krishna or Radha, Rama or Sita. Some were landscapes, Arcadian glades in gentle blushing twilight or great sublime escarpments illumed by lightning-lit clouds. Some depicted creatures from far climes—lions and serpents and beasts with myriad arms that stretched like cords. Others were portraits, stately men and women in formal attire, eyes open and mouths closed tight. Many of these resembled Lord Hugh and Lady Augusta, though the fashions and attire and styles seemed to differ from painting to painting.

At last, they arrived at a vast banqueting table, so long it could never have fit in Biju and Archana's house, comfortable though their home was. They were directed to their seats as Lord Hugh and Lady Augusta likewise sat down.

"You cannot imagine how many formalities and ceremonies accompany a dinner in this house," Lady Augusta laughed airily, leaning toward Archana as though in confidence. "I shall instruct you in our silly English ways in time for tomorrow's dinner party, my dear. For today, however, you have persevered quite long enough, I am sure."

Trays were brought forth, covered in silver domed lids so pristinely polished they looked like bent mirrors. When the servants lifted the lids, Archana was shocked to see *erachi varutharacha* on her plate, with *parotas* stacked neatly on the side. The scent of beef and coconut was released as the lid was withdrawn, and it wafted welcomingly up to her.

"You are far from home," Lord Hugh said. "We took the liberty of researching your cuisine. Tomorrow you will dine in the English style, but I hope that today you may find some of the flavors of home."

Biju nodded. "We humbly thank you, sir," he replied.

Archana echoed her husband's thanks, though as she ate, she found herself only reminded of the great distance that separated her from home. The meal was like a faded image of Kochi's cuisine. The sauce's colors were muted, less vibrant than the *erachi varutharacha* her mother had taught her to make. The *parotas* were dry, the meat chewy, and they had substituted a foreign amalgam of spices in the sauce, far blander than anything she would have allowed in her own kitchen. The result was disappointing, yet how could she be angry at the attempt?

And Archana enjoyed listening to the Crofts, even if her English was insufficient to catch every nuance of their speech, for their syllables rang like a strange music to her, almost intoxicating in its sibilance. She enjoyed looking at them, as though they were artifacts more than people, dolls or paintings come to life. When they asked of life in India, Biju answered their questions, as she had hoped he would, for her ignorance of their language weighed heavily upon her.

So she listened and watched politely as the evening passed, while outside the walls the sunken sun's setting yielded the countryside to darkness. When at last the final courses were served and the conversation waned, Lady Augusta invited Archana into the drawing room, where they sat by the fireplace in salon chairs set upon the wine-red carpet. At first Lady Augusta sat, simply staring deeply into the dancing flames, and Archana saw them reflected in her still, pellucid eyes. When she spoke, it was in a soft, melodic murmur.

"Speak to me of your land, Mrs. Abraham."

"I fear I am not . . . clever with your language, my lady," she replied with painful precision. "My husband—"

Lady Augusta looked up abruptly, almost sharply, and grabbed Archana's hand. Her grip was not painful, but under its pressure Archana could feel her own pulse tapping. The lady's burning glass eyes were now directed almost imploringly into Archana's own.

"Seldom have I strayed from the wolds of Lincolnshire, and never ventured beyond the Thames, and yet I hunger for the life of this grand earth. Have you never longed for anything, thirsted for a draught when you were dry?" The gray eyes glistened, the voice almost vanished. "Tell me of the beauties of your world."

Lady Augusta relaxed her grip, though her pale fingertips still rustled on Archana's brown knuckles. Archana inhaled as one plunging into deep tides, then she spoke.

"The sun burns bright in the sky of Kochi. From my house I can sit in the shade of a *neem* with leaves, green but thin. Then I look out to the west. The banyan trees spread out like many strong arms. I feel sometimes that they embrace and protect my church beside them. And then, there far away, I see the ocean. It is blue and green and alive—alive with animals, alive with boats, alive with people from far away—and alive with *my* people."

Lady Augusta nodded. "Yes," she sighed, "yes, I can see it. Alive." She brought her hands down and folded them in her lap, though not before running one gently across her abdomen. She was so close that Archana could feel the moist warmth of her measured breaths.

But the stillness was breached by a sound like a muffled cry, then shouts from the direction of the foyer. It was a man's voice, hoarse and frail yet forceful, and at first Archana only heard it as guttural growlings. As it grew nearer, though, she could make out a piercing groan. "Death! They bring death! They must die!"

Lord Hugh rushed out of the dining hall, with Biju not far behind him. Lady Augusta's breathing paused, and she rose, one hand upon her chest, one pressed back toward Archana, as though in protection. From the other end of the sitting room Archana saw a figure stagger forth. He wore a frayed dressing gown that may once have been luxuriant velvet but now was tattered and stained. She thought that everything about him looked dry: thin, wispy hair like kindling grasses, rutted skin the color of beach sand, and cracked lips that parted to bark in parched vehemence. Still he shouted of death and judgment, and of all the fears Archana had known since her sandaled feet first stepped off Kochi earth, this was the profoundest and most visceral.

The man was staggering, gesticulating wildly, yet for a moment he stopped to gather a breath, and in that moment his eyes caught Archana's, and they were not what she had expected. His eyes were green—she was too far away to see if they were the green of the sea or the green of the *neem,* but she could tell that they were wet and alive. They were also, she somehow knew, wide as the caves in the jungles to the east, wide in wild horror as they looked at her.

Then Marlow, the Crofts' dour manservant, scuttled into the sitting room and wrapped arms around the old man with such casual force that it was clearly an action at which he was well practiced. The gaunt, desiccated body resisted as Marlow said softly, "It's all right, Master George. You're all right there, sir."

To Archana's surprise, Lady Augusta walked forward in even strides until she came to the frenzied form, and she too looked into those torrid, florid eyes. She took the sallow, hollow cheeks in her cupped hands and kissed lightly the brittle forehead. "You know you must rest, dear. No one here means you harm. There is naught but love for you here."

The antique face fell, and his screams turned to whimpers, like a frightened child's sniffling. The man allowed Marlow to walk him back toward the foyer and the stairs, and Lady Augusta turned back to her guests, a wan, weary smile on her countenance.

"You must forgive my father," she said quietly. "He has lived with us many years, and he is very old. Sometimes he misremembers himself, even us. I know that in your land you value family. Surely you are no stranger to such unfortunate experiences?"

"We understand, ma'am," replied Biju somberly, and Archana nodded, thinking of her own mother's last days, how she would run out of the house and dig in the ground until her fingers bled, how she would weep like an infant when told to stop.

"He could not hope for a better home in these difficult days," Lord Hugh said. "We ensure that his every need is provided for. Even though his situation will never cease to grieve us."

"You have had a taxing day to end a long journey," Lady Augusta interjected, returning to Archana and taking her by the hand. "You will be shown to your rooms, and it is my sincerest desire that you are able to rest well this evening."

Archana followed Biju in thanking them for their hospitality, and they were eventually led up a staircase and through corridors, until at last they were brought to two grand adjoining rooms. The notion that they would sleep separately was one of the greatest surprises in a day of surprises; back home, large families might share a single room no bigger than one of the Crofts' closets. Archana gazed up at the high, paneled ceiling, then down at the door that opened to her husband's room as a young maidservant, perhaps seventeen years of age, tentatively drew near her.

"Who are you?" Archana inquired. She felt the question sounded rude in her staccato English, but she did not know another way to ask it.

"I'm Bridget O'Halloran, Ma'am," the maidservant replied. She was pale as milk, though a flurry of freckles flecked her face. Her hair was orange-red, coarse, and quite obviously long, for strands of it escaped recklessly from what was supposed to be a tight bun. "Lady Augusta sent me to take care of you. I never been a lady's maid before. Most houses, they won't even take folk like me from Ireland, so it's a right honor to be here. And what do I call you by, ma'am?"

Archana was flustered, unprepared to have to introduce herself once more. The stately, precise English of the Crofts was difficult enough for her, so she lost much of what came rolling off the rapid, inflected tongue of young Bridget. "Archana Rachel Abraham," she replied, unsure of what else to say.

"That's quite the mouthful, isn't it? Rachel, you say? That was my grandmother's name."

"It is my baptismal name," Archana told her. "You may use it, if you like."

"Truly? Thank you ever so much, Missis Rachel."

Bridget smiled sheepishly, but Archana flinched as the girl reached for her *chattayum mundum*. The maidservant froze at her reticence, hand still suspended in midair.

"So sorry, Missis Rachel," she said. "I was sent to help you into your nightclothes. I meant no harm by it."

Archana blinked and brought a hand to the white cotton on her shoulder. "I—I know. Perhaps I will undress myself this night . . . Bridget."

"Of course, ma'am!" she nodded vigorously. "Your nightgown's there on the bed if you want it, ma'am. And I'll see you in the morning, then?"

Archana made herself smile. "In the morning, yes."

Bridget bowed hesitantly, looked around, then shuffled out of the room. Archana sat down; her stomach felt unsettled, perhaps from the English attempt at *erachi varutharacha*. She rose again, removed her garment, and hurriedly put on the nightgown—she knew she was alone, yet the bedroom was so much vaster, so much more open, than any room she had ever stayed in, and she felt small and vulnerable inside it. The gown was long, rippling with frills and lace, though the cotton felt little different against her skin from her customary attire, and her discomfort subsided.

Feeling freer now, she walked across the bedroom and opened the door to her husband's room.

"Biju?" she inquired tentatively, and at once she saw him stride over to her. He wore a white nightshirt, not unlike her gown, though more austere. In many ways its color and simplicity differed little from the *mundu* he had been wearing. Yet something of the cut looked so strikingly dissimilar to her that she almost shrank back as he took her hand.

"Are you feeling well, *priya?*" he asked, and Archana's taut muscles loosened at the sound of words in Malayalam.

"Yes . . . mostly," she replied. "And you?"

Biju smiled widely, gazing around at the wide walls and high ceiling of his room. "It is more than I could have imagined or hoped for. I cannot say why such people would grant us hospitality, but surely this will benefit my career."

Archana glanced around her, at the same walls and ceiling her husband saw. To her they were both frighteningly vast and curiously constricting, like a hunting ground. "Biju, do you not feel a . . . misgiving of sorts? I cannot deny that they have been kind, and there is so much that is beautiful in this place. Yet it echoes in my thoughts like a song out of tune somehow. I miss Kochi."

"Of course you do, *priya,*" he said. "It will always be our home. And we will return soon enough. But we may enjoy this first, yes?"

"I do not wish to hinder you, Biju," Archana insisted. "Perhaps I am merely fatigued from our long journey. I do not understand why I was invited."

Biju sat down on the side of his massive bed and beckoned for her join him. "I would not desire to be here without you. How could anyone, even an Englishman, fail to be enchanted by you, Archana?" He gently stroked her temple, drawing his finger down to the nape of her neck. "Even now I always see you as I did at the *minnukettu,* when I was placing the pendant around your neck. Do you know how much I practiced tying knots to get it right?"

Archana touched the *minnu,* then the knot at the back of her neck. "Still there, I see. It seems your practice paid off." She looked again into her husband's eyes. "There are many wonderful things to see in the world, and I do not wish to deny them to you. But do not in your haste for novelty be ashamed of our own land."

"The Englishmen have a proverb: 'There's no place like home.' My home is with you, wherever you are. But I have no greater wish than to be with you beneath our *neem* tree in Kochi."

Archana smiled and nestled into Biju's arms, and they stayed that way for some time until at last she rose. For a moment, she hesitated, thinking perhaps to remain in the room with him; but they were guests, and she had been given a room, and though she already missed the touch of his hand on her skin, she quietly relished the prospect of a night without his snoring. Fatigued in her bones and body, she yawned and shuffled back to her chambers, blew out the candles, and settled into her bed.

Archana slept peacefully, the miles of their travel and the cares of her days in distant lands melting into the voluptuous softness of the mattress. She did not dream, save for a wall of pale whiteness that rose up in her thoughts. She must, however, have moved in her sleep, for she woke up many hours later, on her back looking up at the gauzy red canopy above her. She felt dry; the skin on her fingers was itchy and red in some places, her lips had tiny cracks in them, and her tongue stuck to her palate. Her body, she realized, missed the wetness of her land, the ocean and the rain and the sweat that she could not bring with her to Lincolnshire.

"Are you awake, Missis Rachel?"

Archana sat up to see Bridget standing solicitously by her bedside. She nodded, sitting up and smoothing out the curls of her black hair. Keeping her lips pursed, she tried to gather up enough spit to moisten her tongue before at last answering, "Yes, Bridget. I am awake."

"Mistress has sent a dress for you today, ma'am," Bridget said, smiling. "You want I should . . . Shall I . . . leave it here?"

Archana wanted to say, "Yes." But she looked at the wide, darting, ingratiating blue eyes of the girl, and all she could say was, "You may dress me, if you like."

Bridget's grin grew wider, like a waxing moon, and she at once set to work. Archana had seen the intricacy of her host's dress the night before, yet Lady Augusta had glided across the grounds as though her costume were a part of her person. But upon removing her nightgown, Archana soon found herself overlaid in more clothes than she had conceived it possible for a single person to wear. Chemises, drawers, petticoats, and all manner of cotton materials were layered upon her, with a corset tied tautly around her torso and her legs and hips rounded in the whalebone cage of a crinoline. It was some time before Bridget finally came to the outer garment itself, a deep purple-red frock that rippled and shone like wine. Archana's feet were encased in black boots laced halfway up her calf, her hands in gloves up to the elbows. Then Bridget tied her hair into a loose bun, with ringlet curls spilling down like rain drops to her shoulders, topped with a little lace cap.

When at last the process was complete, Bridget led Archana to the mirror. She could scarcely recognize herself, sealed as she was within these coverings. Yet the roundness of the crinoline somehow made her want to spin, and as she watched the burgundy dress flare out with the movement, she marveled at the alien ingenuity of it all. Archana had never thought herself beautiful, save in the eyes of her husband, but she felt that now, enfolded within the beauty of her costume, perhaps others too might see her that way. She could not say if it was a good feeling, but it was, to be sure, a new one.

"Will you come down for breakfast now, ma'am?" asked Bridget.

"My husband?" Archana inquired. "Will he . . . ?"

"Right this way, ma'am."

Archana followed slowly, each step in her unfamiliar boots a subtle calculation. She found that her wardrobe demanded similar attentiveness to keep the circumference of the crinoline clear of obstacles. She longed for the easy drapery of her plain *chattayum mundum,* its grace so different from the intricate beauty of this dress that seemed to swallow her. But there was a pride too as she moved without stumbling, as she showed to Bridget and would show to Biju that she could master even this foreign trial.

Biju emerged from his room with a manservant at his side, and he wore a black lounge suit with a cravat, and a tall black hat perched upon his head, out of which the curls of his hair spilled with abandon. At first Archana almost laughed, but she stifled the sound, unwilling to wound his pride; and as she gazed more at him she could not deny that the attire lent him a certain exotic allure.

"You look lovely, my dear," he said to her in English.

She blinked, paused, replied, "You look handsome, sir."

Biju's manservant remained stoic as stonework, but Archana could see Bridget scarcely able to contain her giddy good humor. Together they all descended the staircase to the main foyer, where Lord Hugh and Lady Augusta awaited them.

And so began a day more curious than any Archana had known, whether on her travels through diverse countries or in her twenty-one years in Kochi. Pale-fleshed men and women adorned in splendor arrived, two by two, within the walls of Golden Grove. They smiled courteously and laughed, the women's voices ringing like bells about the halls. Perhaps at times their eyes darted askance toward one another when they saw the brown skin of the Crofts' guests, but in speech they were ever unfailingly polite, their words chosen with care as they glanced from their hosts to the Abrahams. How, then, could Archana not smile herself, for how could she help but see that underneath the ruffles of fabric she was as beautiful as they were, perhaps more so? And watching Lady Augusta, Archana knew that her hostess saw it too.

There was much conversation Archana could not follow, talk of Lord Palmerston, of the Queen and the Prince, of the ending of the Crimean War. Biju had sometimes spoken to her of such things, but they felt remote from her days in India and no less remote here. Yet the women also asked her about Kochi, asked as though they might indeed be interested, and so she talked to them of home, as she had done with Lady Augusta, who herself listened, rapt and voracious, to the tales. To Archana, *England* was rich and strange and glimmering with dangerous mysteries. Yet to the English women with whom she spoke, it was the soft white beach sand and wheeling fronds of coconut trees—the sights to which she woke each mundane morning—that were captivating with the allure of the unfamiliar. So she talked on, increasingly heedless of last night's discomfort, as the minutiae of her days were transmuted into legend. Even some ladies' husbands, pensively stroking their pointed beards, inclined their heads in her direction to attend upon her words.

The day passed as a litany of such conversations, interspersed with food and meals at bewildering intervals. After a time, though, the men adjourned to hunt, while their wives remained behind. Lady Augusta had tables arranged outside, with tea and cucumber sandwiches and scones. The banter continued under a modest white sun that perched over the undulating lawns that surrounded Golden Grove. From time to time in the distance Archana heard the harsh crack on gunfire from the hunting expedition. After a few such shots she taught herself not to wince, to forget what such sounds meant when she heard them back home. Here they were sport and conviviality, her husband joining Lord Hugh and the other gentlemen in civilized pursuits.

"How marvelous to speak to one another in a mysterious, mystical tongue like old Sanskrit," intoned a woman of middle age at the table.

"In Kochi we speak Malayalam," Archana replied with the veneer of a smile lacquered upon her countenance. "Sanskrit is—"

Her voice, and the voices buzzing around her, cut off sharply. Beneath their feet the ground trembled as if in a spasm of terror or ecstasy. Archana felt it shudder, through her toes up into her limbs, while the teacups rattled in their white saucers. The tremor was accompanied by a low, profound rumble, nothing like the hard report of the hunters' rifles. And the noise seemed to come not from the distant hunting grounds nor from the house but from close by, in the earth beneath the folly. Archana kept her eyes upon it, though nothing appeared amiss, and the quaking soon ceased. Behind her, coming from Golden Grove, she thought she could hear muffled cries, like those of Lady Augusta's father, shouting phrases that were mostly incoherent, though she imagined she heard the word "Death."

Lady Augusta smiled, laughed, as though a tremendous jest had been uttered. "These lands are queerly prone to such convulsions—'subterranean movements,' as Sir Charles Lyell would call them. Nothing to fear, but quite dramatic. I could hardly have staged things better if I had tried. Who knows what deep secrets may be 'sealed within the iron hills'?"

The company of ladies took their cue from her and laughed, an incongruous chorus of fluting and fluttering, yet Archana found herself joining in the chorus, however quietly. She felt like a lone leaf, caught in the current of a river, following its flowing toward some great gulf. What could she, prone and green, do to resist this movement? And why should she want to resist? Here she was become an object of fascination, of worth even, and of value to her husband's aspirations. One day she would return home to the tide-like rhythms of Kochi life, in her plain white robe where she was simply another woman among thousands. But might she not for this day yield to the pleasures of weird belonging afforded here at Golden Grove?

No more "convulsions" wracked the landscape, and the echoes of the outcries faded from the house. The hours passed as though earth and air had known nothing but placidity. In the blue sky, only freckled with white clouds, the sun carried on its way, shining forth at its zenith before beginning its westward arc down toward the horizon, the guests' shadows all stretching darker and longer as evening drew near.

Eventually the men arrived from hunting. They had collected dozens of red grouse, and Biju sauntered excitedly up to Archana, holding a bag.

"I have never thought of myself as a hunter," he confessed, "and I was not very successful. But I did catch this one."

Archana nodded, smiling gamely as her husband opened the sack to show her his kill. It was a small creature, curled into a ball, the raw red wound of Biju's bullet barely visible beneath its cinnamon plumage.

The afternoon proceeded with much preening on the part of the men, delighting in their successes while their wives indulged their vanity. There was more talk, Biju extoling the virtues of Kochi's bureaucracies and listening while the men spoke further of Parliament and palaeontology and the playthings of their lives. There was, indeed, so much *talk,* so many words—words prancing and flouncing and spilling from loosened lips into ears eager to hear (or pretend they were hearing). They talked as they sat, then talked as they walked back into Golden Grove, then talked as they traveled to the table in the dining hall.

This meal had nothing of India. Course after course after course was laid before them, such that Archana imagined Ravi Varma himself could not have dreamt its splendor. She dined on a mushroom consommé, and a venison pie flanked by cherries and chestnuts, and a bone-white blancmange that quobbed and quivered on the spoon and in her mouth, and countless other dishes, all while answering anew the same questions she had been asked thrice before. Did the unfamiliar foods please her or disgust her or perplex her? Did she love or loathe the languid chirp of the evening's conversation, which grazed from topic to topic while never leaving the same field? By the end she could not even say, save that she spared glances when she could toward Biju, who sometimes caught her glance and on other occasions was lost in colloquies all his own. Through it all she felt an unaccountable numbness in her toes, and behind and beneath all the voices was the laughter of Lady Augusta, like the fluting of a *bansuri.*

In the wild, spinning array of the evening Archana grew regardless of the hours, which crept or hastened—she could not say which—as her belly grew full to the brink of sickness and her throat became raw from the speech and the food. Gradually, two at a time, the guests made their obeisances and their departures, and she smiled and nodded and returned their gestures, desperately effecting the pretense that she could recall their ungainly and discordant English names. The night drew on, and she could see the sky blackening behind the reflected flare of candles in the window panes.

Finally only Lord Hugh and Lady Augusta remained, and the lady once more took Archana's hands into her own, though in the torpor of the late hour Archana felt her own arms rather unresponsive. Lady Augusta's gemlike eyes had a glazed, sheened look, her head tilted at an acute angle as she met Archana's quizzical gaze.

"Are you well?" the lady asked, and in the simple question seemed to roil layers of pelagic undercurrent.

Archana did not answer at once, gathering her thoughts as though they were scattered sand. "Yes," she replied at last, "but tired. I am glad of the night's ending."

Lady Augusta's pale eyes glistened golden-orange. "This night is far from ending, my dear."

Archana did not understand this, and she thought to look toward Biju, but an unaccountable lethargy had settled upon her every muscle. She felt sleep like a summer monsoon wash over her, sliding over her limbs, pouring even into her brain. Her eyes blinked twice before shutting altogether into a darkness deeper than any flood or storm.

She woke to the light of great flames around her, a brightness that seemed to dance with heathenish abandon. The light hurt her eyes, and she moved to rub them but found that she could not do so— something prevented her. Squinting, then forcing her eyes fully open, she saw that her right wrist was bound, shackled in chains of a metal that was orange with a rust that was coated in a layer of faded red stain. She looked around her and saw, to her surprise, that she was inside the round, austere interior of the folly.

But this was not the folly as she remembered it from her brief visit on their first arriving. It was illuminated not by a lonely lantern but by a series of brazen lampstands ringing the perimeter. She smelled a belligerently pungent incense rising from them alongside the light. The brilliance of the fire glared off the gloss of the room's white paint, though it could not exorcise lurid shadows from the walls and floor. The artifacts from across the globe, including their own *sleeva,* remained mounted in their positions. But the plain central dais was gone now. In its place was a yawning hole of a depth she could not discern from her position. From it she could see only darkness, but a noise like the bubbling of viscous slime every so often erupted from it.

Archana saw now that she was chained inside one of the alcoves that had been empty on her first view. Her body was still cocooned in the burgundy dress, and the lamplight scintillated over its silken surface. Across the room she saw Biju, still in his British suit and cravat, though the hat was missing. He had awoken and, like her, was fettered to the alcove, tugging at his bonds. After some time he paused, panting, and looked dejectedly up at Archana.

They did not speak, for between them stood Lord Hugh and Lady Augusta. They too remained in the day's attire, and they both wore smiles—Lord Hugh's broad and vibrant, Lady Augusta's subtler, almost melancholy. Nearer the entry stood the stoic Marlow, gaunt frame erect, features ashen and passionless.

"What are we doing here?" Biju demanded, his normally deep voice close to cracking in a higher register.

"Indeed," replied Lord Hugh. "We have not been fully forthright, I fear. You have been our honored guests, to be sure, and we have sought to accommodate and please you at every moment of your sojourn. In this regard we have been wholly honest. But for most obvious reasons we could not speak of what will happen tonight."

"What do you mean?" Archana asked. She could feel tautness in her breast and sour bile in her throat as she spoke.

Lady Augusta looked directly at her, and the smile had melted on her face into something that looked akin to pity. "Oh, dear Archana, I confess you have made this far more difficult than it often is. Yet I am ever so eager for it as well, knowing you now as I do."

The ground beneath their feet shook, more violently than it had in the afternoon, and Archana knew somehow that this was no ordinary quake, that its source lay buried beneath their very feet. Lord Hugh clasped his wife's hand inside his own and continued.

"I do suppose that no man is impartial where his home is concerned. But I may truthfully say that the grounds of Golden Grove are unlike any to be found elsewhere across the globe. For here alone may be found the home of the being we call The Visitor."

Lord Hugh released Lady Augusta's hand and walked over to the great cavity at the center of the folly. As he neared it the floor trembled yet again, and Archana saw *something* on the verge of the pit. It was long and lean, organic but inhuman, with the slender, whiplike undulations of a serpent, though its copper-coral flesh was lined with pink discs like a squid's. Looking at it, Archana was certain it was the source of the sickly burbling noise she heard. A smell like infected meat crept out from that hole, causing her to gag.

"We discovered it some time ago, in the days before this building, when this part of the property was nothing but overgrown sedge and cowslip. Augusta and I were walking through the fields with little Charlotte, our . . . daughter." He hesitated, as though the world itself had ceased for instant, then resumed. "It burst forth from the earth so suddenly, we had no time to move. We tumbled and sought to shelter our child, and a strange light and warmth then seemed to bathe us. The Visitor, we found, sheds this force from its body, and it wrapped us within its glow.

"After a time of great fear and great stillness, we looked around to see that it was gone, returned to its subterranean residence. And in our arms we saw little Charlotte, lying lifeless before us. Desperate, we tried what measures we could to revive her. Doctors, apothecaries, prayers—all remedies failed us. The Visitor, this hideous terror, had wrought death upon our household!

"Yet not death only. Gradually, in the midst of our mourning, Augusta and I understood something even more vexing, and more wondrous. Our daughter's body had been emptied of life, but *our* bodies had been filled. When we knew what we were seeking, we discovered that somehow, by means beyond the ken of our medicines, Charlotte's life had passed into us. We were now the stewards of that life, the beneficiaries of it. And though we grieved her still, there throbbed inside us a vitality that no other person can ever have known."

Lady Augusta stepped forward. She had wandered distractedly while her husband was speaking, but she looked now down into the pit, and the flame of the lamps cast asymmetrical shadows across her porcelain countenance.

"I cannot convey to you what was this feeling within, even as the sorrow gnawed at me as well. But regardless of the sensation we despaired of knowing it again—until The Visitor emerged once more." She ambled over and reached a hand out to the squirming snakelike appendage, as though she would grasp it. "We learned, over time, that it favors this place, returns to it again and again, regularly, like the migration of animals across the earth. We could predict its coming as surely as an astronomer can chart the Zodiac's progress across the night sky."

"Why would you not destroy this monster?" Biju asked, the first words Archana had heard him speak since their awaking. "If you could predict its arrival, then you could prepare to kill it."

"Kill it, my dear Mr. Abraham?" Lord Hugh looked at him with an expression of alloyed bemusement and incredulity. "Why the devil should I want to kill it?"

"Why would you not?" Archana demanded. "You said that it murdered your child."

"Hardly murder," Lord Hugh retorted. "I cannot say whether or not The Visitor is rational, but certainly it does not seek out the death of any man."

"That is simply an effect of its strange, unknowable nature," Lady Augusta mused. "Why do its energies kill some, and why do they replenish us? It is not hereditary—we share no direct ancestry, and the child of our bodies was not spared. Surely there is a law of nature that might explain these mysteries, but we do not know it."

"What I *do* know," Lord Hugh said, "is what I saw on that day. I saw my daughter dead. I saw that her eyes were empty objects without thought or joy or sadness behind them. Her body had been a machine—a beautiful, adorable machine—and it ceased to function, and all that she was and had been was lost forever. And so it is for me, for my wife, for you. You trust in the promise of a spirit that endures, a life beyond this vale of sorrows and tears? You are betrayed; we all are.

"I learned then the most important lesson in which I have ever been instructed—indeed the only true lesson there is. We will only ever know one life, *this* life, and death is its ending. No sum can be too costly to stave off that ending. I would fain pay any price to preserve my breath and my being for another day, and—if you'll pardon my severity—the man who thinks otherwise is a fool."

And he smiled with a look of wan glory, like crescent moon on the horizon. "So no, I will not kill The Visitor. The Visitor gave Augusta and me the most important gift we can ever receive—life in our bodies. And tonight you will provide us with more of that life."

"Why us?" Archana asked as she tugged and strained at the chain that bound her. "In a world of millions, why did you choose Biju and myself?"

Lady Augusta glanced back at the pit, then moved forward to Archana, almost within reach, a melancholy ecstasy lighting and shadowing her features. "The time is nigh at hand," she said, her quiet voice almost subsumed beneath the bubble-babel of The Visitor's abode. "I do not believe—I hope it is not—as painful a trial as you fear, darling Mrs. Abraham."

She looked up and around at the walls, where the artifacts of so many hands hung like museum pieces. "In the early years we relied on locals, men and women, whose absence would scarcely be remarked upon by authorities. And they were suitable for our purposes. I venture to say; they probably contributed more to the goodwill of human progress in their final sacrifice than they ever had in their lives to that moment. We welcomed their lives, grateful for that sacrifice."

"Over the years, however," Lord Hugh said, "we learned, as we embraced these diverse lives, that every tribe and nation has its own distinct . . . savor, shall we say? And after a time, drawing into ourselves one Lincolnshire peasant after another became downright intolerable. It would do their lives a disservice to call them monotonous, but I cannot deny that we craved a certain vigor that, it seemed, could only be found abroad.

"So it is that we embarked on our grand adventure, summoning to our humble demesne men and women from all corners of the globe. We cast invitations to the tropical jungles and the dark continent and the far Orient, and though some declined, many, like you, took us up on our offer. And like you, they were granted a singular sojourn in the beauty of the Lincolnshire wolds at the heart of this unparalleled empire, before finally arriving here, in the folly, on a night like tonight. I assure you both, you join a long and illustrious company."

"What do you mean?" asked Biju.

The stones beneath Archana's feet shook, and several of The Visitor's appendages flexed forth from the cavity in the folly's center.

"We no longer think of time the way other people do," Lady Augusta answered. "But there is a day I cannot forget—June 17, 1764, the day we first encountered The Visitor."

"Good Lord," gasped Biju, "that was almost a century ago."

Lady Augusta nodded. "Yes, it was. It has been no mean feat to retain our status across the years without arousing undue suspicion. However, there is little that cannot be achieved when the twin dispensations of wealth and social advantage are well marshalled."

Archana thought back to the terrifying old man with the gleaming green eyes. "But what of your father?"

At this, Lady Augusta stared off at the white walls of the folly, a hand absently rubbing her abdomen. "Another misdirection, my dear," she acknowledged. "George is not my father—he is our son. He was born ninety years ago, two years after The Visitor appeared. I could never trust him to The Visitor; I did not wish to watch another child die. And yet . . ." She paused, swallowed, continued, "And yet, we *will* watch him die in the end."

Archana wanted to show strength and poise in the face of this hazard, but she could not keep back all the tears as she stared at the Crofts, still straining at their restraints.

"You cannot be this evil!" she cried, her voice echoing across the folly walls, drowning out for a brief moment the grotesque squishing sound of The Visitor from underneath their feet.

"There is only the domain of this earth," Lord Hugh replied, and disgust smoldered beneath the aloof note of his voice as he spoke. "And this earth knows nothing of evil or good, holiness or hell. This earth knows only survival. And *that* is what the Lady Augusta and I excel in."

An even more profound quaking commenced, and the volume of The Visitor's unctuous quobbing intensified. Biju, Marlow, the Crofts— they all turned toward the monster that was emerging, tentacle by tentacle, from is abode beneath the swards of Wingarden. Archana too watched with a panicked disbelief, but she knew also that this panic would avail her nothing unless it were harnessed. So she poured every last drop of her terror into the ache of her muscles, which strained with strength and deep instincts she had never known she had.

Perhaps in her own power her effort would still have proved insufficient. But she was not alone: to her labor was added that of all those who had come before her, the men and women whom the Crofts had bound and who had themselves strained at those same shackles across the century. Beneath the whitewash, the mortar of the folly's alcove was crumbling, the iron of the chains rooted now only tenuously. Archana felt the loosening as she tugged, until finally, with one impossible effort, she tore the links out from the edifice, and she was free, a tangle of rusted metal dangling from her right wrist. But the noise of her release had been swallowed by the thunder of The Visitor, its molluscan limbs thrashing with a wild, sentient hunger. Marlow stood sentry by the folly exit, while Lord Hugh and Lady Augusta held hands near the threshold of the monster's chthonic dominion, all their eyes fixed on its advent.

So surprising was her abrupt liberty that Archana hesitated, stupefied; for an unthinkable instant the horror gripped her, and she prepared to flee, to race past Marlow into the wolds of Wingarden, never to stop until somehow Kochi was in her sight. But her eye caught Biju, still straining, and she inhaled a cloying breath in the dense incensed air, which somehow steadied her. And whatever the peril, she knew with awful clarity what she must do.

Archana ran, loping awkwardly in the laced boots and stiff crinoline that still engulfed her, but she did not need to travel far to reach her first goal—the jade axe that hung on the wall as one of the Crofts' mementos. The wood was coarse yet comforting in her grasp, though she did not pause or even slow her pace as she grabbed it. By now, Lady Augusta and Lord Hugh had turned in her direction, and Marlow too seemed aware that something was amiss. But The Visitor partially blocked their view, and they were briefly paralyzed in disbelief at seeing her thus. Archana knew that this moment of opportunity would soon pass, and she hefted the axe as she reached the opposite alcove, where Biju stood.

Her life in Kochi had been an active one, but the rituals of her days demanded little of the muscles she needed now, and she doubted herself. Yet there was no time remaining for recrimination, only time to pray and to swing. The smooth tropical green axe arced down to the stone of the alcove, where Biju's chains were attached, and through the wooden handle of the weapon she felt a surge of connection to all her predecessors, to the many victims whose lives had been sacrifices to the snakelike arms and voracious vital lust of the plutonic kraken before them. They had died resisting, struggling, fighting, as Archana herself now would.

And as it had been for her, so it was for her husband. The axe-head struck the stone of the folly where it joined the tarnished iron of the shackles, and here too, the work of those prior captives had worn away at the wall. With a quiet cracking, Biju's chain tore off and his arm was free.

A twitching contortion of rage traveled along Lord Hugh's face, beneath which lurked a fear like bone beneath flesh. Marlow remained composed, his sallow visage stoic as stone. But both men advanced upon the Abrahams now, circling around The Visitor while guarding access to the folly door. Lady Augusta remained motionless, her glassy eyes wide, though she absently ran a delicate hand along the puckered folds of a tentacle.

"I see you prove most accomplished in your resolve," Lord Hugh said as he strode toward them, but he could not conceal from his casual words the undercurrent of baleful frenzy.

"Please," Biju implored, "why will you not release us?"

"You have learned nothing," Lord Hugh snarled, the pretense at last effaced. "It is your life or mine, and I will always choose mine."

He rushed at Biju, but Archana did not have time then to see what happened next, for Marlow was running toward her. In his hand the old butler brandished a Bowie knife, the lamplight glimmering over its steel blade. He limped as he ran, and for the first time Archana noticed a diagonal red scar on his ashen face, and he gripped the blade loosely but securely, with the confidence of habitual use. More than the ghastly alienness of The Visitor or the turbid revulsion in Lord Hugh's anger, the callow ease of Marlow's knife grip soaked Archana with the fear of death.

The line between thought and act blurred as Archana moved. Before Marlow could close the gap, she jumped behind one of The Visitor's twisting arms, so that the servant needed to shift his position. For an instant Marlow was forced to pivot on one leg, just a few feet from Archana but not quite in stabbing range. With a shriek of fright or wrath or exertion, a cry that echoed over the appalling noise of the creature beside her, she darted forward from behind the tentacle and swung the axe in the old man's direction. He raised his arms to protect his face, and the glade-green blade struck his hands instead, causing the knife and blood to fly clattering and spattering to the floor.

Marlow had lost his weapon, but now Archana was off balance, and the butler leapt forward to grab her. She tried to roll away, but he was able to wrap one arm around her throat, grabbing her axe hand with the other. He slammed that hand against the stone floor, and the sharp pain jarred her fingers loose, causing her to release the axe. She could feel the constriction of his arm around her neck, and each breath was gained through a layer of pain.

And worse, she could feel inside her a very different sort of pain, the weird malignity of The Visitor's unthinkable biology as it worked within her. She grew starkly aware that spirit and breath were two very distinct processes: Marlow was robbing her of the latter, but the squirming entity beside her was slavering after the former. How often had she spoken of spirit in the liturgies of her worship, not knowing what she meant? Now she knew the truths she had uttered unthinkingly, for she could feel in her the withering of her very self—the Archana who had looked at Arundhati deep in the night, peering at the skies as though they were her truest home. It was the essence of her, toward which word and image could only gesture, and it was desiccating like famine-parched farmland.

When she heard the scream, she thought at first that it had come from her own lips. But then the great pressure on her throat eased, and her bruised hand was released, and she realized that it was Marlow who had screamed. There was blood on her face and in her hair; it seeped invisibly into the deep red dress she wore. The blood was Marlow's—he was staggering away, dripping, his Bowie knife protruding from his throat. Archana saw a frail white hand webbed with blue veins reach out to her, and she looked up. It was the hand of George, only son of Lord Hugh and Lady Augusta Croft.

She still wasn't certain what was happening, but she extended her left hand and allowed him to pull her up. She looked beyond him across the folly to where her husband and Lord Hugh were grappling. Each bore wounds, and each grimaced with the strain of channeled passions. Lord Hugh's fist lashed out and struck Biju in the jaw, causing him to tumble backward until he was at the foot of one of the cressets that lit the room. Once again the serpentine limbs of The Visitor flailed past, and Biju scurried back farther to avoid its reach. Archana moved toward her husband, but Lady Augusta interposed herself between them.

"I cannot permit you to leave," she groaned in desperation, and it seemed to Archana that she was weeping as she spoke.

"Mother," George said, his hoarse voice dripping softly like water after the rain has ended, "please do not do this."

But Lady Augusta held her place. Archana, almost without a thought, took up the axe and started crossing the room, but even as she did so she could see what her husband was doing. Rising to his feet, his brown eyes wide with a sudden strange knowing, he grabbed the lampstand beside him and ran toward the perimeter of the pit.

Lord Hugh, blocked by a tentacle, hesitated only for a moment—but it was enough. His eyes widened in a very different sort of recognition, and he cried "No!" with an animal's desperation. Biju had thrown the cresset into the abyss, upon the living flesh of The Visitor.

There was a brief, uncanny stillness, in which every individual stood motionless as monuments, all eyes staring in macabre curiosity at the center of the room—save for the open, spiritless eyes of Marlow's prone corpse. Archana wondered what might have happened, and in her mind she began to plot a route by which she could evade Lady Augusta and bring her weapon to deadly use against Lord Hugh if he should resist.

Then The Visitor screamed. With most of its bulk hidden, Archana had been uncertain whether it even had the physiology to produce such noises, but there could be no doubt that the great subterranean beast was the source of the wailing. Yet though the wild ululation was clearly biological, it was also unearthly, vibrating in notes that Archana could never have imagined before she heard them. The horrid voice seemed to echo endlessly back and forth across the folly walls, slithering more into her marrow than her ears. The monster's hideous members writhed and writhed across the floor, and everyone had to leap back toward the walls to avoid their force.

The Visitor was on fire. Biju's desperate charge had succeeded: the oil and flame from the lampstand had seeped into its sticky, slimy flesh and found hellish purchase there. Archana felt the swelter of its ignition heat the thick air of the room, and chunks of smoke billowed from the thing's blistering skin.

From The Visitor, Archana turned her attention to the Crofts. Lord Hugh was screaming too, and though his voice was human, it seemed to carry the cadence of the creature as well. He grabbed at his side, at his chest, at his face, and a century of agony coursed through his youthful features. His brown hair exploded into white before falling off and fluttering down, while his flesh softened and moldered like putrid fruit as he collapsed to the ground. The delicate face of Lady Augusta was still weeping as the years took their hold, though there was also something akin to relief in her fading eyes. She staggered as her skin creased like drying wet paper, and her frail son caught her in his arms. Her graying head bowed, and George gently kissed it before she became a dress full of bones that clattered to the floor.

The air around them rippled with the infernal heat, and The Visitor lashed burning appendages as it wailed its outlandish death cry. George spared a final glance at the remnants of his mother and father, and he and Archana and Biju all hurried past the floundering beast until they reached the only door. They passed through a veil of dark smoke across the threshold and emerged into the clear air of a deep blue night.

When they were finally some distance from the chaos, they all turned back to look. Flames like great jaws devoured the folly, melting the layers of whitewash from its walls, until, in a sudden burst of noise and fire, the imperial tower crumbled to the earth. A deeper rumble poured through the lawn beneath their feet, and the land around the folly's foundation erupted in a last red blaze before falling deep into the world's dark substrata, leaving only a smoking crater, silent save for a low sizzling of buried embers.

Then they were all weeping, and to a man standing from a distance, perhaps it would have appeared absurd, but Archana could think of nothing more logical in the moment. She had fallen on her knees, absentmindedly rubbing her abdomen as she cast out her tears on the English soil—tears of anger, or relief, or joy she could not say. Biju was down in the dewy grass beside her, his arms around her shoulders, his face against her cheek so that she could feel his own tears. He took his right hand and ran a finger along the *minnu* around her neck, the pendant dangling at her throat.

"Still there, I see," she said in Malayalam, with a laugh that somehow seemed wholly appropriate. She could feel Biju laughing beside her.

Nearby, George was still crying. Archana looked up into his *neem*-green eyes and, trembling slightly, she took one of his bony hands into hers.

"Forgive me for what my family has done to you, for what they have done to so many—what I allowed them to do." His voice was quiet, yet far more lucid than it had sounded on the previous day. "They were my parents, and I believe they loved me, and I had to love them. You understand, I think. But there is no assuaging the harms they have committed."

"Perhaps," Archana replied, her choked voice barely a whisper. "But thank you all the same."

George pressed the palm of her hand, and Archana felt something inside it. She opened her fingers to see the little banyan cross, the *Mar Thoma sleeva* that Biju had handed to the Crofts upon their first arriving.

"I could not watch it burn," George told them. "Please take it. It rightly belongs to you."

Archana nodded, and then they all rose and started walking back to the house. Golden Grove stood, grand as ever in the darkness of the night, its windows empty save for a few sporadic lights inside. George's pace was slow, and at times he seemed confused. More than once he glanced back at the smoldering wreckage of the folly. But when he turned back to Biju and Archana as they neared the façades of the front entrance, he spoke with measured assuredness.

"Ask what you will of me. If it is in my power, I will grant it you."

Biju did not hesitate. "I simply want to go home, sir. I know we have hardly been here in England, but you will not blame me for wanting to return at the earliest opportunity."

He looked to Archana, who nodded vigorously. "Yes. You and I in our little house in Kochi. And . . ." She paused, touched the hem of her torn and bloodstained dress. "Might we have our clothes again?"

As they entered Golden Grove, they heard a patter of footfalls, and a bleary-eyed but sprightly Bridget O'Halloran scampered down the stairs.

"Missis Rachel . . . Master George? Beg pardon, but what's the commotion?"

"We will provide you every answer we can in due time," George said. "For the moment I ask only that you bring our guests their robes."

Bridget looked nervously at George, then turned her guileless eyes to Archana. "Missis Rachel?"

Archana nodded. "Yes, please."

Bridget hesitated, then grinned. "They've just been cleaned, ma'am. I'll be right back!"

She hurried back up the stairs. As she went, Biju squeezed Archana's hand and turned to face her. "You were right, *priya,*" he said in Malayalam. "I am sorry I did not listen to you."

"Well," she confessed, "I had doubts about this place, but I cannot say I expected any of *this.*"

"Even so, I would be wise to listen well to you."

Archana laughed, this time a laugh without tears. "I cannot deny it. But know still how much I love you."

"And I you, *priya.*"

At this point, Bridget returned, carrying their clothing, her face still bearing a perplexed expression.

"Come, Miss O'Halloran," George said, leading her down the foyer. "I believe our guests may be allowed some privacy. I will tell you what I can."

Bridget acquiesced, while Biju and Archana found the nearest room with a door. Together they shed the clothing of their hosts, which fell in wet tatters to the floor, and Archana felt the freedom of the open air on her skin as she shed the layers of red cotton and the rigid whalebone crinoline, until only the *minnu* remained. She let her husband drape the *chattayum mundum* over her, relishing the touch of his hand across her waist and her shoulder, and she in turn helped him into his *mundu*. He lightly kissed her fingers where Marlow had bruised them and her neck, where she had been choked.

At last they left the room and found the entrance to Golden Grove ajar, with George and Bridget standing just outside. Together they joined them. Bridget looked at Archana, and beneath her freckles was a sorrow that had not been there before.

"Can't say I really understand all that's happened, but I'm sorry for all your troubles, Missis Rachel."

"The estate is mine now," George—*Lord* George—murmured, as though in disbelief. "I will see to it that you are both brought home to India as soon as the passage can be arranged."

Out of the corner or her eye Archana saw the abysmal desolation where the folly had once stood proudly. She looked at Biju, and they smiled at each other—Kochi smiles, alive like the coconut trees, wild like the ocean. She touched the little *sleeva* in her hand and looked out to the eastern horizon, where the first arc of the sun's gleaming gold nimbus was cresting over the hill, its brilliant rays lighting up their robes.

TERMINATION SHOCK

We sail past Earth, to dust of rust and war,
The world of blood outspread in channels dark
And barren, where in some great ancient age
Flowed fresh blue water streams into small seas,
Before the force of nature stole the sky
To make proud rage its savage sovereign king.

Yet just beyond his realm, we find the king,
The true king staring toward the stars, his war-
Like eye a gloamy red in stormy sky.
He rules the solar system; in the dark,
The grandeur of his cloud-brown crushing seas
Of gas proclaim him ruler of the age.

His feeble father draped in pallid age
Lies bound in iridescent rings, a king
Himself in aeons past, when frothy seas
Shook with the surge of bestial, lordly war,
And bloated from his children's bones, the dark
Cruel titan loafs in mottled yellow sky.

Far farther still, behold primeval sky
Lie mute and impotent in quiet age,
The mage and mystic in the diamond dark,
The frigid father of the slav'ring king,
Now hidden since the frenzied first old war
And stretched across the silent cyan seas.

A leap 'cross night we see the lord of seas,
Ferocious grandson of the slothful sky,
A child and soldier of titanic war,
Yet also cold and blue and wet with age;
With stoic gaze the ice and crystal king
In dwindled rays peers through unfathomed dark.

And what cold chthonic god reigns in that dark?
Though smaller than the lords of vaporous seas,
In his dominion he, th'abysmal king,
Holds sway in that last deathly step—the sky
Of dreaming maculae, who from his age-
Long sleep may rouse in prophesying war . . .

Beyond, the shocking leap into the dark:
At first, the empty warring chaos seas,
Then brilliant sky, the blinding cosmos' age . . .

A Glint amid the Corn

"I can't believe Adam isn't texting me back."

Sofia watched as Chrisleigh sighed in exasperation and stared into her phone. Matt tried one more time to start the car, again to no avail. Sofia pulled out her own phone and checked the time: 4:45. Practice would start in fifteen minutes.

Dante put his arm around Chrisleigh. "Come on, babe," he said, "he's probably already at the field."

Chrisleigh finally tore her metal-gray eyes from the screen. "God, Dante, how are we going to get to there in time? I don't want to be late again."

Sofia glanced at the profusion of green maple and oak trees around them, shading the gravel parking lot where Matt's black-finished car now rested, angled awkwardly beside a row of SUVs. He had just managed to get it off the road before its final sputtering fume-fueled lurches. Sofia clenched her teeth to keep from castigating her boyfriend, who had passed two gas stations en route to the school practice field. She could see that he was panicked enough as it was.

"Who else might give us a ride?" she asked. "Maybe Ava—"

"Hell, no," Chrisleigh shot back. "We're *not* asking her."

"We're so close . . ." Dante trailed off, peering toward the woods. They were at the edge of the park, next to a green-and-tan plastic playscape from which they could hear children crying out excitedly. Nearby, a scarlet smear marked the trailhead that meandered west. Sofia could see the park sign, plastered with the ubiquitous warning that displayed the speckled and garish red form of a spotted lantern-fly, declaring unsubtly, "STOP THIS INVADER!"

But the trail would not help them; they needed to get north, not west. Dante was right—they were achingly near their destination.

"Let's cut across the Fisher farm," Matt interjected suddenly. He took Sofia's free hand and began leading her across the lot toward the north end of the park.

"Matt, we can't do that," Sofia objected, holding back. He released her hand and looked back at her, his hazel eyes squinting quizzically.

Ahead of them, past the playground, the park property ended. The high school was only a couple thousand feet beyond. But between the park and the school lay the wide cornfield of the Fisher farm. Zephaniah Fisher had inherited the land when his father passed away, and the Fishers grew all manner of crops on their 75 acres, which ran adjacent to the school. The other plantings stretched north of the park border, however; only the late-summer corn separated the four young athletes from the garish green turf of the football field.

"Sofia, it'll be like ten minutes if we hurry," Matt replied to her. "The corn's so tall, they won't even see us passing through it."

"Man, I'm with Sofia," Dante piped in.

This time it was Chrisleigh's turn to insist. She grabbed Dante's hand and began tugging. "Matt's right, babe. If Adam won't answer, this is our best chance."

Dante kissed her gold-sheened hair but then arched an eyebrow. "Are you serious? Sure, let's have the huge black man trespassing on an Amish farm. What could possibly go wrong with that?"

"We'll all be with you," Chrisleigh groaned, the impatience near panic in her voice now. "We'll all be together. Sofia, you're friends with them anyway, right? If somebody sees us, you can just put in a good word."

"I can't do that," Sofia maintained, pulling Matt closer to her and away from the park border. "I know Joelle a little, but I don't want to walk through her family's land."

Chrisleigh released Dante's hand and moved to Sofia, looking directly at her. Through a break in the tree shadows, the lowering sun's light made her eyes look more blue than gray for an instant. Sofia realized that in three years of doing cheerleading together, she'd never really seen Chrisleigh's eyes before. They were always either cast down at her phone or out toward an audience. Now they rippled, through glare and incipient tears.

"You don't understand," Chrisleigh said in a raw, sob-choked voice. "You get A's in your classes; you've got your music and your family. Cheerleading . . . this is all I've got. I can't get in any more trouble with coach."

"We've got to do something soon," Matt prompted. "Look, we can keep trying to text people, or we can walk the long way around, or—"

"Fine," Sofia sighed. She looked out at the park boundary as if it were a perilous realm, though she usually loved the sight of crops. They made her think back to visiting her *abuelo's* plantain farm outside Ponce before he had been forced to sell. This was an illusion, perhaps: the great frondy leaves of plantain trees only resembled cornrows from a distance. Still, Sofia felt more kinship with the agriculture than many of her classmates, whose preferences pulled them toward downtown Lancaster. "But Matt's right. Let's just make it quick. And try not to be seen."

She desperately didn't want the Fishers to know she was trespassing. The quiet reserve of Amish farmers could scarcely be more different from the voluble, gregarious life of her grandparents in Puerto Rico, let alone the boisterous existence her parents had carved out for their family in Pennsylvania. But Sofia saw Joelle at their family's stand week after week in the farmer's market, and one shy sentence at a time, they had grown to be something like friends.

Dante rolled his eyes and sighed resignedly, though he still looked nervous. Chrisleigh pulled his head down far enough to kiss his cheek, and then they began to jog to the back of the park. In moments they were at the chain-link fence that separated the properties. Matt didn't hesitate, scrambling up and over the perfunctory obstacle and beckoning for the others to join him. Dante, inhaling deeply, looked back at the dark wood of the park, then climbed over. Chrisleigh followed suit, waving off Dante's chivalrous attempt to help her. So now it was only Sofia, and she wanted so much to run the other way, to kick Matt's car once more and hope it started, or to follow the road around the farm's perimeter, or even just to skip cheerleading practice for one damned day. But of course, she did none of these things. Instead, she leapt the fence nimbly and landed gracefully on the far south boundary of the Fishers' land.

Across that boundary, directly ahead, the corn stretched out before them. To the east on her right it was planted as far as the road, across which lay a larger industrial soybean farm. To her left the west side sloped upward, disappearing from view, though if Sofia squinted she could see the Fishers' house and barn up on the rise. She thought she even saw a small iota of human movement, but she turned away quickly from it; if someone was nearby, she'd rather not know.

She tried to run through the ripening corn, but it was difficult, the thick green stalks giving little room for her feet to tread the ground. Her head was submerged beneath the stalks' tasseling tops, and she could just barely see Matt ahead of her, though he was less than a yard away. In the light late-summer breeze, she could hear the rustling whisper of their leaf blades rubbing up against each other. There seemed to be another sound beneath that riffling, however—a curious hum, like the steady whirring of a machine, though Sofia couldn't trace its source.

But she wasn't paying much attention to the noises anyway; she was simply trying to stay calm. Matt was still visible nearby, but she had lost Chrisleigh and Dante entirely. She couldn't see anything around her but the stalks' towering green, and with even the sun occluded from sight, she wasn't certain they were moving in the right direction.

"Sofia? Matt?"

She heard Chrisleigh's voice above the wind to her left, and she fought through the crowding corn, but still all she could see were rows of green and the red sliver of Matt's T-shirt between them.

"Chrisleigh, where are you?" Sofia inquired.

"We're right here," came the reply, but Sofia saw nothing.

"There's an open spot in the cornfield this way," Dante added. "Let's just keep talking, and we'll meet each other there."

"Sounds good," Matt replied.

"Here we are," Chrisleigh said. "You can find us now, right?"

Sofia kept tracking them, and she knew she was getting closer. Yet something was complicating her task: the once-ambient hum around them seemed to be getting louder, so loud that it threatened to eclipse her friends' words. And as she walked on she felt a strange prickling against her skin, a different sensation from the slightly coarse ticklish rubbing of the leaf blades. This was sharp, even a little painful, and so surprising that it caused a surge of fright to gather inside her. She looked frantically around, and as she did so Matt took her hand in his, and the two hastened on until finally they burst out into the clearing that they sought.

It was a little open patch in the waves of corn, close to seven feet by seven feet, Sofia thought, though it wasn't quite square. The ground was lower here, with some grimy, pooled-up water in a declivity near the center, and she guessed that a heavy rain at planting had washed out the seeds in this spot months earlier. Dante and Chrisleigh were already there. When they arrived, Dante pointed to Sofia.

"What's that on your shirt?"

She hadn't noticed anything, but at his words she looked down at the Eagles jersey she was wearing. There were tiny holes in several places, and she now saw blood beading up in those spots. It occurred to her that she was bleeding in exactly the places where she had felt a prickling moments earlier. Almost by reflex, she dropped her duffel bag and began batting at the tiny rents in her fabric and her flesh. As she did so she heard again the peculiar hum and saw strange flashes of movement shimmer past her, zipping out toward the cornstalks.

Even as she was doing this she noticed in her periphery her friends making similar motions. When she was afforded a moment, she saw that each of them had similar tears in their shirts. Now the air was alive with the preternatural humming, and she caught bright glints amid the corn as the lowering sun struck its dazzling upon the bizarre dots that skittered around them.

"Okay, what the *hell* was that?" Matt demanded as he continued to check his red shirt.

Chrisleigh knelt down to the barren spot of earth at her feet and took something between her thumb and index finger. "Look," she said, rising.

They gathered around her to see what she held. It was a dead bug of some kind, but although Sofia thought of herself as pretty good at biology, she certainly couldn't identify this species. It was an insect, six legs and segmented body, perhaps just shy of an inch in length. Its carapace was black like night in the countryside, so shiny it might have been made of chrome. But it was also covered in a profusion of sharp spikes, even on its wings, extending all the way to its head. That head made up over half its length, dominated by a wide jaw that ended with a pair of serrated mandibles.

"I've never seen anything like that before," Matt said.

"I've never even heard of anything like this," Sofia mused, taking the bug from Chrisleigh. "Could it be some kind of endangered species?"

"If it's endangered, it's doing pretty well for itself here," Dante said. He nodded toward the field, and they followed his gaze.

All around them they could now see that the cornstalks were teeming with the insects. The daylight washed across their lustered shells, making them look like a shower of sparks from a welding torch. Most crawled across leaf blades or used their pincers to burrow into the corn ears, but many flitted and flew around.

"That's some weird shit," Matt acknowledged. "But whatever. We've just got to go, man. We must be almost to the practice field by now."

"I can see the sun over there," Dante pointed. "That's west, so north must be that way," he added, sweeping his arm in a 90-degree arc.

"It's easy enough to say that here," Chrisleigh retorted. "But we could get lost again as soon as we step back into the corn. I'm not taking any chances. Follow me."

She pulled out her phone to use as a compass and purposefully strode up to the north perimeter of the clearing. But even as her phone's screen lit up, the insects' hum transmogrified into a roar like thunder, and a cloud of thick darkness descended upon her. The creatures swarmed over Chrisleigh, and she screamed as they did so. Sofia wanted to run to her friend and claim her from them, but trembling wracked her frame and the terror subdued and paralyzed her, and she stood as still as a grave is still. She glanced at the boys; Matt froze, helpless, mouth stupidly agape, while Dante shuffled forward tentatively and uselessly, trapped between desire to act and vexation at the horrid deathliness of it all.

And so it was that they all stood by and observed while Chrisleigh died. She thrashed and swiped at the things as they congregated over her, and she tried to run, but their jaws stripped the muscle and sinew from her legs, and she collapsed to the earth. Still she flailed, and still she screamed and screamed and screamed, senselessly and horribly at the shock and the betrayal and the pain. They gathered and gorged themselves on her skin and on her blood, and farther into the deepest regions of her body, though Sofia only caught glimpses of this in little bursts of fluid spurting from the ground. Mostly, what she could see was a vaguely human form, shrouded by a shadow of an army, thousands upon thousands, cutting and swarming and hopping and destroying.

Chrisleigh's cries turned to whimpers before they were silenced, but all this occurred in seconds. Sofia quietly, slowly edged backward, terrified that they would move on to her, but when they had eaten their fill the insects turned back to the corn rows, though not out of her sight. Their mouths, fresh from the flesh of her friend, returned to the crisp crops as though there were no difference between a girl and a grain. Beside Chrisleigh's bag and phone and flayed clothes, they left behind them only jaw-notched bone with splinters of nail and strands of golden hair—and, beneath it all, a small damp piece of soil.

"Oh, God," groaned Matt. He doubled over and vomited, a lumpy pink mass of soda and pizza, though even then he kept his eyes up toward the field.

Dante was crying as he stared at Chrisleigh's remains—Dante, whom Sofia had never seen in sorrow before, weeping, the tears and the snot dribbling down his face.

"This doesn't happen," he muttered. "She was just here, talking to us, doing her thing. My baby girl is dead." Then, wet eyes glaring, he looked down at Matt. "This was your idea, damn it! This was your *goddamned* idea!" He reached down and took Matt by the shirt, then struck his puke-stained face, splitting his lip. "Chrisleigh's dead because of you, you stupid bastard!"

Matt's frame hung limp in Dante's grasp, his head nodding vigorously, and the tears were in his eyes now too. "You're right, you're right, this is all my stupid fault."

Dante brough his fist back for another blow, but at this point Sofia jumped in and grabbed his arm. He hesitated, looking over at her.

"That's enough, Dante," she said. "Please just stop. It was a stupid idea, and you're right . . . Chrisleigh's dead. But we—I mean, we've got to find a way out of here. Beating the hell out of each other isn't going to help." She inhaled a great breath, then exhaled solemnly. "We just have to . . . think."

Dante released Matt, who crumpled to the ground like a half-empty sack.

"Yeah. Yeah, sure, right. We've got to think."

Matt looked north again, the direction marked out by Chrisleigh's bones. "We're so close. Maybe we should just make a run for it."

Dante looked back down and squinted. "Man, are you serious? I can run a four-six forty, but not with those cornstalks, and not with those . . . things."

"Why did they kill her so quickly?" Sofia wondered. "We were walking together for a while, and only a few of them attacked us. What was different?"

She hated to talk so clinically, to act as though her friend's death were simply an event to be analyzed and not a grief to be mourned. But she knew the time for her mourning was not yet come; they needed their minds in these moments.

"There might be more of them on that side of the clearing," Matt suggested.

"I don't know about that," Dante replied. He motioned south, the direction from which they'd come, and they could see countless dark specks wriggling about the fibrous green.

"What, then?" Matt asked.

Dante looked back at fragments of his girlfriend and abruptly closed his eyes. "Her phone."

"We've all got our phones with us," Matt reminded him.

"Yeah, but none of us were using them. That's seriously the only difference."

"They didn't eat her phone."

Dante glowered at Matt, and Sofia jumped in, "Yeah, but he's right. Who knows, maybe the power it was using set them off, or the light from the screen. Somehow it agitated them."

"So we might be safe to try running if we keep our phones off."

"Matt," Sofia interjected, "do you really want to risk that? They may not be going after us now, but they don't exactly look like they've calmed down to me."

Dante's brow creased. "Why *aren't* they going after us? Why is this spot clear?"

Sofia wondered that too. A few intrepid scouts were ambling at the perimeter of the clearing, but most of the swarm remained amid the corn.

"There's no corn here for them to eat," she said. "But we're here now. Why didn't they come after us once they'd finished . . . ?" She trailed off, not wanting to trace her thought back to its origin.

"What about the water?" Matt asked, pointing to the puddle beside him. "I toss stinkbugs and June bugs into the water all the time because they can't deal with it."

"You might be right," Dante acknowledged. "But I don't know how that helps us. This is just a puddle, and I don't think I've got enough Gatorade to chase off a million of them."

Sofia paced the small bare patch of dirt, eyes up into the blazing blue of the summer sky, trying to keep her gaze from the death and the danger that lay feet from her, though those dangers prowled about in her thoughts. This day was not the first fear of her life, yet the alienage of the enemy, the sheer eldritch horror of their situation, rippled through her gut and her soul.

"Who's down there?"

She heard the new voice descend, like a plumb line plunging to the infernal abyss in which she lay sunk. It startled all three of them, so unexpected was it to hear someone else speak within their desolation. The voice was a shout from some distance, female, with the throatiness of a slight Pennsylvania Dutch intonation. The boys looked baffled, but Sofia knew in an instant who it was.

"Joelle!" she shouted back.

Joelle Fisher stood upon the crest of the rise to their west, beyond her house and near the edge of the cornfield. The light of the sun behind her cascaded across her plain lavender dress and even danced a little on the brown hairs that strayed from beneath her white bonnet. The light fell like flame upon the dark glasses that concealed her eyes as she peered down at them intently.

"Yes," she replied. "I am Joelle. Who are—?"

"It's me, Sofia Morales, from the market."

"Sofia?" Joelle sounded surprised, yet less so than one might have expected. "What are you doing in our field?"

"My friends and I . . . we're trapped," she called back, and she explained what had happened as concisely as she could. While she spoke, she could feel the seeming outlandishness of their situation weighing upon her, the implausibility catching on her tongue like an acrid and bitter flavor. And she was no less aware of the awkwardness of having to shout every syllable to the diminutive Amish girl who stood demurely so far away.

But when Sofia was threatened with thoughts on the absurdity of their condition, she needed only glance once more to jumble of white bone in the right corner of her vision. She could imagine Chrisleigh's mother and sister and stepfather waiting in vain for her to return from cheerleading and her night shift at the diner. She could know that the two of them would never again stand outside school on a cold winter afternoon debating the relative merits of reggaeton music while waiting for their boyfriends to arrive. She knew that every breath of her friend, the irritated sighs and the caustic laughs and the sudden, unexpected tendernesses and tears, had all been abruptly swallowed up by the earth and these interlopers. One by one, she could see those miniscule soldiers growing braver and creeping past the threshold of the field. Thinking on these things, Sofia raised her voice free from reticence so that Joelle might hear it, clear and loud above the buzz that surrounded them.

"Can you get help?" she concluded, desperately looking from Joelle back to the insects. They were encroaching in greater numbers now, staying on the ground, still avoiding the water, but massing even as she spoke. She and Matt and Dante all gathered as close to the puddle as they could get.

"My family are all away," Joelle answered. "It is only me and my little brothers, until tonight."

Sofia's stomach tightened at those words. Matt took her hand in his, tenderly, not the way he had when he pulled her out toward the field just a few minutes earlier. She squeezed it back in return as she cast her sight back toward Joelle, the purple cotton of the girl's dress framed in the burnishing of the sinking sun.

Then an abrupt change fell upon Joelle's demeanor, a kind of stateliness Sofia hadn't seen before. She appeared to rise, though she had always been standing, and she shouted down to them, "I know what to do. Be ready!"

A new fear gripped Sofia. She wanted to live, voraciously and desperately, not to be ribboned in agony like Chrisleigh. But even now, even with bile swelling in her throat, she couldn't bear to imagine Joelle dying for her. The Amish girl must have been Sofia's age, yet she felt somehow years younger, and so there seemed a particular sacrilege in the thought of that shy, slender body being sacrificed to the swarm.

"Don't come after us!" Sofia cried out. Matt and Dante looked sharply at her as she spoke, and Joelle held her gaze.

"Don't worry!" Joelle called back. "Just be ready to move. When the time comes, it will be quick."

She turned away, skirt flaring from breeze and from motion, and she ran back toward the house and the barn, her bare feet kicking up dust.

"What the hell's she talking about?" Matt asked.

"I don't know," Dante replied, "but she said to be ready, so let's do it."

"What does that even mean?" Matt demanded.

Sofia looked around her, saw the rim of their small haven growing dark with a tightening ring of carapaces. Set against the spiky shells that encased the bugs' inner parts, the skin uncovered by her summer shorts and jersey felt appallingly exposed.

"Quick," she enjoined the boys, "pull out whatever clothes we have. Let's put something between us and their teeth."

"It won't make much difference," Dante responded, though he was unzipping his own bag. "Our practice uniforms are short too."

Sofia removed every fabric item in her own bag, and fortunately, she had stuffed it full of clean outfits that morning. Instead of putting the clothes on, however, she began wrapping them around her limbs.

"It's not much," she said. "But I don't know . . . we need to do something."

Matt nodded. "Okay, but if we're doing this, let's really do it." He pulled in a deep breath, then knelt down into the puddle. "I don't know if they're really avoiding the water, but it's worth a try."

"Sure." Sofia kissed Matt on his damp, muddy hair as he got up before crouching down to do the same herself. It seemed humiliating, yet the touch of the cool water on her clothes felt oddly comforting. Dante briefly hesitated, but after one more glance at Chrisleigh's bones he too immersed himself. Were the insects slowing their ghastly progress as the three splashed water about them? Sofia thought they might be, though she didn't trust her own perception. Slow or not, they certainly weren't stopping: an army of dark arthropods writhed nearer and nearer.

"Is there anything else?" Sofia asked. "Anything else we can do?"

"What about our phones?" Dante suggested.

"Dude, you're smarter than that," Matt castigated. "That's what got Chrisleigh . . ."

He trailed off when he saw the tempests in Dante's glare. For a terrible instant Sofia thought he would attack Matt again, would spatter his blood in the soil and leave him there for the bugs. And Dante clenched a fist—but then dropped his arm to his side.

"I don't mean keep them with us," he said. "When the time comes, we turn them on and toss them as far as possible. They didn't eat the phone . . . but they were drawn to it. It could be a distraction."

Matt hung his head. "Yeah, let's do it." Then he looked up. Wiping the blood from his mouth, he met Dante's gaze without flinching for the first time since Chrisleigh's death. "I am so sorry." He glanced at the bones, then turned to Sofia. "I'm sorry for all of it."

Sofia embraced him, her head on his shoulder, and she could hear his heart rustling through his damp shirt. Dante sighed, rolled his eyes, and looked away.

"It's okay, man. I mean, it's not, but . . . It's all right. We've just got to stay alive now."

Sofia glanced at the Fisher homestead, then back to Matt and Dante. Even knowing their proximity to death, she almost laughed. Under other circumstances they would appear comical, most of their bodies wrapped like bargain-basement mummies in sopping athleticwear, their exposed faces dripping in mud and sweat. She did not feel like any kind of hero or soldier; she felt like a scared, silly girl, and not far beneath the bravado Matt and Dante looked like frightened boys.

She heard it before she saw it, but not long before, because it came in so quickly. There was a sound like flood or flame, rolling down from above on the hillside, emerging from beneath the rays of the westering sun. The source of the sound was a harvest wagon, a simple assemblage of gray boards on large metal wheels hitched up to four bay Belgians. Their massive forms had been doused in water, and the late-day light frolicked across their taut muscles as they galloped. And standing at the front of the wagon, her slim hands firmly gripping the reins, was Joelle Fisher.

Dropping down from the crest of the westward hillside, the wagon accelerated on the descent as the horses tore through the green cornstalks, somehow trampling them down enough to let the cart's wheels roll across the field. At the rate they were traveling, the horses would draw the harvester toward their clearing in seconds.

"Our phones!" Dante yelled, and Sofia and Matt needed no prodding. With all the skill of long use, they snapped on their devices—then hurled them southeastward. A plume of roused black beetles followed the arc of the phones, and their buzzing increased to a noise that rivaled the great reverberance of horse hooves in the farm soil. Yet many of the insects remained behind, closing warily but steadily toward the center of the clearing.

Joelle slowed the horses slightly as she approached them, but Sofia could see the swarm moving toward the wagon. It was clear that the wagon wouldn't stop when it got to them. The boys to her left, Sofia braced herself for its arrival, knowing she might get no other chance. She saw a couple of intrepid bugs dart toward her face, and she flicked them frantically away. Then the curtain of corn was torn free, and she could see the brute, beautiful pectorals of the four charging draft horses.

The three friends shuffled parallel to the horses for a moment, but they couldn't keep alongside very long before the dense field started up again. The wagon was narrow, but Sofia was able to jump onto its side, with Matt right beside her. The two reached out and steadied Dante as he leapt with all his force onto the back. Sofia could feel him in her grip, his muscles straining as he sought not to fall backward; Joelle kept her focus straight ahead, and Sofia knew she would not be pausing. Quite the contrary, as soon as the horses passed the threshold of the clearing, they accelerated into a gallop that seemed even faster than their speed when they came down the hill.

Matt and Sofia helped Dante pull himself fully onto the well-worn boards, but now they could hear around them the great rattle of myriad wings. The insects were in Matt's hair and on his face and smeared across Dante's back, and she could feel them burrowing into the bare flesh of her cheeks. Each of the three rolled on the moving wagon, thrashing and flailing as Chrisleigh had done, and Sofia despaired at the thought that it was too late, that the army had sieged her body and would consume it, that all she knew of life would now cease in a few scattered seconds of torment.

But whether by the rate of their movement or the efficacy of their precautions or some outworking of fortune and providence, their tiny assailants had not gathered in the same multitude by which they had devoured Chrisleigh. Sofia's actions sent them fluttering off her face and scattering away from her clothes. In the rush of towering stalks that now engulfed them, she could still see their chrome-like bodies looping and whirling, and some approached her again. She persisted in waving her arms, looking like an idiot no doubt, yet her seeming foolishness warded them off. Matt and Dante were similarly abasing themselves, shedding their vanity for the sake of their lives.

Then, like a chariot in victory, the harvester burst free from the field, and they were suddenly on the road east of the Fisher property. Joelle silently directed the horses to follow the road north, and though they slackened their pace slightly, their gait retained a dread urgency. To the south Sofia saw the great horde of insects, whose interest had returned to the crops. There, a few yards behind them, a great column of shadow occulted the road at one point. Sofia realized then that the bugs hadn't started on Zeph Fisher's land. They were pouring into it from the massive farm across the street, where the once-flourishing rows of soybeans had been stripped bare. Now the great galvanized steel grain bins in the distance towered, glinting, over acres of ravaged plantings.

Joelle turned the wagon back onto her property once they were clearly beyond the margin of the cornfield, and the swarm had not reached this place yet. She brought them up to her house at the top of the hill before finally releasing the reins and allowing the Belgians to rest, their huge brown chests heaving. Her bonnet and her lavender cape dress had been torn in several places, with blood welled up around her shoulders and neck. Quietly she stepped down from the wagon to stand behind a spigot, planting the sturdy black shoes she now wore onto her ancestral soil.

Sofia stepped down too, beholding the same sight. Her body ached in a thousand sites from tension and adrenaline, but she gave thanks for the ache, for the pain meant she was still alive.

"What are they?" she asked as she watched the pall spreading over the green corn rows.

Sofia hadn't really expected a response, so she turned with a start when Joelle answered her.

"I saw them somehow, in a dream," she declared in a soft, otherworldly voice that wafted like flame on the wind. She took the glasses from her face, and for the first time that day Sofia saw her eyes, blue like the heavens, as they surveyed her family's ancient lands, lands upon which generations of Fishers had toiled. "I saw them, and I saw you. I dreamed the other night that you would come like this, and so would they, and you would be here."

Sofia had never heard Joelle talk like that before—cryptic, oracular, quite unlike the reserved, practical Amish girl she met on weekends. She spoke so earnestly that they all—Sofia, Matt, Dante—turned away from the field to look at her.

"What do you mean?" asked Dante, and in the reddening sun his earthy eyes seemed to sparkle like stars.

"It's the judgment upon the land," Joelle replied intently, as though the words were being poured into her.

She said nothing more. Sofia glanced at Matt; his customary crafty grin had been effaced, supplanted by a bedrock-deep solemnity. She took his hand, felt the tackiness of the blood that had been drawn from it. Then she felt a pressure on her right palm; Joelle was clasping it, even as she now held Dante's hand on the other side. The four of them gazed across the countryside beneath the crest of the hill.

"Good Lord," she breathed.

Below them was a vision like blood and fire, the swarm pluming like a column of smoke as, one by one, a thousand thousand minute mandibles devoured their way through the growth. They stood there, the four of them, in the arterial glow of the sun, shocked and sorrowing in their rent garments, beholding the reckoning of a mighty scourge over the earth.

THE LADY IN THE WOOD

He traveled toward the lonesome wood
Beyond the gardens and the glades.
Upon a high place then he stood,
Looked down where winter snows in flood
Melt off in liquid braids.

Descending to the valley, he
Returned into that gloomy green
And found the path that wound through tree
And shrub, the human highway, free
Inside the sylvan scene.

He saw the lady on the road.
She wore a dress of blue brocade
That from her fulsome figure flowed
Beneath a belt of brown, and showed
Her shoulders unafraid.

He did not move, but yet she turned
And looked on him with diamond eyes
That gleamed in shards of sun, and burned
Like ice on flesh, a gaze that churned
The air in wild surmise.

She spoke sweet words in lilting tone,
A song that swelled, like pulpy fruit,
Enticing, lyrical, a moan
Meandering in a tongue unknown,
Melodious as a lute.

He took her in embrace and kissed
Those rich red lips which late had sung
Their faerie song; she took his wrist
Within her slender grasp to tryst
Him toward the elm, where clung

The vining ivy twined around
The coarse gray trunk. Her lips, they oped
To sheen-white teeth. Without a sound
These strangers sunk down to the ground.
Her pall-pale fingers groped

Into the small of his broad back.
And then his own great jaws gaped wide:
He bared his fierce fangs in attack,
His flesh convulsed in hunger's wrack,
As hellishly he cried

And brought his teeth down toward her throat.
Yet then she rolled upon the path
From out his grasp. A piping note
Of glee escaped her lips afloat
The air, as in her wrath

She proffered then the silver blade
Concealed within her graceful gown.
Her blue-clad arm, in silk arrayed,
Arced through the shadows and the shade
And struck the monster down.

And so, eyes wide, his clean-shorn head
Rolled toward the margin of the road
As from his sundered neck was shed
The stolen blood, which now outspread
In rivulets that flowed

Into the thirsty earth. And she,
The lady in the wood, then smiled
And cleaned and sheathed her sword, now free
To head for home, once more to see
Her husband and her child.

THE ACHE OF BONE AND JOIST AND PAGE

I first woke to life on an autumn morning, the sky a gray slate of clouds, but bright clouds, with the sun glowing through them, and outside me the fields laden with harvest as Keats's mists and mellow fruitfulness. The first words I heard were *his,* speaking a language nowhere else in my mind, syllables tripping in strange feet that owed nothing to the iambs of the English or the dactyls of the Greeks, lilting and lyrical and terrible as a Sapphic ode. Until that moment I had sat for centuries, lonely and dumb and unthinking, a strong and beautiful slab towering on the hill, looking down upon the crops and the boughs of the tenants and the patchwork landscapes of grass and cultivated groves of maples and beeches. He it was who gathered my scattered thoughts, a library's worth of knowledge from across the millennia, and bound them into a consciousness, turned me from a lifeless estate of mortar and oak into a being rich in sentience, thinking with the mind of thousands upon thousands of sages and scholars, their learning and wisdom gathered into myself.

Day after day after day he returns to my brain and my heart, the library nestled windowless deep inside my body, and here he takes into himself a page at a time all the wisdom that I freely grant him, for in so doing I feel joined to him. These tomes are my speech, and though it is a rhetoric rich as Seneca and Cicero, I long to have my own voice, that I may communicate freely what his magic has unwittingly achieved. On most days he opens grammars of Herodian and Varro, Septuagint and Vulgate and Hexapla recensions, and scripts of Ugaritic and Aramaic, antique tongues of men with truths and stories set down through century upon century. He studies the winged words of Homer, the hexameter of Virgil, the pentameter of Shakespeare and Milton ("Sing, heavenly muse"), the poetic measures in whose time my hearts beats. And there are histories of Herodotus and Thucydides, Livy and Tacitus, Plutarch, Josephus, and Eusebius, manuscripts accounting for the wild and vile and glorious deeds of mankind through every era of the wide world.

For many months he remains, nestled entirely in my thoughts and in my bosom, straying only at need to my great belly of the dining hall by the adjoining kitchen, where the remnant of his late uncle's servants bring him the austere victuals that, like St. Antony in the wilderness, are all he desires. Only in the darkest hours of the night, when the sunless sky blinds my sight to the grounds, does his last lone candle traverse the veiny corridors to his bed. On difficult days, when translations elude him and interpretations wander and err, when he mutters in melancholy to himself at his inadequacy, he may seek out an old wine from deep in my bowels, the cellar carved out centuries ago and so often neglected. In these moments, how I long for a voice, to cheer him in his good work, to call on him to gird his loins for the great battle against ignorance and oblivion.

On the day he first leaves, summons his phaëton whose steeds take him over the southeastern hillocks and beyond the prospect of my glass eyes' gaze, I roil and question and mourn within myself. Now only those dull-witted, cacophonous servants crawl through me, little better than the mice or the mites that nibble at my bones and my body, infesting and infecting me. I am desolate as Medea and Dido, bereft as Achilles and Priam: he has departed with no word of destination in my hearing, and I wonder, will he ever return to my acreage? I have stood for centuries, steadfast across years of tempest and turmoil, but only at his arcane words did I become aware of the time in which I am embedded, the march of minutes and stream of seconds that roll over me. Each hour is as an aeon without his presence, an aeon I cannot escape or flee, for I am forever rooted in my foundations to the green lawn of this antique property.

When his carriage returns at long last—after how many sunrises and sunsets of barren agony I spend in his absence?—I rejoice with the rejoicings of my heart, for as Sappho would sing, is this not true beauty? He emerges into the light, and I cannot deny that his sojourn has been good to him, the pallor of his skin changed to the ruddy robustness of health, the shadows and irritation of his eyes replaced by a wide blinking twinkling. Yet he does not emerge alone; at his side is another person, a lady with raven tresses coiled in dark serpentine braids atop her head. I cannot see her as comely in the manner of Aphrodite or Helen or Iseult, her features too dark, too sharp, her lips too dry and pale, and her green dress does not disguise that her frame lacks Diana's slenderness beneath the taffeta. Yet as they walk down the path toward my arcades, they do not look at me, but peer into one another's eyes with wild surmise, not silent, speaking in soft and sibilant syllables.

Of what do they speak? Their converse is occupied by trivialities and superficialities, talk of weather and fashions and the pages of the *Daily Telegraph,* not of eternities or the scope of man's vast learning and achievements. Oh, here and there escape some words of beauty and erudition, turns of phrase that may evoke Homer's winged words or Marlowe's mighty lines, and do I hear an allusion to *Lysistrata* escape the lady's lips? But more than anything, they are speaking of love, of plans and preparations, and he regales her with commendations of her beauty—yet these encomia are poorly phrased and banal, with little in them of Catullus, Petrarch, Sidney, Spenser, or Keats. And worst of all, they are lies, precious flatteries, protestations against a manifest reality, for she is no Galatea or Beatrice or Laura or Stella; she is rather a dark lady, nothing like the sun. How can he betray the glory of his learning in such a way, lavishing trite tribute on this interloping harlot?

In the days that follow, he leads her through my body, and the renewed motion of the once-idle domestics now skittering in service itches in me as a rash must itch. He takes her through all my hidden places, casting bare before her gaze my most intimate parts, disclosing secret spaces that at one time I alone shared with him. When dawn's rosy fingers rise and warmly tickle my stone skin, the two of them frolic in the idylls of the pastoral grounds, as though he has forgotten "Et in Arcadia Ego," though I can never forget the crypts in which lie the moldering memento mori of his bloodline. And all throughout, they speak of wedlock, of vows and nuptials, and the nectar of blooming pomegranates, and I can hear in their furtive whispers fleshly vulgarities to shock the cultivated intellect.

It is then that I see her for who she is—Jezebel, Lilith, Duessa, a temptress of Folly and Fortune whose honeyed words have led his heart and passions astray to the paths of destruction. The force of this truth shines forth on me, brilliant and terrible, a light of knowledge that transfigures all that I perceive, and I feel that I have torn off this Calypso's veils to show out her countenance as it really is. How is it, though, that my young man cannot see what I see so clearly—how he has failed to follow his admirable learning, the minds and pens of so many great intellects, to open his eyes to this reality? And in the light of this epiphany, the scales falling from my eyes, I see—I see, I truly, truly see—what I must do.

I must needs await my opportunity, but I am patient with the centuries of my stony hide and hidden, aching, enduring joints and joists, and I *can* wait. Yet I cannot wait too long, for my scholar is not an ancient being like myself, but a young man finite and fleshly, and the carnal sacrament of his nuptials draws ever nigher. So I wait, alert, as they roam about my arteries and frolic and plan the plans of their incontinence. How it enrages me to see him brought to this perilous pass, this dark valley of shadows—he must be released, and he cannot do so of his own accord, so upon myself I take this high burden.

At last the moment arrives. They are together sporting in my mind, in the library, though the pages of poets and philosophers and historians remain trapped on the shelves as they speak only of airy vanities and grotesque, bubbling appetites. Were my body as theirs, I would vomit forth the sick and sticky vile bile of my viscera in disgust at this superficial folly, these chases in arras and gilded emptiness. After a time, however, the tenor of their intercourse alters, and my man begins confiding in his trollop about his occultic researches, his penetrations beyond the unreasoning mask, the painted veil that those who live call life. They stand, and he brings her to the shelves that hold my deepest thoughts, and together they pass by tomes of Dionysius the Areopagite and Paracelsus until they are standing by the fine folios of his antique esoterica. His fingers fondle the spine of the very text by which he drew me from inorganic imbecility to glorious rationality, and I know the time is right.

For weeks I have been rehearsing for this hour, harnessing the potential energies of my ancient bones; for if I cannot speak with the tongue of my mouth, perhaps I can communicate with my sinewy braces and beams, flexing forth the foundations of my form. I tremble in the majesty of my wrath and my righteousness, tremors rippling through the walls and floor and ceiling, setting the shelves to shuddering. Thus will I crush the whorish intruder, the frail flibbertigibbet who flirts at my wise man's side. Great heroes are born from loss and trial, and I will give him the suffering he needs to become truly noble, and the only cost will be the small life of a sensuous coquette.

Yet, alas, I had not reckoned on sacrifice, on the draw of his heart to the dark strumpet upon whom his gaze and his dreams have been fixed. The shelves, and the texts that they bear, begin to topple like teetering towers, and they would strike the harlot, yet my man casts himself in the shadow of that weight, pushing her clear of its heaviness. Instead, the broad oak frame and its ranks of lore and learning collapse upon his prone body. Aghast, I hear the sharp cracking of his bones and, a moment later, feel the sticky moistness of the blood seeping from his torn flesh, soaking into the damson carpet and the wooden floor beneath. I hear the deep, panicked inhalations and exhalations of his beloved, and I listen in vain for his own breath.

Yet I feel another agony as well, a pain less sharp but more visceral than the extinction of my man's spirit. Not shelves alone have fallen in my mind; the shaking has dislodged the candles by which he read those volumes. And the flames from these weary wicks leap free to the dark red threads of the carpet that covers the ancient stained timbers of the library floor. They erupt in torrential tongues of fire, like the high circles of Dante's Inferno, the air curling in heat like doomed Sodom or pompous Pompeii. The devilish woman strives to attain to the corpse of her man—*my* man—but the shelf and the books are engulfed, consumed in the raging blaze, and there is no avenue toward him, so she flees, weaving a wary way through the archipelago of fire. She has escaped, as my man had hoped in his parting sacrifice, and the servants too scurry like the vermin they are out of my orifices and onto the grounds.

I am left alone with my scholar as his mortal veil is rent, and his spirit—to what heights or depths does his spirit travel? I know only that our bodies are burning together in the funereal pyre that my brain has become, a hecatomb to our love. And I realize that I am screaming, screaming in what manner I am able, in a voice that sounds out like the inarticulate thunder of a passing storm. The many books that form my thoughts, the wise sayings and stories of great men, the long line of human accomplishments, they are devoured a page at a time by worms of flame. If I cannot exult in an incarnate union of our lives, may I not glory in this final consummation as in Hercalitean fire and ash we are reduced to our elements and slough off this prisoner's garb of flesh and stone? I, his one true home, will make of my foundations our marital bed and warm him in eager welcome as our last embers flicker far beneath the diamond-studded sky.

The Mermaids Keep Their Own Counsel

The sailors stalk the deck about the bow
And gaze with prurience upon the froth
Of frenzied ocean flindered by the wrath
Of testy tides on wandering rocks. Below
The bleak blue breakers, green glints sparkle through
The wending waves—the sheen of scales beneath
The water: women swimming in a swath
Of current, caught in sunset's solar flow.

The mermaids do not sing for men; they slide
Through reefs and grottoes, still and hidden, hushed,
The silent sirens of the sacred sea.
They live their lives aloof from men, who've pried
In pride and dusty lust: they'll not be crushed
But thrive through deeps divine, together free.

THE LIME KILN

Esther Good adjusted the pins on the thin lace oblong of her head covering one more time before checking her phone to see if anyone had texted her, but there were no new messages. Tugging at her T-shirt, she sat down on a half-rotted oak stump and reached over her striped skirt to double-knot the laces of her sneakers, then began her pacing once again. Isaiah was only ten minutes late, but he was usually early, so her heart raced even faster than it would during a *normal* day with him.

To pass the time, she looked around her, observing more closely than she ever had the features of the forest. She heard the sharp, lyrical fluting of robins and the unhurried, unembarrassed rush of the creek deeper in—the perennial chorus of a south Lancaster spring. Her eye caught a web, diaphanous and glistening in splinters of sunlight. A spider was approaching from its perimeter toward the center, where a lone wasp lay, beating its wings. To her surprise, with a twist of its torso the wasp tore through the sticky filaments, thrusting its stinger into the spider's body, again and again and again, until the paralyzed spider folded in upon itself and became the prey.

She watched with grotesque fascination until a strange sensation pulled at her attention, a ripple through the breeze like a sharp whisper. Out of the corner of her eye she thought she saw an unnatural violet shade, but when she turned, only the deep green of the wood met her view. The odd noise was gone, and all she could hear was a typical Susquehanna wind, and now her heart beating above it.

"Esther."

She turned with a start to the north. She hadn't expected him from that direction, for the little patch of gravel where she had parked was south of the woods. He emerged though a thick crowd of choke-berry shrubs, his favorite faded red T-shirt standing out from the green and the brown. His face bore its usual wry, lopsided smile with-in the thin frame of his ruddy, freshly shaved countenance. Not for the first time did she wonder what it might be like to kiss those dry, wryly smiling lips.

"Were you trying to scare me?" she asked, arms crossed, chan-neling her energies into a gaudily artificial scowl.

"I found it," he replied. "Through the woods that way. I'll show you in a minute."

She raised an eyebrow. "Seriously? I'm impressed, Mr. Yoder. I figured it had collapsed after all these years. Show me! We've only got a few hours before volleyball at the church."

"Yeah, sure. It's not far this way. But I wanted to show you some-thing else first."

He fished around in the pocket of his jeans. They were tight on him—*Not their least endearing feature,* she thought—and it took him an awkward moment before he could get what he was fumbling for. At last he pulled out a pendant, shining in the sunlight that trickled through the trees into the woods, which he carefully placed in her hand. She held it up into the morning light and saw on the end of a necklace the glinting form of a dove, sculpted from tin, its wings spread as though in embrace of the sky.

"Isaiah, where did you get this?"

He shrugged. "I made it. Mr. Zook let me use the equipment af-ter my shifts were finished. He's not *that* bad, you know." He hesitat-ed, looked around at the trees as if listening to them, then added, "I wanted to give you something memorable, and I figured you'd prob-ably be okay with it, but maybe it's too much like jewelry. I don't know what your folks would think. It's not a *ring* or anything, but you don't need to wear it if you don't want, you know . . . It's just, I was planning for today to . . . Oh, crap, this is all turning out wrong."

Esther pulled a stray strand of earth-brown hair away from her hazel eyes so she could look at him. He was breathing deeply, and his usually steady arms appeared to be trembling. "Isaiah Yoder, are you asking me to marry you?"

He nodded, seemingly relieved that she had understood him. "I don't think I'm doing it very well, not like how I practiced it, but yeah. Um, Esther Good, will you marry me?"

She handed the dove pendant back to him. "Here, help me put this on." She brought her shirt collar below the line of her clavicle and, lowering her head, used her left hand to pull to one side some rebellious wisps of hair that had slipped from her bun, leaving the nape of her neck bare. With care and precision, even reverence, Isaiah fastened the necklace in place. Esther paused, caught in the moment like a bird on a breeze; then she let her hair fall back down and turned to face him. The smile burst from her mouth, inevitable as the rising sun. "Yes, I'll marry you." She almost added, "you big idiot," since that is what she'd usually say, and she knew he'd receive it in good humor. But she also knew somehow that this was a distinct time, a time for solemnity to leaven her joy.

She pulled out her phone. "Okay, we need a selfie. Just for us, no one else."

Isaiah smiled gamely and crouched beside her on the left. She stretched out a hand toward a clearing in the trees until they were both in the frame and then took the picture. The lighting was uneven, a swath of shade dimming the right-hand side of the image, but their faces showed clear enough through.

"Now," she added, "are you going to show me what you found?"

He grinned eagerly. "Yeah, it's this way." He led her through the underbrush, for there were no trails here. They walked past posted signs reading "Private Property: No Trespassing," though she couldn't see any fences or boundary markers.

"Who owns this land?" she asked.

"Technically, I think it's the Brubakers. Hank Brubaker, not Abram. But he's too old to do anything with it, so he's going to pass it on to the township. He wouldn't mind me being here. And it's the perfect time to check it out, before anyone from the Historical Society gets the chance to explore. We should have plenty of time before volleyball."

Here the grade of the ground sloped sharply, fading clusters of henbit and deadnettle crowding a declivity of dry dirt over an outcropping. Isaiah took Esther's hand and helped her down to the next tier. As the soles of her sneakers found purchase, she glared playfully at him, one hand on her hip while she left the other in his.

"Isaiah, do you really believe I care that much about volleyball? On a day like this?"

"I never underestimate how seriously you take your volleyball," he responded. "What would a weekend look like if Esther Good didn't get in a few kills?"

"It can wait," she insisted. "We're engaged. Let's just enjoy that. And . . ."

"And?"

"And so you found it? There's really a lime kiln?" she inquired excitedly.

"Yeah."

"And is it a double kiln?"

He nodded. "Just like you said."

Esther thought the day couldn't get better. Since she was in diapers, she had been listening to her grandfather talk about the history of the area. As a girl, she would scutter off as soon as her chores were done and start digging in the back yard, convinced that a relic of her ancestors lay one more dig beneath the grass or the soil, even just an old coin or a nail—something that would connect her across the centuries to the communion of souls that had passed before her. When she was old enough, she visited any local history museum she could find.

And that was how she learned about the old Wolff estate. For decades, from the waning of the eighteenth century to the dawn of the nineteenth, it stood adjacent to the property of a Zimmerman clan, but unlike the Zimmermans, the Wolffs had not emigrated for religious reasons. The reclusive Wolffs were odd neighbors for the gregarious Zimmermans, and their respective houses were almost a mile apart. But in the manner of the day, they had for practical reasons constructed a shared lime kiln on the boundary-line of their properties.

As time passed, the Wolff line died out quietly, while the Zimmermans abruptly and enigmatically moved eastward shortly thereafter, and the land went to the Brubakers, who for almost two centuries showed no proclivity to cultivate or develop it, a striking neglect for landowners of the day—and an irresistible mystery for Esther to solve. She was a research nerd of the sort that baffled most of her peers, and Isaiah already knew that she was as comfortable in an archive as she was in a kitchen. But today she just wanted to see the kiln.

And then, after fifteen minutes of navigating a maze of oak and shagbark hickory, they arrived. The kiln had been built into the side of another descent in the landscape, and Esther could see why it had been lost to time. Dogwood and ferns, along with encroaching soil, had crowded from view most of the two top chambers, the great pits into which the families would have dumped large blocks of the limestone from their land. She and Isaiah clambered down the slope side until they were looking directly at the front of the edifice. From this point, it became clearly visible as an artificial structure, quarried gray stones mortared tightly together to a height of some twenty feet, with twin stoke-holes four feet high and rounded like sockets at the base. It was here that, some two centuries ago, the Zimmermans and the Wolffs would have lit the lower fires that burned the limestone poured into the chambers above until it crumbled down the shaft and became quicklime: fertilizer for their crops and protection for their wood. On one side the interior of the kiln had completely filled with detritus across the years, but the other looked clear, and Esther crouched down.

"This is it," Esther said.

"This is it," affirmed Isaiah.

Esther gave a couple of quick, excited claps, then ducked further until she was able to shuffle into the open stoke-hole.

It was in that moment, as she crossed the threshold of the little portal, that everything around her shifted. A noise like a scream redounded within her temples, a scream with no voice yet agonized and seemingly without end. Her body felt as though it were suddenly caught in a strong current, though she knew she wasn't moving. But she was being immersed in *something,* in a turbulent flow of images, sensations, memories, carrying her and spinning her, not across acres but through centuries—perhaps even eons. She floundered, her limbs thrashing at the walls of the kiln, until her hand caught the steady hand of her own Isaiah, who pulled her out of the stoke-hole. Only then did she realize that she too had been screaming.

Isaiah, kneeling, held her close to his chest, stroking the hair outside her veil, as he never had done before. "Esther," he gasped uneasily, "what happened?"

She swallowed, tried to remind her lungs how to breathe again, and though it broke one of the rules they had set themselves, she let Isaiah keep holding her. Her eyes roamed the terrain, the spring's glorious eruption of growing green, and the brilliant blue sky beyond. And there before her, the cold gray frame of that hateful kiln.

"I—I know it now," she whispered, her words just barely audible above the wind and the buzz of woodland life. "The Wolffs, the Zimmermans—I know what happened here."

She was shaking, as if a January chill had caught her, but she gently removed herself from Isaiah's tender hold. Then she crawled back toward the kiln entrance. Isaiah stayed close by but didn't move to restrain her. She reached her hands into the stoke-hole, running them through recent dirt and older layers of fallen quicklime, feeling it beneath her fingernails as she dug, and there seemed a burning on her skin, though the ground was cool and dry. At last she stopped, pulling both her hands out. She held up her right hand so that she and Isaiah could see clearly: between her thumb and forefinger, still caked in a matrix of soil, was a human molar.

"She's here," Esther said. "She's still here, after all these years. And so is *it.*"

Isaiah's attention turned from the tooth to Esther's face, and she looked back into his eyes, blue as the sky. "What are you talking about?" he asked softly.

She gently placed the tooth on the ground beside the kiln, then took his face in her hands. "I love you, Isaiah," she declared, as she had so often before, but she had never uttered the words with true urgency, with the thought that these words were sacred and cosmic. "You know me. You know who I am. Can you trust me?"

"I mean, sure, yeah. But what are you . . . ?" Then peering at her, at the resolve that now glowed like a nimbus from her round face, he said simply, "I love you, Esther, and I trust you."

She nodded, rising to her feet. She held out a hand and helped him stand beside her. "Thank you," she sighed. "I promise I'll explain it to you while we walk."

"Where are we going?"

"To the Wolff house."

"Why are we going there? We just got here," he started, but Esther was already moving. He scrambled up the slope into which the kiln had been built, trying to keep up with her. Soon they had ascended back to the ledge upon which they had stood together just a few minutes earlier. She forged out in a different direction, westward through pathless oak and hickory and crowding shrubs.

"Jerusha Zimmerman," Esther began once they were passing through more level land. "She was seventeen, living with her family on the homestead here, two hundred years ago."

"You never told me about her."

"I didn't know," Esther replied. "No one knew. I learned just now, down there in the lime kiln." She didn't stop but turned to Isaiah beside her as they walked. "When I stepped in there, it all poured in on me. She shared with me her memories, her experiences, her desires. For a moment, I knew everything she had known."

"You met—what, her ghost?"

Esther drew in a breath nervously. "I didn't want to say the word because . . . because I was afraid if I did, you'd think I was crazy."

Isaiah reached out and took her hand, and they paused their trek.

Once more she peered at him with iridescent eyes, lips parted as if she would say more. She searched for mockery or incredulity, for a caustic grin fluttering at the corners of his mouth. But his slightly angular features and his wide, clear eyes were firm.

"Esther, you're about the smartest—and the wisest—person I know. You're a step ahead me every day. I'm just a welder from Providence Township. I meant it—I trust you." He turned back toward the wood and resumed walking. "So let's get going, and you tell me about Jerusha Zimmerman."

Jerusha Zimmerman, hair pouring like maple syrup, snuck away from the house as sunset neared, looking for Julian. She knew his father would be out at town, and she sighed in relief to think of it, her breath clouding into the cold early evening. Gregor Wolff frightened her, with his wild wide brown eyes and billowing, tumultuous white beard. When she saw him outside, he so often seemed to be scanning the land, sunken in an abstruse gloom; when he was in the house, she sometimes heard him muttering syllables in some tongue that was not English or German or Dutch.

How unlike Gregor was his son, willowy Julian, shining hair like an alchemy of blent gold and silver, free of word and mien, relentlessly curious. Jerusha knew that her father mistrusted the Wolffs; though he joined funds with them years ago for the building of the kiln, he did not know their faith and held in scorn any who would not work their fields with their own weather-beaten hands. Why he even tolerated them, she could not say.

Lantern in hand for the journey back, Jerusha approached the Wolff house, its two-story masonry looking almost like a castle on its hill, set against the blazing scald of the orange sun behind it. Most of the windows were dark, save a guttering sprig of luminance in one on the first floor. She walked to the east-side entrance, casting glances about in hopes that she might not be seen by their servants. Then she opened the door, which, newly oiled, did not creak on its hinges. The little light was coming from the family's study—a vain extravagance, her father would think—into which she strode with caution and confidence.

The room seemed empty at first, no movement save the pale, frolicking flame of a candle on the desk. But Jerusha perceived more light deeper in, seemingly sourceless, and then she saw that it was emanating from the back wall. A shelf of books had been displaced—it was, she realized, a door, behind which were stairs that led down, beneath the first floor of the Wolff house and into the marrow of the hill. She had ever been wily but never hesitant, and with care she quietly peeked down the steps and into the glowing cellar.

Here were books, ancient books with flaking, weathered spines whose musty smell of centuries wafted with the scent of candle-smoke up to her nose. On shelves they ringed the small room in a riot of brown, the brown of dry, fallow soil. A small, simple table stood in the center, its surface concealed by books and papers, and sitting at the table, his fair hair gleaming, was the man she sought.

"Julian!" she exclaimed, enthralled, for she had half feared she would see his father. She loped down the stairs as he looked up from his books, smiling, his crystal eyes hidden in the sheening glass of his spectacles.

"My darling Jerusha," he said, "have you come all this way for me?"

"Of course. What else might bring me hence?"

He closed the book he had been reading, wisping atomies of dust into the air as he did. Removing his spectacles, he seized her hand. "Then let us make the most of our time."

Esther's strides ceased abruptly, and she looked around her at the great overstory of oak and maple.

"Have you actually *been* to the Wolff house, Isaiah?" she inquired.

He shook his head. "No. Why? It seemed like you knew where it was."

"I know the land as Jerusha knew it, which was different. And I'm still trying to fit together everything she was showing me."

A movement caught their eye, and both Isaiah and Esther turned their attention northwest. Through the trees, some fifteen yards distant, they saw a strange glow well up like a pustule in the air. It came as a distension of dark purple light—not the purple of royalty or of exquisite storm-clearing sunsets but the purple of a bruise, swelling with sour and sticky infection. Then, seconds later, it burst, and the wood was clear again. Yet not quite clear, for the whole atmosphere it left behind it looked altered in some unnamable way, and they could see little deaths within its ambit—spring leaves now autumn-crisp, bark peeling like burnt skin, bees tumbling unceremoniously out of the sky, a gray-yellow warbler plummeting stiffly to the ground.

At once Esther was walking again, tugging at Isaiah's shirt as she did.

"Do you know where the house is, then?" he asked. His baffled gaze still lingered on the aftermath of the bizarre disruption, but he never failed at keeping in stride with her.

"I'm not sure, but I hope so," she answered. "We have to hurry. It's breaking free."

"Meet me at dawn at the lime kiln," Julian had said to her. Father was already feeding the animals, so Jerusha could creep out of the house without raising much concern. It was even colder than last evening, and the stars were fading as black sky washed into deep blue, with a blush of white on the eastern horizon. Lantern in hand, she carefully edged down, the frosty dirt crunching beneath her feet.

True to his word, Julian stood by the mouth of the kiln's upper chamber, where a thick vapor rose in the frigid air. He was smiling as he helped her down to his level, and the touch of his hand was warm upon her cold fingers. He lifted her chin with his other hand, lightly kissing her lips, and she could smell the bacon of his breakfast on his breath.

"Thank you for coming, my dearest," he said. "I did not know if you would."

"I would fain travel anywhere for you, Julian," she replied.

He nodded. "That is well." Licking his lips, he added, "I had not expected to see you last night. Perhaps it was fortuitous, portending great things . . . though not as I once had hoped."

She regarded him quizzically, puzzling out his cryptic words. And then, without warning, there was a tugging at her arm, and by the time

she knew that Julian was pulling her, it was too late. He thrust her to-
ward the great column of pallid smoke until she plummeted into the
vertical shaft of the kiln, and all she had time to think was, How can
this be? Why would he do such a thing? Then the ghastliness of the
pains took hold—the yielding of bone as her feet hit the pile of lime-
stone fragments, the choking stench of the gases invading her lungs,
the horrific mindless burning as the flame from the stoke-hole be-
neath her rose through her flesh. There was nothing to see, nothing
to do, in those mindless minutes but flail uselessly in the agony of her
blinding, senseless death.

The Wolff house stood at the crest of a small hill when they found it.
From afar it appeared as Jerusha would have seen it, but the landscape was altered. The chestnut trees had died out decades ago, leaving a vacant gap gouged out of the forest, and the grass was tall and
unruly. Any trace of the track on which their carriages would have
driven had long since been swallowed up by an orgy of weeds.

Esther could see Isaiah's disgust as she told him what she knew.
He held her back when she spoke of Jerusha's death, a sickly pallor
across his usually suntanned face.

"What happened to her . . . is that what *you* felt when you went
into the kiln?"

Esther looked up into his eyes and nodded.

"But I don't understand. I mean . . . why?"

Once again, she started walking. "We have to keep moving," she
insisted. "Julian and his father, they were both . . . sorcerers, I guess
you'd call them. They learned some kind of magic from these old
books they had. But they used it in different ways. Gregor Wolff just
wanted some land to be farmed, and when he came to Pennsylvania,
he found this little patch that no one had claimed, and no one wanted
to. And there was a reason no one wanted to."

"What kind of reason?" Isaiah asked as they began the climb toward the brow of the hill and the house. The closer they came, the
more the wear of the centuries stood out in crumbling masonry and
lichenous fractals.

"There was something here already," Esther replied. "Something old, something not part of our earth but that had lived here for . . . a really long time. A monster, or a force. Isaiah, I don't know what kind of word to use for it. Whatever it was, it scared people away. So Gregor did some kind of magic, and he trapped it, and then the land was safe and good for a farmer. And cheap, which is probably why Levi Zimmerman jumped in next door."

"But what about Julian?" Isaiah persisted.

As they continued further up, leaving the thickest trees behind them, Esther said, "Julian didn't just want a quiet farm like his father did. That thing—it was powerful, and he thought he could catch it and use its power. He wanted to be some kind of great man, to do whatever he wanted. But for that kind of magic, he needed . . ." She trailed off, choking back the panic that filled her as she remembered the appalling betrayal of Jerusha, which Esther had known and felt herself. ". . . a sacrifice. He needed a sacrifice."

When they reached the house, they found it boarded up, a padlock on the door, its windows occluded by planks, like obols on the eyes of the dead. But the boards had been put in place years ago, and Isaiah soon found one that was rotting at the screws. He and Esther stuck their fingers into the gap where the cheap wood had curled from moisture and time, and together they pulled. With a splintering sound the obstruction gave way, falling to the overgrown grass below. Isaiah kicked out the remaining glass, and the two crawled into the window. They set their phones to flashlight mode and walked into the Wolff house, the first people in years to breathe its oppressive air.

Esther knew others had entered it since the day Jerusha died, yet the dark interior looked surprisingly as it had then, for most of the old furniture remained. But it was an enclave of frayed shadows now, as the bright blue-white light from their phones caught scalene angles and great tapestries of cobwebs. Immense, long-concealed spiders scurried away from the light, and Esther could hear the burbling crack of their bodies being crushed beneath her shoes as she advanced. Perhaps a day ago the seething teeming of lightless life would have disgusted her, but now she had known horrors far worse than any scuttling arthropods.

Isaiah coughed from breathing in the dust, but he stifled the noise, looking hesitantly around. Esther marched forward into the study until she found the shelf on the back wall. She carefully set her phone on the filmy floor and began to tug, but it held fast. Isaiah saw what she was doing and set his phone down beside hers. Together they pulled, yet without effect.

"Wait," Isaiah told her.

Grabbing his phone, he shone the light closely at the shelf until he found a tiny latch, concealed behind a moldering book. With a little jiggling it came free, and the shelf door swung open on its hidden hinges. Esther already had her own phone ready, and she descended the stairs into the Wolff house's cellar, Isaiah a step behind her.

Here was a wealth of arcane lore, the dark researches of millennia, now crumbling like stale bread in their rows along the walls. The work of Gregor's life, and his son's obsession, the envy of any true magician, was yielding to time and humidity and worms and bacteria— to the ineluctable procession of nature that the younger Wolff had striven so hard to conquer.

In the center of the cellar and its ring of disintegrating lore was a simple table. Lying head down at the table was a body, dressed in a rotting wine-dark tailcoat with bone buttons over a waistcoat and linen shirt. The features of the corpse were remarkably well preserved; the skin was pale as chalk, though dry and rubbery, but Esther could see no sign of putrefaction. And the face was one she now knew all too well.

"Julian Wolff," she said.

It did not end with her death—she moved from one terror into another. As Jerusha's flesh crumbled with the quicklime, her soul remained, ensnared once again by Julian's ravening, thirsting cruelty. He had woven a great web of words, casting them forth to trap the fetid power that had stalked these lands for five thousand ages. That net, when at last released, caught more than the entity toward which it had been thrown—it caught and held Jerusha too.

She was stuck, the store of her self now tangled in the tacky fila-ments of her lover's incantations. The elder thing thrashed against its restraints, but what could Jerusha, once a girl on the cusp of young womanhood, do against such magic? She squirmed and twitched, but the cords held fast.

And so, that which endured of Jerusha Zimmerman could do nothing but wait and exist and learn, in the dread education of the centuries. She felt impossibly small beside the vast bulk of the pres-ence, yet her very smallness preserved her from worse harms, for the energies of the thing were all concentrated on shredding through Jul-ian's web. Most days the magic held firm, but once in a while a preda-tory appendage would tear free into the world she had known. And day by day, year by year, the net grew slacker, more tattered. Two hundred years was an eye-blink in the time scale of this power, and soon, she knew, it would free itself wholly from Julian's ill-conceived work. But two hundred years to a human soul still seemed intermina-ble, so Jerusha explored the strange boundaries of her new world and studied the beast beside which she was trapped. And all the while without ceasing she screamed, praying that someday her voice might be heard.

"Esther, what is going on?" Isaiah pleaded, putting an arm around her in the night-black circle of the cellar.

"He thought he could hold it," Esther murmured, casting her light on the dead man's horrified waxy face. "He thought his magic was strong enough to control a monster. He killed Jerusha because he thought he could control it." She laughed a hollow laugh, like the echo in a well. "And of course it didn't work. The thing reached out and destroyed him on the same day."

"Now what?" Isaiah asked.

Esther looked down at the table where Julian lay, its surface bare but for two objects. Beneath his left arm was a vellum volume, clutched in his stiff fingers. His right hand lay extended toward a small parchment, upon which were scrawled words in Latin and some other language. Esther breathed minimally to keep from inhaling the noxious dust that thickened the air, but she could feel the percussion of her heartbeats as the fear entered into her. She saw now what she needed to do.

She grabbed Julian's left hand and pulled at the fingers until they cracked, releasing the book, and then she picked up the sheet of paper to his right. Once more she was in motion, trusting Isaiah to keep pace as she ran upstairs and climbed out the window.

"Do you keep matches in your truck?" she queried.

"Yeah, I'm sure I've got some in the glove compartment," he told her.

"Good. We'll need them." She spared him a glance as she began running south toward his vehicle. "Julian used the book to summon that thing. But before that, this little note has the words Gregor Wolff used to restrain it in the first place. Gregor's magic isn't like Julian's magic; it's simpler, more like a prayer than a spell. Gregor never wanted to *use* the power; he just wanted to take this place back from something that never should have been here. So we need to use Gregor's words to get rid of the thing."

"I don't understand. Why not just do it here and now?"

Esther slowed a moment, her breath rasping from all the running she had been doing, but she kept going. "I wish it was that easy. But we have to remove Julian's trap first. And there's only one way to do that: to burn his book at the place where it all started."

"You mean the lime kiln."

"Yes."

Isaiah didn't ask again how Esther knew this, and she almost cried in gratitude that he didn't. She had always been studious, always seeking and learning for the sheer joy of immersing herself in the gift of the cosmos, and that quality sustained her now, but this knowledge was of a different order. It was both learned and instinctive, dripping into her soul like rainwater through layers of soil. She was also just as certain that the entity knew her plan; its malevolence stretched over her like the shadow of a looming cloud.

And then it was there. Like the claw of a tiger reaching through cage bars, the entity burst into the woods with them. It came once more with a purpling distension of the air and the earth, an ichorous discharge of dynamistic alienage. Behind her ears Esther heard a sound like a bellow or a laugh or an earthquake as her environment ruptured. It happened beside her, so quickly that she scarcely saw the moment it swallowed Isaiah. He was pushing her away from himself, and he had no more than a second to cry out in pain and fear as his body was subsumed within the entity's bourn.

She was perhaps three feet away, and she stumbled back from the rippling wall of negation. The emptiness that gouged her heart felt worse than any pain she had known on this day. Her Isaiah was simply gone. Isaiah, who shared his macaroni and cheese with her when her parents sent her to their Mennonite school with carrot sticks; who snuck out of metalworking class even though he loved it just to catch a glimpse of her at study hall; who smiled goofily without defending himself every time she teased him for tripping over his words. How much had gone into the making of him in his nineteen years, the building of the strong, muscular body she desired and the gentle, ardent spirit she loved? All so that he should be elided like an afterthought from the universe of things?

There was no time for Esther Good to think. She dropped the book and the paper. Touching a finger to the pendant around her neck, she ran into the inky blot beside her, hand outstretched. Inside she felt a great cold—not the cold of a Lancaster December, but the cold of the great voids between galaxies, where stars cannot be seen. For some iota of time she knew earth as the entity knew it, as earth had been when the power first arrived from its own dimensional abysms in search of new prospect, prowling hot, shallow Cambrian seas amid spiny, scurrying *Olenellus* trilobites and voracious, undulating anomalocarids.

Esther felt herself plunging into the great gulf of deep space and deep time inside the primeval membranes of the hungering atrocity, and with it the awful inexorability of death that a falling person feels—until a little gleam of soul beckoned to her like a pole star. It was a dim flicker in that darkness, but any light is a victory, for darkness is only an absence, and in that glinting she could see just enough to reach forth into its maw and grab Isaiah, pulling him free from the frost and fire of the antinatural thing.

They stumbled into the sharded light of the sun sneaking through oak boughs, and Esther felt the refreshing itch of nettles on her palm as she tried to rise. Isaiah lay beside her, looking stiff and sickly, like Julian in his cellar, and, *Oh, God,* she thought, *is it too late?* Kneeling down, she yanked him further from the bilious indigo beside them and, running her fingers through the curls of his rusty auburn hair, she kissed him in an agony of desperation. And in so doing she rejoiced, for those lips that had tripped so often over words now were warm lips through which hot breath was escaping.

His eyes opened, not gradually or flutteringly but wide with the horror of the deeps they had seen. But those eyes saw her, and their blue grew tranquil as a tide pool, and the lips smiled and said simply, "Esther."

Esther was weeping with the joy of it, but she was not still, for the entity had not vanished, was indeed transgressing close again upon their space. Isaiah coughed and rose unsteadily, but peering into the deep excrescence from which he had been rescued, he scrambled to his feet as Esther scooped up the book and the parchment, and they ran. By now her lungs were beginning to burn from the strain, yet she ran faster than ever, for she had known the pain of Jerusha's suffering and the primordial dismay of the universe's dark spaces, and now any earthly pain seemed dull and stagnant by comparison. Isaiah must have known it too, for he ran by her side as they dodged maples and oaks and hickories, moved up and down sedimentary declivities. Her sneakers trod over moss and ferns and white clover, no doubt crushing spiders and caterpillars and wasps in their progress. Around them more and more shafts of slimy violet light burst into the sylvan landscape.

Over a rise and through a dense line of white and amber honeysuckle, they emerged at the little gravel rectangle where Isaiah's truck was parked. The windows were down, the doors unlocked, and he whipped the passenger side open so hard that it almost cracked at the hinges. He rifled through insurance cards and sundry tools and a flashlight until he found a small box of matches. Leaping down, he joined Esther as they re-entered the forest.

The entity was never static around them. It might vanish from one patch of ground, leaving an incongruous scar of deathliness carved into the spring verdancy, then appear ten yards away in its shadowy pestilent glow. Every minute it probed the weakening of Julian's magic, pulling at the threads until they split. At any moment it might reclaim this whole unhallowed ground as its own dominion.

But the lime kiln was not far, and soon they came to the stokehole at its base. Esther flung Julian's book into the pit of dirt and quicklime, turning to Isaiah.

"Get ready," she warned. "There's only one way to catch this thing, but I'll have to release it from Julian's spell first. Do you understand what I'm saying?"

He nodded. "We're setting it free."

"Exactly." She looked back to the ragged tome in the kiln and drew in one more breath. "Okay, Isaiah—light it."

He struck the match without hesitation, and an orange flame jumped to life at the end of the little stick. There was a grace in the smooth motion by which he brought forth that flame and set it to the book: if there was one thing Isaiah Yoder knew, it was fire. And the text burst forth with a violent red burning well beyond what its matter could have sustained, so hot that Esther and Isaiah had to leap back.

In seconds the book was gone, and the sky darkened at the flexing of the festering force in its sudden freedom. Holding Isaiah's hand, Esther read the words from Gregor's paper, not even comprehending them in full but uttering them like a plea or a petition, casting her voice into the void against the chaos that was swelling up on every side of them. As she was speaking, she could feel *it* gathering, drawing near, and she almost choked at the thought that it could swallow her before she had finished speaking. Yet something was holding the darkness at bay, a tiny spark in its midst, and as she read on she knew it was the same light that had guided her out at Isaiah's rescue—it was Jerusha Zimmerman, her spirit at last free but remaining here in the kiln for one moment more to shield them from the frothing spite of the entity.

Esther spoke the last word, and now she heard a new scream—not the tortured cry that Jerusha had been wailing since her death but the hideous inhuman shriek of the cosmic interloper as it was bound once again. Esther could not know whether she had sent it to its home or its prison, or even if there was a difference between them. The echo of its hate shuddered in her soul, and its last outlashing hurt like a venomed sting. But the echo faded, and the hurt subsided, and she was now surrounded by trees and flowers and innocuous bugs and creatures of the great calm.

She shuffled further from the lime kiln and then lay on her back at the foot of it, breathing deep breaths, eyes closed, an inexplicable rest settling like a blanket upon her. How long she lay this way she couldn't say, but when at last she opened her eyes again she saw her Isaiah, lying beside her, and above them the night sky, brilliantly shining in through a round clearing in the canopy of the dark wood.

"Isaiah, are you here with me?" she whispered.

"Yeah, I am."

Past all the terrors she had seen on this day, Esther smiled. "I'm sorry we had to spend our engagement day like this."

Isaiah, still looking up, shrugged his shoulders against the cool earth. "I guess we'll never forget it," he chuckled. "We're just getting started. They say marriage is an adventure."

One hand to the necklace at her throat, she reached out the other and once more caught hold of Isaiah's. "I love you," she murmured, and they both laughed. Laughed—the woods rang with it. And together they looked up again, beyond the woods and into the piece-bright paling of sky and all its sparkling stars.

THROUGH ENCHANTMENT

The journey passes through the darkened wood,
The well-worn path a slice of gathered green
Shard-shadowed at the margins, thick as blood
And bark. Here goblins grow in stones, unseen,
As dryads dance to please a fairy queen,
Who reigns in rage and revelry, while elves
Flit feyly from their firelit haunts between
The boles and knolls and deeper diamond delves.
The people passing on the path themselves
Thread through the thicket where the sunrays slant.
Perhaps they see past shadows to the shelves
Where fair-folk flock and spirit-sprites enchant.
They crowd in crowing wrath and languid laughter—
Then, past this path, we find our ever after.

THE CARTOGRAPHER

> Here, then, is the pattern in my carpet, the sense of the eternal mysteries, the eternal beauty hidden beneath the crust of common and commonplace things; hidden and yet burning and glowing continually if you care to look with purged eyes.
>
> —Arthur Machen, *The London Adventure*

> Down the way, the road's divided
> Paint me the places you've seen.
> —R.E.M., "Maps and Legends"

Caleb Graff had known something was wrong when he saw the lines on the map begin to move. At first he had dismissed it as a trick of the eye or the rustling of the old parchment in a summer breeze passing through the screen door. The ink was faded, the terrain it described unfamiliar, so it would hardly be surprising if he lost track of the contours of its features. But after a third glimpse he could deny it no longer: the river boundary had definitely shifted position, as had the image of the peculiar flower that appeared beside its banks. It was at this point that he knew, if there had ever been any doubt, that this was no ordinary map.

And that was why he found himself where he was now, taking his pickup up 222 to the Pennsylvania Turnpike until it reached the Vine Street Expressway, where, crossing the Schuylkill River, he hopped on I-95 just long enough to get to exit 20. It was a measure of his desperation that he found himself now heading toward Ellsworth, because he was no fan of driving anywhere in Philadelphia, let alone South Philly. He avoided it when he could, except when the business of the farm demanded it. His last sojourn into the city had coincided with his last date, an occasion far more memorable for the food than the company.

It was late afternoon, and he had factored in time for traffic, but not enough time, and he was already running behind schedule before his desperate search for a legal parking space began. Finally, testing the patience of several irate drivers behind him, he managed to parallel park (by a loose definition of the term) several blocks from his destination. Gathering up his material, he hurried out into the sweltering hazy sun and checked his phone to confirm the address. He strode by block after block, trying with a spectacular lack of success to look as though he belonged in the neighborhood before arriving, twenty minutes late, at the address. Squinting down at the phone, he confirmed once again that he was at the right place. He wasn't sure what he had been expecting, but it certainly was not this simple red-brick apartment building without any business signs. And even though his odyssey had taken him two hours of anxiety and stressful driving to get here, he almost decided to head back to the truck. Then he thought of Josh, and of Rebekah and Karis and Luke, and sucking in an unsteady breath, Caleb rang the doorbell.

The door was opened by a balding Lebanese man of perhaps fifty with a thick black beard that covered his face and his neck. He looked intently and unflinchingly at Caleb with penetrating eyes.

"Are you . . . Mr. Khouri?" Caleb inquired hesitantly.

The man paused before turning his head back into the house and shouting something in what Caleb assumed to be Arabic. A woman appeared at the door and afforded the man a brief withering glance before rolling her eyes and turning her attention to Caleb. She opened the door and gestured for him to enter.

"Come in, please," she insisted. "Forgive my husband's manners. He gets grouchy at this time of day. Would you like some tea?"

Caleb shook his head as he cautiously entered what was clearly the kitchen of a residence and not the shop front he had somehow pictured. "I'm sorry," he said, "I just want to make sure I'm in this right place. I'm looking for a certain D. Khouri."

The woman sighed and shook her head with a smile, as though Caleb had uttered a rare and profound truth. "Yes, of course you are, Mr. ——?"

She looked at him expectantly, and he stammered out, "Um, Graff . . . Caleb Graff. I was led to believe that this was the address of D. Khouri, a—cartographer."

This time, it was the man who rolled his eyes; his wife only nodded and replied, "Yes, that would be Dina."

"You're not embarrassing me, are you?"

This was a different voice that came from a room beyond the kitchen. Caleb's gaze followed the voice, which was high, like the upper range of a flute. When the speaker emerged, he saw that she was a young woman, barely five feet in height, with black hair in a rather unkempt ponytail. At first glance she looked singularly girlish, but her light brown eyes were old and full of mysteries. She had a dark red stud in her nose and wore a loose black R.E.M. shirt and artfully torn blue jeans.

Caleb felt he had spent enough time already looking foolish and baffled, so he determined to respond levelheadedly. "So *you're* the person I'm looking for."

The younger woman, Dina, smiled. "That's right. And *you're* late. I was just about to pencil you in as a no-show. You'd be surprised how often that happens."

"I'm sure I would be," Caleb responded, perhaps a trifle disingenuously.

"Fortunately for you, I myself have rather idiosyncratic opinions about time, so I'm willing to give you a pass. Shall we step into my office?"

"Sounds good," said Caleb, keeping his resolve. He followed Dina through a short, narrow corridor until they hung a left and passed through a door from which a sign bearing her name hung beneath a poster declaring, "It's the End of the World as We Know It (and I Feel Fine)."

It was clearly an office, with a filing cabinet whose drawers were half open and a desk on which sat an old computer, an assortment of loose papers, and innumerable blue sticky notes, all presided over by a St. Thomas Aquinas bobblehead. But it was just as clearly a bedroom, with a twin mattress in the corner surrounded by eclectic film and album posters and reproductions of ancient maps and M. C. Escher prints. A song with Arabic lyrics was playing from a tablet that rested on one of the six bookshelves that crowded much of the room. There was only a narrow avenue available to get to the desk, and Dina had to stop abruptly on first entering, so that Caleb bumped into her inelegantly when they first got there. She gave no indication of annoyance, simply squeezing between a shelf and the corner of the desk until she could sit down. Caleb took the hint and sat in the seat opposite her, which barely fit in the office.

"So what can I do for you, Mr. Graff?" she asked, and she was so close that he could smell the ginger-ale on her breath.

The whole situation felt both bizarre and inevitable to Caleb, moving ahead with the peculiar logic of a dream. He wondered if he should choose to end it all here, flee back to his familiar pickup and his familiar farm, to country roads and feed corn. But he thought then of dying crops, and he remembered again the impossible moving river, and with a shrug he pulled out the map and set it in front of her.

"This is the map you mentioned in your email?"

Caleb nodded. "Yes, Ms. Khouri. And like I said, you might think I'm crazy, but I swear to you—and I'm not the kind of guy who says stuff lightly—I swear the map itself has been . . . changing."

Dina smiled reassuringly as she took the map in her hands. "Mr. Graff, I believe you contacted me because I am the one person around here who *won't* think you're crazy. But I need to know a little more. As strange as all this is—and I totally get how strange it must be for you—people like you don't find people like me unless something more is going on. So what's the backstory?"

Caleb scratched his head, a habit he hated because doing so always reminded him of his thinning hair. "Our farm had been in the family for over ten generations—we still have the deed signed by William Penn's son. And in all that time, it's done well. We've never been rich, but always successful—kind of almost weirdly successful. Droughts, storms, blights, you name it, going back to the eighteenth century, our property somehow managed to escape it all. We're al-most like a running local joke that way. But that changed when my dad died."

"I'm so sorry, Mr. Graff," she said. He looked for irony in her cryptic almond eyes and couldn't see any.

"Thank you." He had exhausted his tears some time ago, but the subject still rubbed his heart with a nettle-like sting. "It was bad, of course. But my brother and I didn't get much chance to grieve. When he passed away, it was like a river that'd been dammed up, and suddenly the dam just burst. Everything terrible that *hadn't* happened to the Graffs for centuries all started happening at once. Crops failed, buildings burned, machines broke. Ms. Khouri, I watched radar of a dark red storm come out of nowhere on a clear dry spring day and level a whole planting in ten minutes, then disappear without a trace."

She was listening, a pen in her mouth, with no sign of impatience, but Caleb felt the weight of the hour. "Anyway, how does this get to you? Sometime in the middle of all the disasters, I got a chance to look through some of the old family objects that my dad had kept locked away in a trunk. I'd always thought we might have some neat stuff, but I never had the time to look through them all, and my dad never volunteered them. There were lots of cool antiques in there: lanterns, jewelry, some old letters . . . but there was also this map. And I don't know why, but when I looked at it, I got the feeling it was important for some reason, even though it's three centuries old, *and* it's in German, *and* I can't read it, *and* I have no idea what it's even a map of."

"Latin, Mr. Graff."

"I beg your pardon?"

"It's not in German, it's in Latin," Dina told him as she shifted her eyes from him to the contours of the map. "And it's a lot older than three hundred years."

"I—wait, what?"

Dina looked back up, though she wasn't meeting his gaze any-more. She seemed to be staring off into either a corner of her room or another world altogether. "Please continue. You have quite the enigma on your hands, and any detail you can give me could help."

"It *moves,* Ms. Khouri. Not like this"—he grabbed the map and started flapping it in the air—"I mean, the pictures or lines on it move." And he explained to her the phenomenon of the migrating river and its flower. As he set it down again, he glanced at the old document. There was a cluster of buildings that resembled a depiction of a city, through which that infuriating river flowed. He could see angles in the north that looked like a sketch of mountains, but other topographical details that resembled nothing he had ever seen in an atlas. At the margins lurked entities that looked like beasts and men, though he could not place the species of the beasts, and the sallow men glared forebodingly at him as if in warning. Between the flower and the city was an umbrous smudge that stood out amid the richly textured decorations of the page, all the more because it appeared curiously deliberate, as if the artist had been covering something dark below the mark. Beside the flower were a series of lines and marks that, despite the differences in notation, were immediately recognizable as musical notes. Caleb had even tried playing them on the piano in the house once, though they made for discordant and unevenly rhythmic music.

Dina took the map back from him and studied it while he spoke, though Caleb didn't get the impression that she was ignoring him. When he concluded she said, "You mentioned that the chest contained other objects. Was there anything . . . associated with this map in there? Anything that you felt at the time might have some kind of connection? In our correspondence, I asked you to bring any object you thought might be relevant."

Caleb hesitated. When he left earlier in the afternoon, he had considered bringing the map alone. But in the end one item had seemed too distinctive to ignore.

"Yeah, this," he told her and pulled it out of his pocket. It was a little rock of a basaltic gray, smooth and polished, at first glance little different from what you might find in the waters of a shallow stream.

Indeed, its very ordinariness was what had first struck his eye about it: why would his ancestors have kept such an unassuming piece of geology side by side with intricately wrought iron, opulent ornaments, and yellowing ghost maps? On further inspection, he had realized that it wasn't entirely smooth; dozens of tiny characters were carved faintly all around it. They might have been letters in an alphabet, but if so, it wasn't like any lettering system his learning could identify.

When Caleb pulled it out, Dina's eyes moved from the map immediately, and she all but grabbed it out of his hand. She never averted her attention from it, though her left hand riffled through her papers until she found an old-fashioned magnifying glass. Caleb was more interested in watching her than in the rock itself, and notwithstanding all the mysteries he wanted solved, he paused to admire the luster of her wide, wise chalcedony eye as the glass doubled its size.

"Holy shit!" she exclaimed, before glancing up at him and sheepishly adding, "Sorry. It's just . . ."

Caleb gave her an awkward interval to finish her statement, but she kept sitting with her mouth hanging open, turning the object around and around in her hand.

"It's just . . . ?" he prompted her at last.

"Where did you get this? Was it with the map?"

"Yeah, they were wrapped up together, as I recall, though I didn't think much of it at the time."

Dina put down the magnifying glass and stood up abruptly, so abruptly that she got her arm caught in the cord of a desk lamp, which plowed through the clutter of papers on her desk. She disregarded the added chaos as she grabbed for her tablet, which was still playing Lebanese music at a low volume.

"This is wild," she said as she began tapping and swiping the tablet screen with her right hand; she kept the rock in her left.

"What?" Caleb asked. "What is it?"

"Okay, Mr. Graff. The good news is, I think I know what we're going to have to do. The bad news—well, I don't know if it's really *bad* news per se, but . . . You've got to understand how weird this all is."

Caleb couldn't help allowing a little smile to escape. "Yeah, I think I'm pretty good on that score."

Dina stared at him intensely, and Caleb, who was never one much for remembering people's eyes, thought that her irises were like another alphabet he couldn't read, like symbols too deep for him to interpret. He knew in that moment that, for all her affected flippancy, she had seen things with those eyes that his rustic brain couldn't even imagine.

She held up the stone as she talked. "Do you know what this is? If I'm right, this is the Sixtystone. And that map? That tells us where it came from."

"Which means . . . ?"

She smiled back at him, and it was an exuberant smile, but also a dangerous one, the kind his old school friends would flash right before they got him into trouble.

"Which means I know why you're having so many problems, and I know how we can solve them. But before we do, I'm going to have to ask you to sign these forms."

That was not the answer Caleb had expected, and he momentarily sat blinking while Dina proffered him her tablet. Squinting, he looked down at the screen and found himself scrolling through several pages of text, filled with the kind of legal jargon he was accustomed to seeing when he bought a new piece of farming equipment or updated his banking policy. One clause that did jump out at him read, "Applicant waives all right to pursue legal action or litigation for psychological or physical harm, including, but not limited to, accidental death or dismemberment."

"Pardon me, Ms. Khouri," he said, "but I feel like I need to know a little more about what exactly is happening before I sign this document."

Dina exhaled through her lower lip, blowing some stray hairs away from her face, then gave a tight-lipped grin before saying, "Sure, I get it. I can't ask you to trust me because we've barely met, and honestly, you'd have to be some kind of idiot to trust anyone who put you into this kind of situation. But I think you have a notion that there's a whole lot more going on here than I can chat with you about in my pathetic excuse for an office. You opened up a family chest and found some stuff that doesn't fit the way the world is supposed to be. And I'm telling you now that that map—that's the tip of the iceberg, skipper. What you're looking for, you'll never find it except by plunging in. So I'm not asking you to trust; I'm asking you to roll the dice. You can try another way to figure out what's going on with that map and that rock, and maybe they'll work for you. But if I may say, I don't think you're going to get a better offer than this one."

This was not living the Caleb Graff life. His life was balancing budgets and tracking crop yields and troubleshooting baler failures. On an adventurous day it might mean taking his niece and nephew to Dutch Wonderland or going bowling with his Sunday school class, maybe hunting deer for a weekend with Josh. He tried to convince himself that the recent misfortunes were coincidence, that the map's rolling ink was a trick of his fancy. Not for the first time—or the last—he asked himself, *How did I get here?* His heart pumped jaggedly in his chest, and he felt a jolt of nausea grip his gut.

And he set his finger to the screen and signed the contract.

Dina took back the tablet. "There's more than a little irony in this because three hundred years ago, your ancestor probably got you into this mess by signing a very different kind of deal."

"What are you talking about?" Caleb asked in exasperation.

"I promise, this part's nearly over. Honestly, this next part is my least favorite, but I really do run a legit business, so I'm going to have to ask you for fifty percent up front. I take checks, and I do accept Venmo or PayPal, if that's your preferred magic, or . . ."

Caleb was ready for this one and handed her a large wad of fifty-dollar bills.

". . . or you can pay me in cash."

"I *am* from Lancaster County, so it's a bit of a habit."

"Fair enough," Dina acknowledged. "We're going to need these"—she picked up the stone and the map and carefully set them in a small backpack, which she slung over her shoulder before squeezing back around her desk and brushing past Caleb. "Now come along with me. I hope you didn't make plans for this evening."

Caleb stood up and walked close behind her through the hall and into the kitchen. The elder Khouris were sitting down at the table now, but Mrs. Khouri looked up and said, "It was so nice to meet you."

Dina kissed each of her parents on the head. "I love you, *māma*, *bāba*. Don't wait up for me."

Mr. Khouri stared dourly at the plate in front of him and said something in Arabic, while Mrs. Khouri sighed once more and said, "I love you too. Please be careful."

Dina hurried out so quickly that Caleb had to thrust his hand out reflexively to prevent the apartment door from slamming shut in his face. He hustled to keep up with her as she walked purposefully down the street.

"So are you going to tell me what that map is, exactly?" he asked.

"I am, I promise," she assured him. "But first: what exactly *is* a map?"

Caleb stopped in his tracks with a groan. "Look, Ms. Khouri, I just want to know what I can do about my home. I'm not here for a philosophy lesson."

Dina halted her progress beside him, though he could see her legs twitching. With a sympathetic smile she said, "I'm afraid you can't have one without the other on this mission, skipper. Humor me. What do you think of when you think of a map?"

They resumed walking as he finally replied, "It's a tool, a way to find out how to get from one place to another."

"And that's a perfectly adequate way to describe maps as we think of them now. But five hundred years ago, that's not the way people thought about maps—at least, not the only way. Sure, an ancient map might tell you *what* a place was, or *how* to get there—but many of those maps were also about the *why*. They were insights into the true nature of places. Places—at least some places—have *being*, Mr. Graff.

Your family has farmed the same land for three centuries. Don't tell me you don't know that spaces can have . . . a soul? An essence?"

Everything in Caleb wanted to cry out against Dina's words. But he held his tongue and thought of the rich, downy soil in his hands, the feel of July nights when the whirl of summer stars across a vast sky mirrored the desire of dancing fireflies as they rose from the ground. Though Caleb did more with the bookkeeping and the machinery than the planting, he knew the spiritual gravity of the earth his family had tended.

"Maybe?" he conceded. "So what kind of cartographer are you?"

Dina laughed a laugh that rang out between a giggle and a song. "Well, I like to think of myself as a metacartographer. I want to get to the essence of the map. But that's probably too many syllables for a good American marketing logo."

"And how did you come to be a . . . metacartographer?"

"*That,* skipper, is a long story, one that involves an ex-boyfriend, a few old back alleys in Sidon, and, of course, alt-rock music . . . *whoa!*"

In the middle of her sentence Dina went tumbling as she collided with a woman who looked to be in her early sixties. The woman had been walking a bike down the street as they turned a corner, and the impact sent both her and Dina sprawling to the pavement. Caleb saw the woman flailing, grabbing at Dina's backpack as she went down in a desperate attempt to check her fall, and his surprise wore off quickly enough for him to extend a hand to try to help her. She grasped and clutched until finally able to catch his hand, which allowed him then to pull her gently to her feet. Dina, meanwhile, was also rising; she had skinned her left knee a little where the jeans were torn but otherwise looked well.

"I'm so sorry, Mrs. Lopez," Dina said.

"*Está bien. No te preocupes,*" she replied as she dusted off her red skirt. "My fault, Dina. You know I am so clumsy."

"I hope I didn't damage your bicycle."

Mrs. Lopez looked at the rusty orange frame and shook her

head. There was a little scar on her forehead, framed by her loose black and gray curls. "No, *pequeña,* it is not broken."

Dina nodded, giving her shoulders a squeeze. "Good. I'll check in with you tomorrow and bring some of *māma's mafroukeh."*

"*Gracias,* Dina. You go on and don't mind me."

Dina didn't hesitate, and she was back in motion soon, Caleb once again struggling to keep pace. He couldn't help looking back as Mrs. Lopez disappeared from sight around the street corner.

"Will she be all right?" he asked.

"Who, Mrs. Lopez? Oh, she'll be fine. She's not wrong when she talks about being clumsy. Do you know how she got that scar? She tripped over her dog trying to get a jar of *salsa verde.*"

Caleb, remembering what became of his grandmother's arthritis, said, "Falls can be bad for people her age."

"I understand, but you have to know, Mrs. Lopez isn't in any danger. She may be clumsy, but don't let that fool you; she's also sturdy as a truck."

Caleb caught up with her. "So . . . maps?"

"Right. Okay, your ancestor was a Graeff, of course. And your family line, they emigrated from Switzerland. I'm going to guess from somewhere near Basel?"

"Um, yeah . . . Yeah, I think that's right. How did you—?"

"Well, it explains a whole lot. In the sixteenth century the University of Basel was home to some pretty interesting folks: Renaissance men, scholars, and a whole bunch of dudes that we might call alchemists. Over time the city became more of a business center and lost its mystical street cred. The scholars scattered for the most part, but some—especially the ones who were already working under the radar—just went underground. And that included the Graeff family. You ever traced your lineage back to the Old World?"

They stopped at a crosswalk, which gave Caleb a chance to catch his breath. He had always envied his brother's physique, though he knew Joshua needed him to concentrate on the more sedentary business side of the farm. Even so, he tried to stay active about the land, whether in puzzling over harvester repair or planning out crop rotation. But he felt singularly out of shape matched with the lithe Dina Khouri, who moved with all the kinetic energy of a barn swallow.

"Not really," he admitted. "We don't seem to be related to Hans Conrad Groff like most of the other folk in the area. I've looked back as far as Albert Graeff, but I always had a hard time finding anything about the line before him."

"Don't feel bad about it," Dina replied as they began to cross the street. "That's the way he wanted it. There was an Albert Graeff at the University of Basel in its heyday, and he was in the thick of all their research. Some of the professors and their students started discovering other places, spaces that are as real as Passyunk Avenue over there but that you wouldn't find on any traditional map. Just as European navigators were exploring what they called the New World, these scholars were exploring new worlds of a completely different kind. Most were content to visit, but Graeff—he wanted something more. He wanted to take the alchemy of Paracelsus and mix it with cartography of Sebastian Münster. He wanted to map out the otherspace—what we like to call the Underroom."

"Why?"

Dina turned another corner, checked her phone for a moment, and then launched down a side street. Then she began speaking again, chattering with the wild abandon of a house wren. "There are two kinds of people in the world—the kind who learn something because they want to *love* it, and the kind who learn something because they want to *use* it. I don't know your family line, but it looks to me like Dr. Graeff drew up that map so that he could get hold of the Sixtystone, so *that* would put him in category two."

"You mentioned that before," Caleb said. "What exactly *is* the Sixtystone?"

"The Underroom has its own physics, its own laws, and the objects there operate according to those laws even when brought to our world. Some of those objects contain types of power that we don't even have words for here. And one of those objects was the Sixtystone. Alchemists at Basel and everywhere else in Europe and the Middle East knew about it and tried anything they could to find it. But it looks like your family beat them to it."

"You're saying my many-times-great-grandfather was connected to these alchemists and somehow found and acquired the stone. And it's been sitting in my family's farmhouse for the last three hundred years without us knowing it?"

"Sounds about right. That little rock you brought with you today? Men have been hunting it for centuries, maybe even millennia. People have died—and killed—trying to find it. No pressure there, Mr. Graff."

Caleb halted, standing still on a concrete sidewalk slab, little strands of weed growing out of the seams at his feet. He looked up at the rows of red brick buildings, listened to the woven chords of conversation in several languages and passing vehicles playing music with bone-stirring bass undertones, and he abruptly felt paralyzed by the alienness of it all. He didn't know what was most jarring: the ordinary yet unfamiliar rattle and hum of the city, the outrageous arcane history to which he was hereditarily bound, or the careless audacity of his fairy-like guide. When peers of his generation complained of the difficulty they had in "adulting," he had always humored them with quiet incredulity. Graffs bore responsibility with the practical, hard-nosed stoicism of their tribe, and it had never occurred to him to perceive life in any other frame. But now he found himself flung into a bewildering gulf, challenges and choices thrust upon him that scant hours ago would have found no purchase in his worldview.

"Why me?" he asked in a whisper, and he was almost surprised that Dina could hear him past the clack and clamor of the urban landscape. "You're bringing me with you. Why?" He didn't want to load his family's curse upon her, yet she seemed casually at ease as she narrated the rules of this bizarre world toward which he was now moving. He had employed her services precisely for that ease—what part could he play in this drama?

Dina stopped beside him, and if a spark of annoyance flashed in her features, it was almost immediately supplanted by a softening of sympathy. She put a hand on his shoulder, and the touch of consolation catalyzed him.

"I wasn't always like this, you know. Most people grow old like Mrs. Lopez, like my parents even—living the life in front of them as though that's the whole measure of reality. America, the West, they make it easy to follow our eyes and our atoms. It took some pretty weird experiences to shake me out of it, and I'm guessing that's the way it is with you too.

"To answer your question: blood means something in the Underroom, and so do guilt and shame. They're not just social constructs or subjective interpretations. Your ancestor took the Sixtystone from its world to make himself prosper in our world, and that created an imbalance. Your family got ten, maybe a dozen, good generations from the bargain, but, suck as it may, the ledger has turned red for you and your brother. I can use your family's map to get us back to the stone's place of origin, but I'm not a Graff; someone from your bloodline will have to return it."

"And what then?"

Dina shrugged. "This is uncharted territory even for me. But my guess is that you'll go back to being normal. You won't live on an eerily prosperous farm anymore, but it also won't be curiously catastrophic. You'll sow seeds and harvest crops like anyone else in the county, with some good fortune and some bad fortune. Will that please you?"

Caleb nodded. "God, yes. Some good land and a little hard work. That's all I ever wanted, Ms. Khouri."

"A good old simple farm boy, Mr. Graff. I will do my best to accommodate you. Deal?"

Somehow he was slightly dismayed by her characterization of him in this way, though she had not misspoken. So all he said in reply was, "Deal," and then they were off once again.

She brought him through byways and alleys, while occasionally she waved at passersby. Caleb didn't know how long they had been walking before finally she stopped at an unassuming structure made of white concrete blocks, its surface sporadically spray-painted with graffiti both beautiful and profane. She went around to the side, beneath a fire escape, to a nondescript metal door with no handle, which she knocked on four times.

"This is . . . ?" Caleb began, but Dina shushed him.

"Not all significant spaces are farmland and firelight, skipper," she rejoined. "Cities have their magic too."

Caleb remained dubious as the seconds ticked by, but after a time the door nudged open, and a middle-aged Italian man peeked out. He had thick grayish-black hair and large round glasses that perched over an expansive mustache, and the brown eyes behind those glasses widened in pleasure when he saw who stood opposite him at the door.

"Little Dina!" he exclaimed.

"Mr. Vitale," she replied. "Have you got anything for me?"

"Come in, child. I see you have a guest with you?"

"We're on a little mission, and I'll need you for that too. But first . . ."

Mr. Vitale nodded and opened the door wider, allowing them both to enter. On the other side of the swelter of summer and the dingy, flaking cinderblocks, Caleb found himself among shelves and shelves of books. The door closed behind him, and though he could hear the hum of air conditioning, the lighting appeared to be all candles and lanterns, which his pragmatic side considered a terrible safety and insurance risk. Yet there was also a bracing aroma of clean dust and ancient paper, rather like the smell of his family's old chest, but fuller and more majestic. Caleb read books, some digital and some print, and he had a well-worn Bible at his bedstand, but he had never understood the love of antique tomes that folk like his second college roommate would report—until now. In the air he could smell, could even feel, the giddy weightiness of pages that were only one step removed from having been trees and even now centuries hence carried the sap of a very different life in them.

Mr. Vitale shuffled over to a cherry wood table, where a very old cash register sat beside a very new card reader. He reached behind the desk and pulled out three texts, pushing them across the surface toward Dina, who set down her backpack and scooped them up with élan. "There you go," he said. "An eighteenth-century edition of the Latin *Nuremberg Chronicle,* an early edition of Amstutz's *De Vera Natura Locorum,* and a July 1940 issue of *Flash Comics* Number Seven."

"And the *al-Mā' al-Waraqī?*"

"Give me some time to find the edition you want, little Dina."

She nodded and pulled out a debit card while Mr. Vitale gently placed the works, each with a little golden bookmark, into her backpack. Caleb couldn't see how much she paid, though he imagined that such a collection could hardly be cheap. On the other hand, neither were her services, so he supposed she could afford such purchases. But he was distracted by the store—if that was what this place even was. Here and there he could see relatively recent texts with computer-printed pages and book jackets that retained some glossiness, but most were earthier browns with lettering composed of hand-mixed ink. Few were in English, fewer still in English after the long ſ character had been dropped from usage. He saw scrolls and parchments and forms of text and documents he had no name for.

"What is this place?" he wondered aloud.

"Just Vitale's is all," the man replied. "My own little book shop, a bit wilder than the Amazon."

"And it just sits here in this old building, no sign, no advertising?"

Mr. Vitale and Dina exchanged knowing grins.

"Vitale's is a floating bookstore, Mr. Graff," Dina told him.

"I take my books where they need to be when they need to be there," Mr. Vitale added. "Usually that's here in South Philly, but it could be Uptown, or King of Prussia, or . . . even farther." Seeing Caleb's baffled stare, Mr. Vitale assured him, "It's not as hard as it sounds, if you know the right words to say."

"Speaking of traveling," Dina said, "I also need an aperture—to the Underroom."

"It's been a while since you've traveled by my shop. What, you think Vitale's not good enough for you?"

Dina gave him a good-natured smirk. "Quite the contrary. Your shop's like a good wine: I save it for special occasions. This is going to be a tricky one." Then she told him—what? At first Caleb thought they were numbers, coordinates. Then he thought perhaps she was speaking place names, locations with which he was unfamiliar. But perhaps she was speaking in another language—or were they words at all? Sounds were coming from her lips, which he watched almost hypnotically, and Mr. Vitale seemed to be cocking his head in recognition. But it was like no set of directions Caleb had ever heard.

"Of course, little Dina," Mr. Vitale said when she had finished. "Follow me."

Dina picked up the backpack, now heavy with her new purchases, and began to follow as Mr. Vitale led them deeper into the store. Caleb once again found himself ambling to keep pace, for the rows of shelves seemed to have no end. They strode through aisles and perpendicular turns, up a staircase until they reached what appeared to be a small, carpeted bathroom.

"What, is this some secret portal?" Caleb inquired, unable to restrain a note of sarcasm.

"Nope, it's a restroom," Dina informed him. "I'm going to use it, and I'd suggest you do the same. The facilities in the Underroom are . . . less accommodating."

And without hesitating, she went in and closed the door, leaving Mr. Vitale patiently waiting beside a gawking Caleb.

"This your first time traveling between realms?" the older man asked, stroking his mustache.

Startled, Caleb turned to face him. "Um, yeah. I think I've had a lot of firsts today."

Mr. Vitale chuckled. "Well, prepare yourself, little man. This probably won't be your last first today."

Caleb was about to ask him what that even meant, but a flush from the toilet interrupted him, and shortly after, Dina emerged.

Awkwardly, almost diffidently, Caleb slipped past her and availed himself of the facilities. Dina was waiting, and Mr. Vitale took them into another side room, where they had to duck under a low door-frame. They rounded another corner, and then . . .

The disorientation was immediate and overwhelming. Caleb felt a gush of gravity in his gut, and for a naked instant he had no breath inside him. All around him the scope of his view was skinned off, as though the little book shop were peeling away like the dark green outside of a cucumber. *This must be death,* he thought, and he cursed himself for trusting the strange young woman with the nose stud and bedroom office.

And then he realized he was on his knees in an actual, physical place, though it was not the place in which he had just been standing. He was no longer in a building at all but outside in an open field, a field so flat and far that at first he wondered if he might be back on the farm. But this was not his home, and as Caleb looked around he saw that he was nowhere he could have even described. His knees were sunk not on plain dirt or grass or grain but on a strange, lichen-ous material of pulsing orange and blue. He touched it tentatively: it was porous and felt damp, though no moisture clung to his hand when he lifted it. The strange bedding spread around him for hundreds of feet, though he could at times see flitting shapes run across it, shadows that looked little like the mammals that roam Pennsylvania pastures. Flying forms zigged and zagged high in the deep blue luster of the eastern sky, but he could not say with any certainty that they were birds.

Caleb gagged, forcing himself to swallow an uncomfortable welling of bile, if only to avoid the shame of being seen as sickly and pathetic. He saw that Dina was crouched beside him, her face momentarily free from its customary insouciance. She reached out her hand to him, and he took it; she was much smaller than he was, but there was appreciable power in her grasp as she helped him to his feet. A rush of dizziness set him reeling, but her hand steadied him.

"Is this . . . ?"

"The Underroom," Dina confirmed.

"Sorry about all the . . . well, you know. Pretty pathetic, I suppose."

Dina's lips smiled gently. "You did better than most. You should've seen my first trip here."

"How did that happen?" he asked.

She lost her smile, and it was as though a dark fog passed over her bright brown eyes. Caleb thought he saw the hand he had just held tremble. "That's not one of my favorite stories to tell . . . even though it led to good things."

Looking past her, Caleb saw something far off on the horizon. The sun had begun sinking in the west, a disc burning distantly in the clear evening sky. Beneath it, as though forged from the drippings of that bronze sphere, he could see the silhouette of a city, a city whose borders began suddenly on the far plain, with walls and towers girdled round and a river bisecting it. This was no sprawling Philadelphia, sitting like a spider in a web of suburbs, nor even Lancaster city, with its orbit of touristed agricultural towns. Its structures had nothing of America's desperate, famished glass and brick architecture, and only a dappling of tiny cottages spread across the land leading up to it, though there *were* roads of a sort across the fields, which it swallowed like a maw whose teeth were turrets.

"What's that?" Caleb asked.

"That the city," Dina replied. "You *don't* want to go there. We're headed *this* way," and she pointed to the deep blue east.

She began to walk toward that way, following an angle that would eventually bring them beside the river. The spongy ground beneath Caleb's shoes gave his steps a bounce, and he found a new energy that helped him keep step with his fey guide. For this he was thankful, as it occurred to him now how overdressed he was. He had journeyed to Philadelphia expecting to conduct a business transaction, forsaking his jeans, flannel, and boots for a white shirt, blue tie, and dress shoes. The shoes still felt tight on him, but the eldritch earth seemed to lighten the load of his body.

For some time they walked together in silence, though the questions crowded around him, clamoring to be voiced. But Caleb had seen the flash of fear in Dina's eyes when she glanced west at the city and heard the quaver that caught in her voice when she spoke of her past travels. So he allowed the stillness its purchase, though it was an outlandish sort of stillness—a kind of quiet for which his own home had no word. It was tense, like the atmosphere of dark-morning deer hunting in cold autumn, but this was no glade or grove; yet every atom of the land seemed callously and casually aware of him. He felt haunted by the presence of the place.

As they approached the river Dina stopped and unslung her backpack, kneeling down and unzipping it. "All right, so let's look at this map your family had," she said. "I recognized the river right away, but now we've got to . . . Wait. Wait a minute. What the—?"

Caleb saw something akin to panic scurry across her features as she riffled through the contents of her bag, pulling out the items from Vitale's, along with the Sixtystone. She reached her hand through the canvas, then turned it upside down, causing loose change, scrap paper, bookmarks, hair elastics, bent jewelry, and other sundry bric-a-brac to tumble onto the turf.

"Damn it," Dina muttered, clasping her forehead in her hands. "No way, no way. I swear, this can't be happening."

"That doesn't sound good," Caleb said. "Where's my . . . did you lose my map?"

"Your map, your map, yeah, I just . . . I put it in here, you *saw* me put it in here. Shit!" she shouted and slammed the ground with her fist, which sprang back unexpectedly as it bounced off the particolored moss.

"How do we get back home?" Caleb asked. "You know how we got here, so we can backtrack . . ."

Dina shook her head and sighed. "No, that's not how it works. It'll be a while before we'll get another aperture. We're stuck in the Underroom for now, so we might as well move forward."

"But we don't have the map!"

Dina nodded. "We'll make it work. Mr. Graff, I swear to you, I really am a professional at this. I can't imagine what you must be thinking about me right now, but I've done this sort of thing—well, something *like* this sort of thing—many times before. I *will* land the plane. But I have to ask you a quick question."

"What is it, Ms. Khouri?"

Dina inhaled, then asked, "Do you have anything to write with?"

Caleb didn't even bother deploying any of the sardonic rejoinders that came to mind. He rolled his eyes and started searching his pockets until at last he found something. "I've got this," he told her, holding out a small bright pink gel pen. He had been practicing writing the alphabet with his niece, and Karis had insisted he illuminate her manuscript in the brightest possible colors.

Dina snatched it out of his hand and picked up one of the pieces of scrap paper. "It'll do," she said, and with that she sat cross-legged and began drawing a map. At first it looked like a random assortment of lines and shapes, little different from Karis's pre-school foray into calligraphy. But somehow, as the minutes passed, a remarkable transformation occurred: Dina brought together the haphazard threads and wove them into a meaningful geography. The features he remembered from his family's map began to emerge from the chaos—stark and rudimentary and, of course, garishly pink. It was not the painstakingly detailed sheet of vellum that had waited across the centuries in the Graff family chest. But the landmarks, the old symbols, were vividly recognizable to him.

"How did you do that?" he asked.

"Lots and lots of practice . . . and a halfway decent memory. Not too bad, all things considered. It should get us where we need to go."

As Dina stood back up and pored over what she had wrought, Caleb asked, "Why even draw it, if you can remember it all anyway?"

"It's like I've been telling you, skipper. A map isn't just about *how*. I have a feeling I'm going to need this soon enough."

Then she was striding again—*Did she ever stop?* Caleb wondered—and they were following the track of the river. It flowed away from them, toward the battlements of the great vertical city, and it flowed slowly but not gently. Its current moved with the wary deliberation of a mercenary. The waters were opaque, not with the toxic pollution of human chemicals—this river had nothing of humans in it—but with an older and deadlier venom. This was no country creek or even commercial canal; it was an alien artery cut into the perplexing landscape. If it was inhuman, however, it was nonetheless alive, alive with hidden life that glared rapaciously at them as it passed by.

"Is everything in the Underroom dangerous?" Caleb blurted out.

"Everything everywhere is dangerous in its way," Dina replied. "But we're more aware of it here. Are you scared? Please don't try to give me some masculine bravado crap for an answer. If you're not, fine, but I'd rather know the truth."

Caleb almost lied, because he hated how she saw his haplessness. He felt like a flailing fish, prone in painful air, about to be skinned and gutted. If only he could be chatting with her next to a harrow in a soybean field; that was a dangerous object he could stand beside in confidence.

"Yes," he said at last. "Yeah, I guess I am."

"Good," she smiled. "You're honest. And I'd be far more worried if you were fearless. I love the Underroom, but I'm never not nervous here." She stopped and nudged him. "You want to see something cool? Look."

She pointed to the heavens. The sun had set, twilight had trickled into the western verge, and night was draped across the sky. Stars were emerging, brighter and fuller than even Caleb, who lived miles from any downtown, was accustomed to. But as he followed the track of her finger, he nearly gasped in shock.

"That's . . ."

"The Little Dipper," Dina confirmed. "And the Big Dipper. Cassiopeia, Leo, the Summer Triangle."

"How are they here, in this world?" he asked.

"We're not as far from Pennsylvania as you might think," she said. "It takes some time to train your brain to accept it."

"Where did you get that kind of training? Do they still teach that in Basel?"

Dina laughed. "I've never actually been to Basel. In fact, I've only traveled to Europe once. I *did* major in geography at Penn State."

"I'm guessing they didn't talk much about the Underroom there."

"I learned some great stuff, and I do still use it. But no, my education in metacartography had to come from some more unorthodox channels."

"I went to Penn State—well, Penn State Berks. Majored in business so I could learn to run the farm better. But some days I wish I knew some 'unorthodox channels' to help me figure out how to keep a family farm alive in the twenty-first century."

Again Dina laughed, and Caleb saw that it was genuine, though with a mournful undercurrent. "We can start by getting rid of the Sixtystone. But I hear you. I guess I'm what you'd call an old soul. I'll take sixteenth-century manuscripts—and family farms—over any fancy new products . . . which I say as I pull out my cell phone."

She turned the flashlight feature on and pointed at the pink sketch she had made. It seemed to glow spectrally in the phone's glare, to take on an unreal look. For some time she puzzled over the paper intently, even as she kept walking, and then she looked up and ahead.

"That's what I was afraid of."

"What?"

"That."

She gestured ahead of them, and at first Caleb couldn't tell what she meant. In the deepening night he didn't expect to see very much, and initially he saw nothing at all. But as he peered more intently he beheld something baffling and unfamiliar in that darkness. Somehow, about a thousand feet ahead of them, the space grew thicker, fuller, *more.* There were no words for the sight; it was as though a great hand had plucked an environment from one location and set it down in front of them. There were, simply put, two places in one. There was the fierce and laminar river that they followed, beside the banks and the filamented plain beyond. But superimposed over it was another terrain, an ecosystem of shadow and rock, like billows of crystallizing smoke. Neither region held pre-eminence; they coexisted in a paradox so impossible it hurt his eyes to look at it. And that was exactly where Dina was walking.

"What am I seeing?" Caleb queried.

"It's a palimpsest," she replied. "I've only seen this a couple of times. Like, this is some next-level magic here."

"Magic? So this isn't a . . . normal part of the Underroom?"

Dina shook her head. Caleb kept following her, but he could see the light from her phone shuddering uneasily. "You'll see some weird junk in the Underroom, skipper, but this isn't natural, even here. If you've got somebody who really knows their crap, a serious adept or magus, maybe he could pull this off. And I'm guessing that's what Albert Graeff did."

She glanced once more at her own little chart. "Most cartographers like me, our skill is in *mapping* spaces like the Underroom. But if you've got someone who has the knack for geography *and* for alchemy, you can make maps that actually *change* the land. And a few of them—like your ancestor, apparently—can create palimpsests. It's what that smudge on your old map was: he overwrote a different place on top of the Underroom's original space. It clogs everything up, and it's a devil of a time to get through. I'm guessing he did this before he got to the Sixtystone, to keep it safe until he could retrieve it. But once he acquired the stone, he just left the palimpsest here."

"Can't we just go around it?" Caleb asked, buoyed by good rustic common sense.

"I'm afraid not. The palimpsest is sort of like a guard dog. It knows when someone's approaching. Don't try to understand it—I don't really get it myself. The only way to navigate a palimpsest is if you have a map of it."

Caleb wilted like a flower in hot July. "But we lost my map."

Dina held up her little scrap of paper. "Which is why we made this."

"So your handwritten sketch will get us through this thing?"

She inhaled deeply, a wry grimace on her face, her brown eyes glinting in the phone light. "I don't see why it shouldn't. Assuming my memory holds . . ." Seeing Caleb's anxious cast, she quickly added, ". . . which it will. But listen—you *need* to follow me closely, and you need to keep up. It's going to get weird, and it might hurt, and if we get lost or spend a lot of time there—well, let's just say *that's* why you signed the waiver."

Caleb stopped, closing his eyes and bringing his hands to his knees. He was not an exciting person, but he had always regarded himself as an inheritor of the inherent fortitude that came with being a man of the land. Despite his spreadsheets and business calls, he also had the oil stains on his jeans and the callouses on his palms, the fresh scrapes and old scars, to witness to his rural bona fides. But he had confessed his fear to Dina, and it rushed upon him like the swollen waters of a summer flood. He set aside his disdain for all things meditative and tried to measure his breathing in the dizzying, unearthly earth upon which he stood. A certain stillness did lap over him, though only intermittently, like a tide rushing and receding. The fear remained beneath it. But he could open his eyes and stand upright again.

Dina looked up at him, hesitating, choosing her words with care. "I don't know if you're ready to trust me, or if we're still in gambling mode. We don't have to do this—but I can only say that your misfortunes will not leave your family until the stone is returned. In this place, that's as much a law of physics as gravity."

Caleb looked right at her, and he was ashamed of the dread he knew she must see in his bland water-blue eyes. But he didn't flinch from the contact. "I'm not even sure if I should, Ms. Khouri. But I'm going to choose to trust you. So *please* don't let me and my family down."

Once again she smiled, not in derision or doubt—rather, the disarming, boisterous grin of a sprite in meadow grass. "Then let's do this. We're almost there."

She wasted no time, striding, almost jogging, toward the great enigma, and Caleb kept pace, though he feared his side would cramp before he even got into the darkness. He kept his eyes down on her sloppy ponytail and the pastel red scrunchy that held it in place. The bright starlight sheened off that hair in the night, a little aureole that kept her visible, even as they crossed the threshold into the palimpsest.

It was not as he had expected, in part because at first they just kept walking. The starlight dimmed somewhat, and he could no longer hear the sound of the running river, but otherwise little seemed to change. But as Dina pressed on, her eyes scanning her makeshift map by the light of her phone, Caleb began to feel the thickness. Each breath seemed to fill his lungs too full, and he coughed coarsely. He tried to keep his eyes on Dina, but in the periphery he started to catch glimpses of the world around him. Even those glimpses hurt—physically hurt—his eyes. A stab of fog like a fractured gem whirled and churned around them, each moment inventing a new geometry to keep its place in the unwilling topography. At times it seemed inert as a picked-clean carcass, only to dance again with a sort of deathly life. Now he felt as though he were traveling through water, or oil, or ice.

"Come on," he thought her heard Dina say, but her voice sounded distant, like the last echoes a drowning man might feel from his would-be rescuer. He was losing sight of her hair in the occlusion of the palimpsest, just a crescent of pale reflection and the fading coral swirl of the embedded elastic. He tried to call out to her, but the palimpsest filled his mouth and stole his voice. Frantically he found himself trying to run in the dense double haecceity of the place, but doing so only forced her further from his sight. All that he encountered now was a burning contradiction that entered his eyes but radiated through his skin. He looked up, hoping to see a shard of the old constellations, but all he saw were atoms of brown dirt and dry grass, as though the whole terrain had flipped and his feet were planted in open sky.

So Caleb Graff screamed wordlessly and staggered on through the slough, the great trap that his own flesh and blood had laid centuries ago. He did not know how long it had been since he breathed, and there was no simple air for him to take in. He dropped to one knee, eyes closed against the ghastly incongruity of the palimpsest, and in that violent vale he prepared to die.

A pressure caught his left hand, so light it felt more like a tickle than a grasp, but it was human all the same. He forced one eye open, and through the mangled panorama he saw the slender hand and black-polished fingernails of Dina Khouri. His own meaty palm engulfed her hand, and he feared he might crush it even as he grabbed it. There was no preternatural strength in the grip she offered, but it provided some force and direction, and his strained muscles followed her lead. For this was something Caleb Graff could do. Of magic countries and cursed objects he was ignorant, but he could throw his body and his muscles into a difficult task; indeed, there was little else he asked of life. He was just a mundane person, like Mrs. Lopez with her bicycle and her little scar. Thinking of plows and hay bales and crates, he plunged breathlessly onward.

And then he was rolling in broad beds of soft, vivid lichen, wisps of air cavorting in his lungs, and strands of Dina's hair caught in his mouth. She had pulled him free, and they had collapsed together into an ungainly heap beyond the perimeter of the palimpsest. Caleb could see it still roiling, tossing out physical impossibilities with dizzying aplomb—but now, most significantly, its chaos lay behind them.

Dina released Caleb's hand and scurried to her feet while he lay, sputtering, shaking, terrified, embarrassed, and most of all grateful. He took a minute to remain on his back and look up into a sky free from the light pollution of Lancaster and Reading, a sprawling spread so thick with stars it seemed to glow white in some spots. Then, tottering, he rose to his feet.

"Thank you," he said. "Thank you for reaching out to me."

"I brought you here. It was the least I could do."

"Do we have much further to go?"

Dina took only the briefest of glances at her map before smiling and shaking her head. "Actually, no. We're not too far off now. With a little luck this will be over soon."

She started on again, still close to the river on their left side. As he unsteadily followed her, Caleb realized just how hungry he was. He'd had a regular lunch that afternoon but had gotten to Philadelphia around dinner time—and that was when this careening cascade of events had begun. It had never occurred to him when he first rang that doorbell at the Khouris' apartment that he was only just embarking on the wildest night of his life—a night full of incident but not of food. He didn't even bother asking Dina; he'd seen her empty her bag, whose contents held nothing more edible than dental floss.

As they continued, the landscape changed somewhat. The bright lichen thinned out, replaced by refreshingly ordinary dirt and occasional patches of a stubby round grass that was just a little too darkly green for comfort. After a time they came to a rise beyond which the long level plain dipped suddenly into a valley. As they approached the edge, Caleb could see its contours laid out beneath them in the radiance of the Milky Way above, though its features were still indistinct. Past a mat of thick green on the near side he could see vertical clusters that must be forest, albeit a forest whose trees writhed out from the ground like agonized men. The river continued down the slope into the heart of the valley, and it was with a shock that Caleb realized that even here it was flowing west, rising up the sharp incline. He marveled at the peculiarity, but without comment, for it was hardly the most unaccountable sight he had encountered.

Dina began to descend, and the way was steep, though not so steep as to require any gear or climbing. There was no clear path, though she stayed close to the river, while a rising moist mist grew thicker and thicker around them. At first Caleb thought little of it: fog, at least, was as natural to northern Lancaster as to the Underroom. But the more it surrounded them, the less he could see. It was not oppressive in quite the way the palimpsest had been, though his heart did begin to pound once again.

And then he lost sight altogether. This wasn't any kind of blindness; rather, it seemed he was immersed in his other senses. On any typical day the hierarchy of his body privileged seeing and hearing, and for hours at a time he might forget the others. Somehow, here that order was flipped. He was flooded with tastes, with a sticky sweetness like barbecue and the soft bitterness of squash blossoms. Scents wafted through him, the fresh green aroma of tomato vines and the sickly odor of burnt blood. His touch was more distant, and each step felt faint and dreamlike as he took it, not knowing where it was leading, only that wherever he was, he dared not stay still. But his mind had forgotten how to see and how to hear, and try as he might, he could not get it to remember.

This time, however, Caleb refused to panic. How often in this past day had he lurched from one helplessness to the next, resigned to his role as the fool in this drama? *I will choose to continue,* he thought, whatever that might mean. He kept his respiration steady and called to mind his mother's simple advice: "When in doubt, follow your nose." It had served him well in fields of manure and hay bales, bringing him home to breakfast bacon and the indescribable but distinctive redolence of old Pennsylvania farmhouses. And resolved to this framing, the wild whorl of smells became intelligible to him, and he caught a trailing wisp that somehow he knew was the reckless, enticing fragrance of the Underroom. His feet were numb, but he willed the muscles in his legs in what he thought to be the correct direction, and in this way, with the stolid, steady gait of a tortoise, he persevered.

It was some minutes before the fog lifted, but it did so with little warning. All at once Caleb felt firm earth beneath his shoes, which crunched on stone and dirt, and the star-speckled black night looked almost dazzlingly bright as his eyesight returned. He had traveled some distance down the valley and now stood ten feet away from the upflowing river on a ledge that dropped rather precipitously fifty feet or so down. As he looked back, the whelming mist drifted across the slope he had just traversed.

In surveying the declivity, he saw Dina's form descending, but with none of her customary pixie-like alacrity. She was wending and wandering down the way, her eyes glazed and unseeing, her arms extended gropingly as though in utter darkness. She was about fifteen

feet away, and with a shock Caleb realized that she was faltering blindly toward the far edge of the ledge on which he stood, and that only a
couple of steps more would send her plummeting into the valley below. Surprising himself with his own urgent agility, Caleb raced across
the dirt and scree toward the tottering Dina Khouri, even as her
sneakers slid on the loose stone and she fell. He caught the straps of
her backpack in his hands, which arrested her motion momentarily,
though her slender arms quickly slipped free. Caleb's action had
bought her time, however, and she was able to twist her body around
and catch hold of the pack. Her chest slammed into the side of the
precipice, but she clung tenaciously to keep from plunging any further, and so she lay dangling above the gulf, while Caleb strained to
keep hold of the straps without rolling off the edge himself.

"Are you all right, Ms. Khouri?" he asked, unable even to see her
from his vantage lying flat on the rocky ground.

"Um, yeah, for the moment," she replied shakily. "Just—just give
me a minute."

Caleb didn't know if he had a minute, but he clutched the backpack. Perhaps his legs were dull from years of desk tasks, yet his
hands could connect wiring and his arms could carry feed and fire-
wood, and he allowed the years of those chores to guide his grip. His
muscles strained as he felt a tugging on the fabric of the bookbag, for
Dina was climbing, and in a moment he saw her head peek over the
ledge. She grunted and growled, vein-lines visible on her arms as she
pulled her lissome little body up to the rock shelf beside him, gasping
and tear-choked.

Even now Dina did not lie long. She grabbed her backpack, then
wiped her eyes and stood up, straightening her T-shirt and tightening
her ponytail. As Caleb rose he saw the scratches on her arms and a
vivid gray bruise on her soiled face, and though his own life was in as
much danger, he longed wordlessly for some way to take on the pain
he knew she was hiding.

She swallowed softly and said, "Thanks. I'm sorry about that.
Let's make our way down to the valley. This is the place."

Caleb didn't ask Dina about the mist they had just passed through as she consulted her torn map sketch by the light of her cracked phone. She located a switchback on the scarred ledge, and gradually they made their way further down. Despite their precarious perch, Caleb could see her regain her confidence as they walked, for she had found her way once more. And here his step was lightened too, for he felt that they were approaching their destination and now surely this mad quest was almost at an end.

At last the path emptied into a deep dale, where Caleb could see the ribbon of the river coil for what looked like miles to the valley's other side. The earth here was carpeted by flowers, some as familiar as zinnias and lilies, others utterly unlike any he might see at home. It was a vast field, livid and vivid with competing colors and shapes, with plants that could have sat inconspicuously in Lancastrian terrain side by side with gaudy blooms and baubles. Amidst them all, perhaps a hundred feet away near the riverbank, stood the map's flower.

There could be no doubt of it. Despite the variety of foliage that populated this side of the valley, only one was this immense, and Caleb could see in it the same dimensions as that strange drawing on the old yellowed paper that had rested so long in his house. It was shaped vaguely like the bulb of a lily, though that bud was larger than he was and protruded directly from a dark green base. The fiery starlight shimmied and shimmered across its surface. But what Caleb did not know was what connection this towering flower had to the Sixtystone in Dina's backpack.

And then the bud opened. It opened the way a lily back home would, eight petals curling outward to reveal what looked like a niche or alcove where one might have expected a stamen. This space was almost exactly the size of the stone. But Caleb only noted it briefly, for his eyes were drawn back to the petals. They were not of any thin, silky texture, covered instead with a network of blade-like barbs and framed by edges as sharp as razors. He barely had time to recognize these features before the flower snapped shut. It continued to open and close before his eyes at seemingly random intervals. As they drew nearer, Caleb could see better the ground around the base of the voracious lily. Here the lush fecundity of the flora grew through death, vines and blooms bursting forth from a ring of bones and skulls and, in some spots, the tackiness of fresher flesh. And when the lily petals curved out once again, Caleb could see a similar layer of ruin upon its inside.

"This is it?" Caleb sputtered. "You can't be serious."

Dina kept her eyes ahead on the flower. "Yeah, I think so. Of course, I didn't know the details. I figured we'd have a hard journey, though I'll admit this is a little rougher than I was expecting."

"Do you want to tell me why the heck I shouldn't just head home as quick as I can and take my chances back on the farm? Ms. Khouri, if all those bodies died trying to get inside that thing, how could I possibly expect to make it out alive?"

"Because you don't need to get the stone *out;* you just need to get it *in.*"

Caleb wasn't fully satisfied with this answer, but he never got the opportunity to say so. For his attention was caught by a movement from behind the giant bud. A human figure emerged, a woman clothed in fluid robes that seemed to coruscate in the light of the stars and a lantern she held in her right hand. The lantern's flame cast her face in a tessellation of shine and shadow; Caleb could see that she looked young and beautiful, black hair tumbling freely to her shoulders, a relaxed, feline smile on her full red lips. But what really caught his attention was the space above her intent eyes, where her smooth bronze forehead was interrupted by a little scalene scar.

Dina saw it, too, and she squinted as the woman approached. "Mrs. Lopez?" she asked hesitantly.

"Dina Khouri," the woman responded, and Caleb could hear in it the cadences of Mrs. Lopez's voice, though transmogrified by the vocal chords of the body before him and woven through with an ancient accent he could not place. "I did not think you would make it so far, especially without this." She held up her left hand, and now Caleb saw that she was holding his family's map.

"You—*you* took the map from me?" Dina stammered.

"Yes. You would never suspect that poor old Mrs. Lopez might know about the Underroom. You would never guess that I have been searching for the Sixtystone since the days when Albert Graeff was a baby wetting his diaper in Switzerland. So many ironies! I have lived in Philadelphia for years, and here I find that the map I could never make myself was a ninety-minute drive from my residence. And when I learned, I took the map from you—except the very thing I wanted the map for was right beside it all along. Right beside it in *that* backpack."

She laughed, and it might have been the frivolous laugh of a teenager savoring a prank, save for the fiery, feral spark animating her eyes. She never averted her gaze but knelt to set down the lantern and the map. Reaching into the fold of her spectral tunic, she pulled out a knife with a curved blade so long it was almost a sword. She extended the blade in Dina's direction.

"Hand me the Sixtystone, *pequeña*. It is all I want. It is all I have *ever* wanted."

"Why?" blurted Caleb without thinking, and then he locked his mouth shut as Mrs. Lopez turned her raptorial attention on him for the first time.

"Go home to your farm, Caleb Graff," she replied with a jovial sneer. "You do not belong in this world of hazard and power. Your ancestor took one of the most potent objects in all the worlds and used it for good luck on a few acres of land. It is time that stone finds its way into the hands of someone who knows what to do with it."

"I don't think I want to know what you intend to do with it," Dina said, edging back slightly as Mrs. Lopez sauntered forward.

"In your most feverish dreams you could never imagine the plans I have for the Sixtystone, little Dina. You walk this realm like a child playing at dress-up with her dolls, a child who truly thinks she is grown up. You pose no threat to me, you and that stupid fat farmer. And so I repeat: if you only hand me the stone, I'll let you play your silly little games here as much as you like. But if you choose to be naughty, you *will* be punished."

Dina glanced at Caleb and then looked back to Mrs. Lopez. Slowly she shrugged the backpack from her shoulders and crouched to the floral soil, where she emptied the contents. Her book purchases and miscellaneous possessions once again lay strewn across the turf of the Underroom, and among them was the little engraved rock. She took it in her hand and rose. As she did so, Mrs. Lopez continued unhurriedly in their direction, parallel to the river, caressing her weapon's blade with her thumb and forefinger, as though it were the spine of a lover.

"The old men in Basel knew so many secrets," she purred. "They had quite the little society to themselves. But there was no place in it for an alchemist from Seville, let alone for his demure little wife. Dina Khouri, you with your scholarship to a university, with your home to return to each day, with your glossy website and a professional headshot—you cannot know all that I have sacrificed to be right here, right now. I have forced the universe to keep me alive across centuries so that I could hold *that* stone."

Dina didn't answer, but Caleb could see her entire body trembling, even as his own was. She began to walk toward Mrs. Lopez with minced steps, and Caleb followed nervously beside her. Dina extended her left hand, the unassuming gray Sixtystone shadowed like a black eclipse in the night. Mrs. Lopez eyed it with an insatiate lust.

Then, with a bird-like rapidity of movement, Dina whipped out her right hand and threw something in the direction of the advancing adversary. Startled though he was, Caleb could see that she was throwing one of the small golden bookmarks that Mr. Vitale had set inside the pages of Dina's order at the shop. He didn't have time to wonder why, for it became evident soon enough: the shining sliver struck Mrs. Lopez on the arm and burst into a spray of light.

"What was—?" Caleb began, but Dina cut him off and shoved the Sixtystone unceremoniously into his hand.

"Go! Take this to the flower and put it back where it came from."

The great torrent of questions rushed in upon him, but he dammed them up. There were uncountable mysteries here in this land of twists and turns, and they stretched around him like a great wine-dark sea. But his weather-worn harvester's soul knew that this was not a moment for talk but a moment for action. He acknowledged Dina's plea by grabbing the stone and running in the direction of the lily, but taking an arcing path so as to avoid Mrs. Lopez. He could see her in the periphery of his left eye—the smoke and smolder of her sleeve where it had blazed, her saber fallen to the green ground.

Dina threw another of the little gold slips at her, but this time she was too quick. She rolled down, avoiding the fleeting flare, then jumped to her feet and charged at Dina. Caleb wondered why she wasn't pursuing *him,* even though he was the one holding the Sixtystone. But he understood almost immediately. Mrs. Lopez did not regard him as a threat. She need only dispatch Dina Khouri, and then she could turn her attention to pathetic, ineffectual Caleb Graff.

Knowing this, Caleb made his choice. He pocketed the stone and pivoted, bustling with silent expedition back toward the two grappling women. Dina now lay on the turf, and Mrs. Lopez was on top of her, knees on Dina's chest and hands encircling her throat. Mrs. Lopez's hair poured darkly down across her flushed face, which had lost its cruel nonchalance. Her rich red lips were twisted in a gouge of hatred, glistening with spittle, and her eyes were narrowed in the force of her rage.

"You little shit," she snarled.

So intent was she on the satisfaction of her violence that she did not see what Caleb could see—that the river was moving, its very banks silently shifting southward toward them all. The great telescoping of her wrath was what gave Caleb the only chance he knew he would have. The flowers under his feet hushed his treading, and setting the full gravity of his girth into the act, he slammed his body into Mrs. Lopez.

Dina was freed from the grip, rising to her feet, gasping hoarsely and clutching at the blue-black bruises on her throat, and Caleb went sprawling beside her. Mrs. Lopez fell backward but lashed out as she fell and managed to grab at Dina's arm to stabilize herself. Still coughing, Dina kicked out and struck Mrs. Lopez in the chest, causing her to stagger backward. But in the process Dina too lost her balance, tottering near the edge of the advancing riverbank. Caleb jumped up and reached out his hand, catching hold of Dina's. She still fell but was able to topple forward, keeping her feet out of the water.

This was not the case for Mrs. Lopez; she didn't plunge entirely into the current, but she could not prevent her left foot from submerging. Six centuries of stoicism kept her from crying out, but Caleb shuddered at the agonized contortion that rippled across her comely countenance. She staggered forward, pulling herself fully back to solid ground, but as she did so she left a tacky red track—for her foot was gone, and only a stump of shin culminating in shreds of blood and bone remained.

Dina squirmed away from the river and Mrs. Lopez, toward Caleb, who was backpedaling. "Thanks," she rasped. "Now go, you idiot. Get rid of that damned stone."

Caleb ran, and even the adrenaline of the moment could not conceal from him how much his body hurt. He had been moving all day; his thighs throbbed, his chest ached, and each breath was bought with discomfort. But Mrs. Lopez was moving too, limping toward him, her lovely face collapsed into a paroxysm of pain and loathing. So Caleb urged himself on, pausing only to snatch up the Graeff map that she had dropped, though he couldn't say why.

When he arrived again at the flower, he remembered once again the great barrier to his success. It was even more terrifying close up, as he heard the crackle of ancient bones beneath his black dress shoes. The petals made a noise like metal on metal as they closed, and when they opened he could see severed arms and heads, the rotting flesh molting and melting into the filamented base of the plant. How had Albert Graeff achieved the Sixtystone when so many had failed? How could he, Caleb Graff, the stupid fat farmer, set things right?

In desperation he glanced at the old map, which was only visible because the stars shone so brightly in the Underroom. The flower was depicted in the simple cartoonish beauty of an illuminated manuscript, with no evidence of its viciousness. He could see the contours of the landscape that he sought to follow, that Dina had so skillfully copied on her piece of scrap paper. Was that not what the map was for? And yet here he was, his journey at an end but still perilously incomplete.

That was when his eyes strayed off to the margins, to the inexplicable bars and dots that he had recognized as musical notation. He glanced from the page to the plant, held his breath, counted for a few seconds, and saw at last what his ancestor had done. The notes were no random, cacophonous melody; they measured out the beats of the lily's opening and closing. If he could remember the music he had played, he could anticipate the ravening motions of the petals. That is what Albert Graeff had learned centuries ago and what he had set down on paper for his descendants to read.

But knowing the pattern was not enough; he would need to act, to *trust* the map. Any hastiness or hesitation, any misstep or miscalculation, would transform him into more lifeless meat at the flower's perimeter. He felt sick in his grumbling stomach, and if he had stood alone in safety, perhaps he would not have had the courage to take that final step. But he could see the enraged Mrs. Lopez staggering toward him, the blade back in her hand, as farther on Dina struggled to get to her feet. He knew the threat this enemy posed, and he knew the curse of the stone; so, counting under his breath he paused, inhaled, and finally leapt into the heart of the lily.

Now Caleb was inside, and he set the Sixtystone with care in the little organic recess at which he stood. As the stone left his hand, a strange sensation washed over him, like a cleansing beneath his flesh. He had not known how dirty his blood felt until that old stain was removed, purged by the simple act of relinquishing a polluted power.

There was no time for him to jump back out. The petals snapped closed, and he was in a darkness as deep as primordial chaos. He was horribly aware of the hard skulls and oozing viscera at his feet and the razored blossoms that caged him. A scent like death and pollen tickled his nostrils. Then the petals split open, but Caleb remembered the tune and the tempo and knew that he dared not move, for they shut again almost at once. Four times they repeated this pattern, and Caleb suppressed the urge to leave, knowing that to do so would mean death but watching as Mrs. Lopez drew ever nearer. At last the petals opened once more, and he knew a caesura had come in their appalling measure, and he jumped out through a gap in the petals, landing in rough relief on the earth outside.

By now Mrs. Lopez was almost upon him, but he realized that her attention remained fixed on the flower. Dropping her blade, she stared at it, and Caleb could see that she was counting. Had she too learned the secret timing of the lily's murderous strokes? Would all his terror and all his work be for naught if she could simply claim the Sixtystone for her own almost as soon as he had abandoned it? For it was with great assurance that she launched herself with her remaining foot toward the stone in its receptacle.

As she did so, a sharp flash struck Caleb's eyes, and it disoriented him so much that at first he didn't know what was happening. But soon he was all too aware. Dina had taken the last little gold slip from Vitale's and flung it at Mrs. Lopez even as she darted forward. It erupted into the back of her robe, and the sheer shock of it threw off her balance. She stumbled and flailed out a hand to try to grab the Sixtystone, but the interruption in her motion was final and fatal: the lily's jaws curled closed upon her, slicing through her midriff as though she were paper. An empty half-torso and mangled legs dropped to the ground, cloven so cleanly that it was several seconds before the body remembered to bleed. Caleb turned away in disgust, though not in time to avoid seeing the petals part to reveal the empty gaze of Mrs. Lopez's face. The desiccation of centuries had reclaimed her flesh beneath rags of brittle white hair, which framed the same cipher of a scar on her brow.

Caleb wanted to lie still, to draw breath deeply in the cooling night air and to forget that he was in the Underroom with its wonders and its horrors. But he found he could not yet rest. He gathered himself and faltered forth around the flower and toward the spot where Dina Khouri lay crumpled next to her backpack. He dropped to his knees beside her.

"Ms. Khouri, are you all right?"

As he asked the question, looking across to her wounded throat, his vision seemed blurred in the starshine—blurred, he knew, from something like a welling of tears. He blinked and furiously wiped at his eyes, suddenly alarmed lest Dina should see him cry. But he was too late, for she raised her head and peered back at him, offering an uncharacteristically shy smile.

"I am," she replied, then added ruefully, "But Mrs. Lopez was right. I've tried so hard to act mysterious and wise and professional, but I really am just a silly little girl, playing with a fire that's going to burn me . . . or other people."

Caleb shook his head, gently but with a vehemence that surprised himself. "That's not true. I honestly don't know what the heck happened today. I don't really know what this place is or what we're doing here. But if you're right, when I get back home to where my brother and his family are lying in bed, we'll have a regular old farm to work on. Crops and dirt and tools and family . . . and no curses."

Dina winced as she laughed. "You get a full refund if it didn't work."

"How do you do this kind of job, living each day like it's an adventure but working with ordinary boring people like me for your clients?"

She shrugged. "You're nowhere near as boring as my father, Mr. Graff . . . and I love him more than anyone else in the world. There's more to life than adventure."

Caleb nodded, then looked up and around him. "So what happens now?"

"We've just got to wait for Mr. Vitale to reopen the aperture. And don't worry—we don't have to get back to where we started. It'll find us."

"Understood," said Caleb. "Or, well, maybe not *understood,* but I guess I can live with it. I mean, if he can create exploding bookmarks . . ."

"He likes to take care of me," Dina chuckled. "He always slips me a few custom creations when I travel to the Underroom. You know what I call them? *Flash cards.* Get it?"

Caleb didn't think the term was quite as clever as Dina did, but she laughed hysterically as she said it, and he let himself laugh beside her. At last she regained her composure, though an elfin grin still graced her face as she said, "Could you do me one last favor?"

"I suppose."

"Just keep an eye out while we wait. I—I think I really need a rest."

A rest sounded ferociously appealing to Caleb at that moment, but he saw the blood welling up in Dina's bruised neck where Mrs. Lopez had seized her, and he heard the hurt in her voice. "Sure," he replied, with only the barest hesitation, successfully hiding his own exhaustion.

And so he sat beside her, feeling the dewy fronds of the field on his palms as she closed her eyes and nestled her head into something that looked like a pillowy hibiscus. He won the war with his weariness and the weight of his lungs and kept guard for a time, though how long he could not tell, for he refused to pull out his phone. He simply kept vigil as the constellations crept slowly across the sky, occasionally glancing down almost reverently at her, but mostly giving the land his full attention. Every so often an unknown shape would occlude some stars or race past on the brow of the valley, but he never saw an animal up close, and no other hunters approached the flower. He rose only once, to gather whatever of their belongings lay scattered across the plain and return them to Dina's bag. As he did so, he took a moment to hold Albert Graeff's map side by side with Dina's copy, and he marveled at the likeness.

The aperture occurred as it had before, without warning, the Underroom unraveling around him like apple skins; and though he knew he would not die, the nauseating whirl felt worse on his taxed muscles. But he had never been so glad to see a shelf of books: even the esoteric halls of Vitale's seemed cheerily familiar to him now. Dina roused as they arrived, and Mr. Vitale was there waiting, helping her to her feet. He looked at her with concern, but she waved him off.

"I'll be fine," she assured him, and when he squinted skeptically at her, she insisted, "Really. It's not like the day we met, not even close. But I did need every one of the flash cards."

Mr. Vitale didn't answer except with a knowing nod. Then he helped lead them through the shop and bade them farewell as they found the exit. The sky looked smaller here, the lights of Philadelphia crowding out many of the stars they had seen in the Underroom, and it was beginning its transition from black to blue. Caleb followed Dina back through the streets, which looked like a transmuted landscape when not lit by the sun, filled with just as much glory and terror as the exotic Underroom. They stayed silent as they walked, through the chorus of cars and stereos until at last they arrived back where the journey had begun, at the unassuming red-brick apartment. A light was on despite the hour, and Dina's mother thrust the door open as they walked up to it. Caleb stood self-consciously, but she beckoned him in, and he awkwardly relented.

It took a minute for Dina to assure her parents that she was okay when they saw her throat, and Caleb wasn't convinced that they fully accepted her protestations. But they let her sit at the kitchen table and motioned for him to do the same.

"Would you like some tea and *fatteh?*" her father offered with gruff hospitality.

"Yes, thank you," Caleb said.

When the bread and yogurt dish arrived, he had to discipline himself to eat it temperately and politely, so great was his hunger, though Dina showed no such restraint. The nutty, spicy, citrusy tea was so hot it almost burned his mouth, but he drank it as quickly as propriety would allow. Occasionally Mr. and Mrs. Khouri would speak to their daughter in Arabic, but otherwise they sat together without words, until finally Dina stood up and Caleb joined her.

"I—I suppose I'll need to be going," he said.

"I'll walk you to your car."

Caleb thanked Dina's parents, and he ambled on the sidewalk beneath the slowly paling sky toward where he had parked.

"Thank you again," he said to her.

"I know I said it before, but I'm sorry I put you through all this."

Caleb didn't answer at first, because he wanted to speak honestly. "No," he said at length, "you don't need to apologize. I think . . . I think it was good that I went there. Maybe I even needed to."

"Well," she said, "for your sake, I hope you never need to do anything like that again. But . . ." She trailed off, as though searching for elusive words. Then she reached into the pocket of her blue jeans and pulled out a crumpled little business card ". . . but if you ever *should* need another adventure, you could, maybe, give me a call."

Caleb took the card and looked at her. He was not skilled at maps and meanings; he had little facility for interpretation. But as he met the gaze of her brown eyes glittering in the deep blue blush of the morning and regarded the smile that frolicked across her lips, he thought that, perhaps, here was one legend he could read rightly.

ACKNOWLEDGMENTS

Countless individuals have helped this book come to fruition, some of whom I will do my best to pay tribute to here.

I am grateful to my sister Alisa Ruddell and my friends Joshua Green and Christian Dickinson for having read and commented on so many of the stories in this volume.

I am thankful to my family for their love and support: my wife, Mary; my children, Greta, Simon, Silas, and Irene; my parents, Dennis and Judy; my brother Andrew; and my in-laws, aunts, uncles, cousins, nieces, and nephews.

My own writing is indebted to countless past writers whose works have shaped my sensibilities. I am likewise indebted to those writing instructors who invested in me over the years: Charles Franklyn Beach, Randy Smith, Zeta Dawson-Godboalt, and Greg Garrett. I have also been in several fine writing groups, most notably the group from my seminary Historiography class (Anita Kobayashi Sung, Adam Eisenga, Catherine Hommes).

I could not have come this far without the support of the team at Hippocampus Press. Derrick Hussey and S. T. Joshi have created a truly remarkable publishing company, and I cannot extend sufficient thanks to them for allowing me to be a part of the Hippocampus catalog.

Many communities have guided me on my intellectual journey, including faculty, students, and staff at Windham Public Schools, Nyack College, Gordon-Conwell Theological Seminary, Baylor University, The Baptist College of Florida, and Lancaster Bible College. Other such communities have included my colleagues at Christ and Pop Culture, as well as such groups as the Mythopoeic Society, the Conference on Christianity and Literature, The C. S. Lewis and the

Inklings Society, The Eighth Day Institute, and Square Halo Books. And of course I have been richly blessed with hundreds of thoughtful and engaged students throughout the years. A special thanks go out to those students who humored me in my course Strange Gods: Religion and the Weird Horror Tradition.

My spiritual journey has been molded by fellow believers at Storrs Community Church, Baptist Fellowship of Columbia, Risen King Alliance Church, Holy Spirit Episcopal Church, Church under the Bridge, Harmony Baptist Mission Church, Damascus Baptist Church, All Saints Church, Willow Street Mennonite Church, and Strasburg Mennonite Church.

And I am grateful to the following individuals, who have read and given constructive input on one or more the works contained in this volume: Shellie Austin, Ian Barrs, Adam Eisenga, Robin Jeffers, Jason Kettinger, Sylvena Loo Suen Ying, Rebekah Mann, Rachel Miller, Rebecca Miller, Joshua Novalis, Ben Petersheim, Steve Petersheim, Cooper Ray, Praveen Rudra, Steve Schuler, Esther Swartzentruber, Timothy Thomas, Joyanna Wakeman, and Matt Wheeler.

PUBLICATION HISTORY

"The Absence." First published in *Penumbra* No. 2 (2021).

"The Ache of Bone and Joist and Page." Original to this volume.

"Adept." First published in *Penumbra* No. 4 (2023).

"Arbitress of Tides." Original to this volume.

"Big Sky." Original to this volume.

"The Cartographer." Original to this volume.

"Désirée." Original to this volume.

"An Edwardian Quartet." First published in *Penumbra* No. 3 (2022).

"Eternal Night." First published in *Spectral Realms* No. 14 (Winter 2021).

"The Folly." Original to this volume.

"A Green Shade." First published in *Penumbra* No. 2 (2021).

"A Glint amid the Corn." First published in *Penumbra* No. 3 (2022).

"A Hellish Thing." First published in *ParABnormal* No. 4.3 (September 2022).

"The Lady in the Wood." First published in *Spectral Realms* No. 17 (Summer 2022).

"The Lime Kiln." First published in *Black Wings VII: New Tales of Lovecraftian Horror*, ed. S. T. Joshi (PS Publishing, 2023).

"MacAdam." Original to this volume.

"The Mermaids Keep Their Own Counsel." First published in *The Mythic Circle* No. 44 (2022).

"The Nightmare." First published in *Spectral Realms* No. 19 (Summer 2023).

"Permian/Triassic." First published in *Spectral Realms* No. 15 (Summer 2021).

"Quartz Contentment." Original to this volume.

"Star Dust." First published in *Spectral Realms* No. 16 (Winter 2022).

"Termination Shock." First published in *Spectral Realms* No. 15 (Summer 2021).

"Testing the Spirits." Original to this volume.

"Through Enchantment." First published in *Penumbra* No. 4 (2023).

"A Voice in the Night." First published in *Spectral Realms* No. 18 (Winter 2023).

"What If Atlantis . . . ?" First published in *Spectral Realms* No. 14 (Winter 2021).

"A Word." First published in *Spectral Realms* No. 15 (Summer 2021).

www.ingramcontent.com/pod-product-compliance
Lightning Source LLC
Chambersburg PA
CBHW061430030726
47503CB00005B/1356